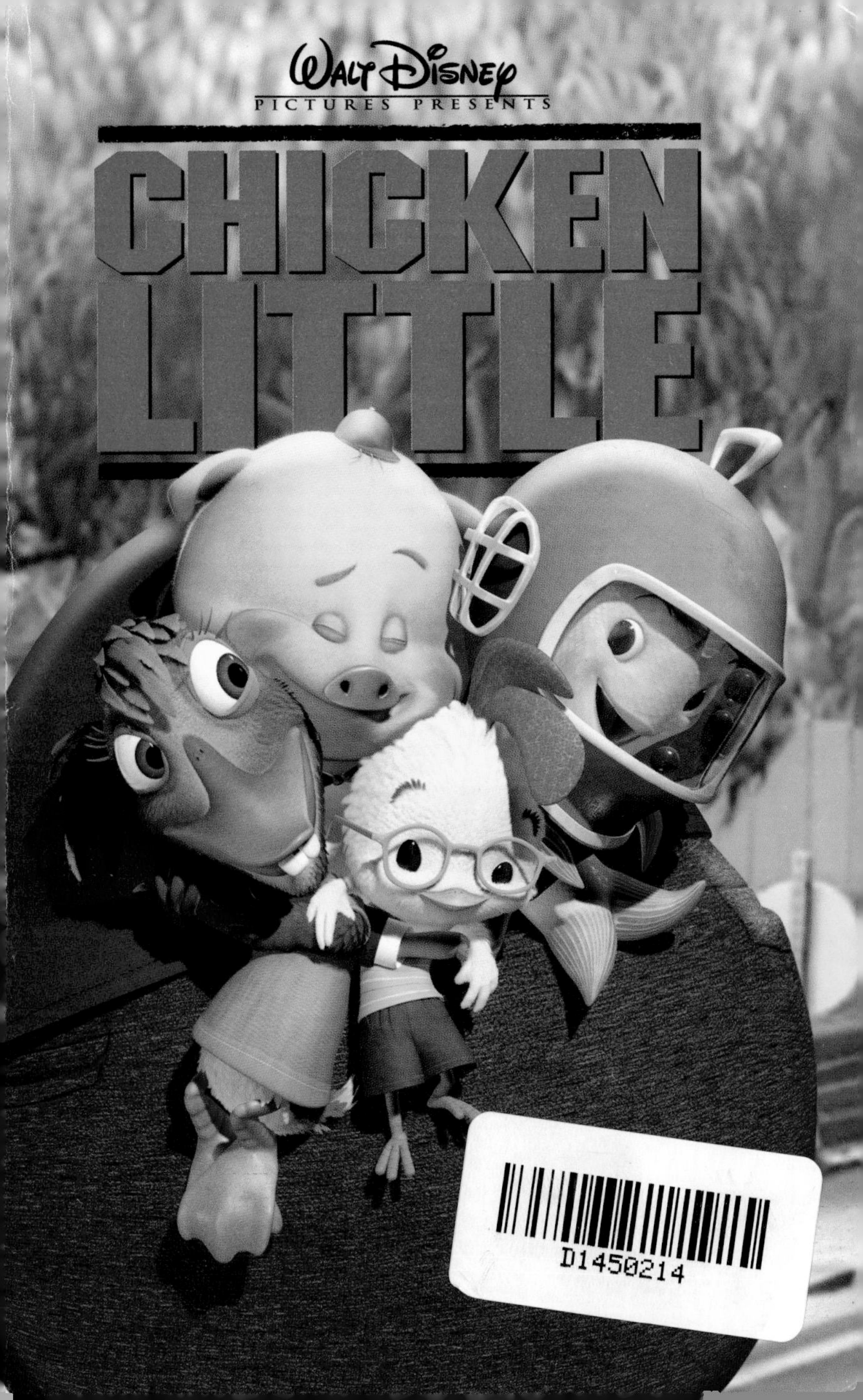
WALT DISNEY
PICTURES PRESENTS
CHICKEN
LITTLE

Editor - Erin Stein
Contributing Editor - Amy Court Kaemon
Graphic Designer and Letterer - Monalisa J. de Asis
Cover Designer - Louis Csontos
Graphic Artists - Anna Kernbaum & Louis Csontos

Digital Imaging Manager - Chris Buford
Production Managers - Jennifer Miller and Mutsumi Miyazaki
Senior Designer - Anna Kernbaum
Senior Editor - Elizabeth Hurchalla
Managing Editor - Lindsey Johnston
VP of Production - Ron Klamert
Publisher & Editor in Chief - Mike Kiley
President & C.O.O. - John Parker
C.E.O. - Stuart Levy

E-mail: info@tokyopop.com
Come visit us online at www.TOKYOPOP.com

A **TOKYOPOP** Cine-Manga® Book
TOKYOPOP Inc.
5900 Wilshire Blvd., Suite 2000
Los Angeles, CA 90036

Chicken Little

ISBN: 1-59532-724-X

First TOKYOPOP® printing: November 2005

10 9 8 7 6 5 4 3 2 1

Printed in the USA

(WALT DISNEY
PICTURES PRESENTS

CHICKEN LITTLE

Hamburg • London • Los Angeles • Tokyo

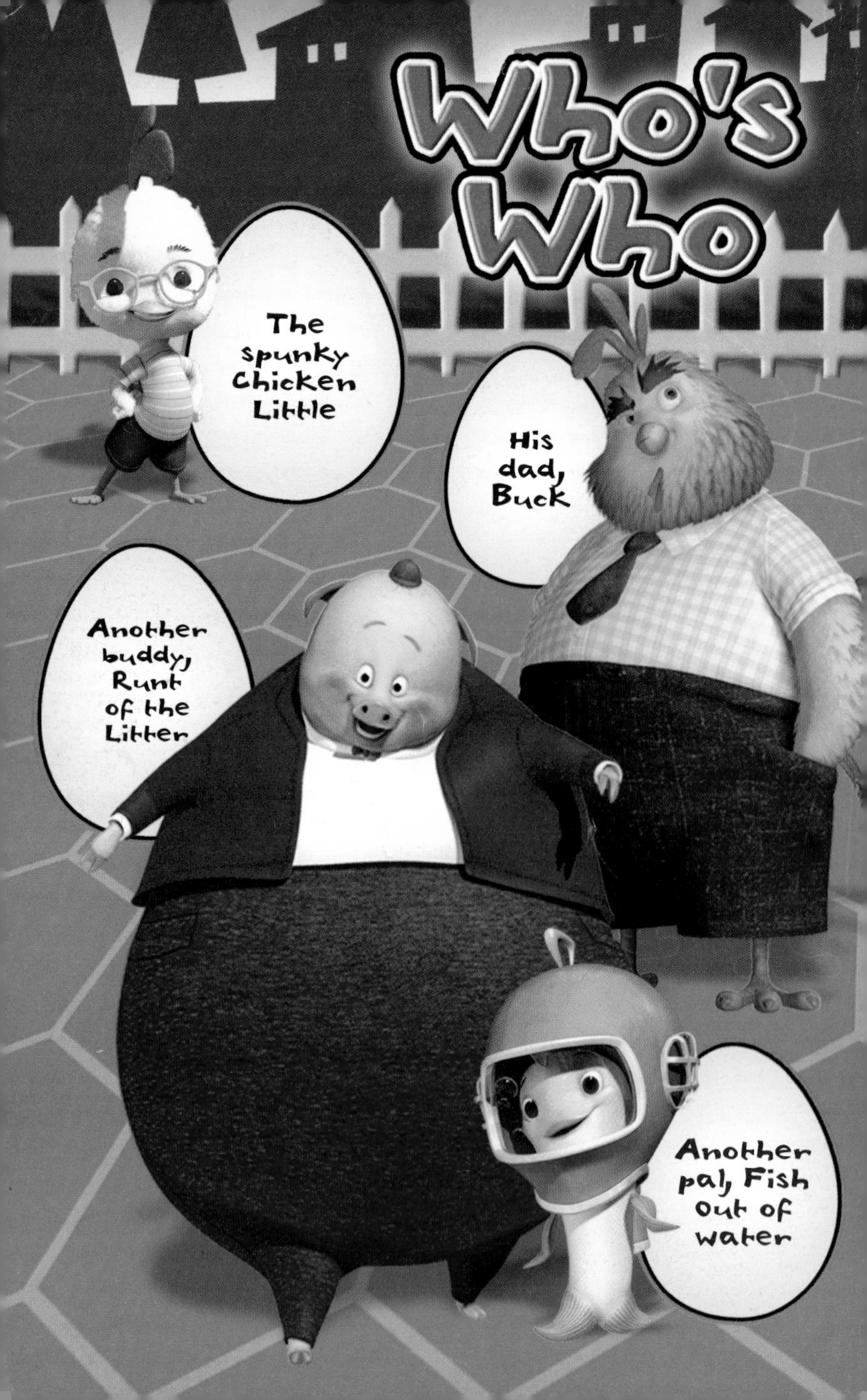
Who's Who
The spunky Chicken Little
His dad, Buck
Another buddy, Runt of the Litter
Another pal, Fish out of water

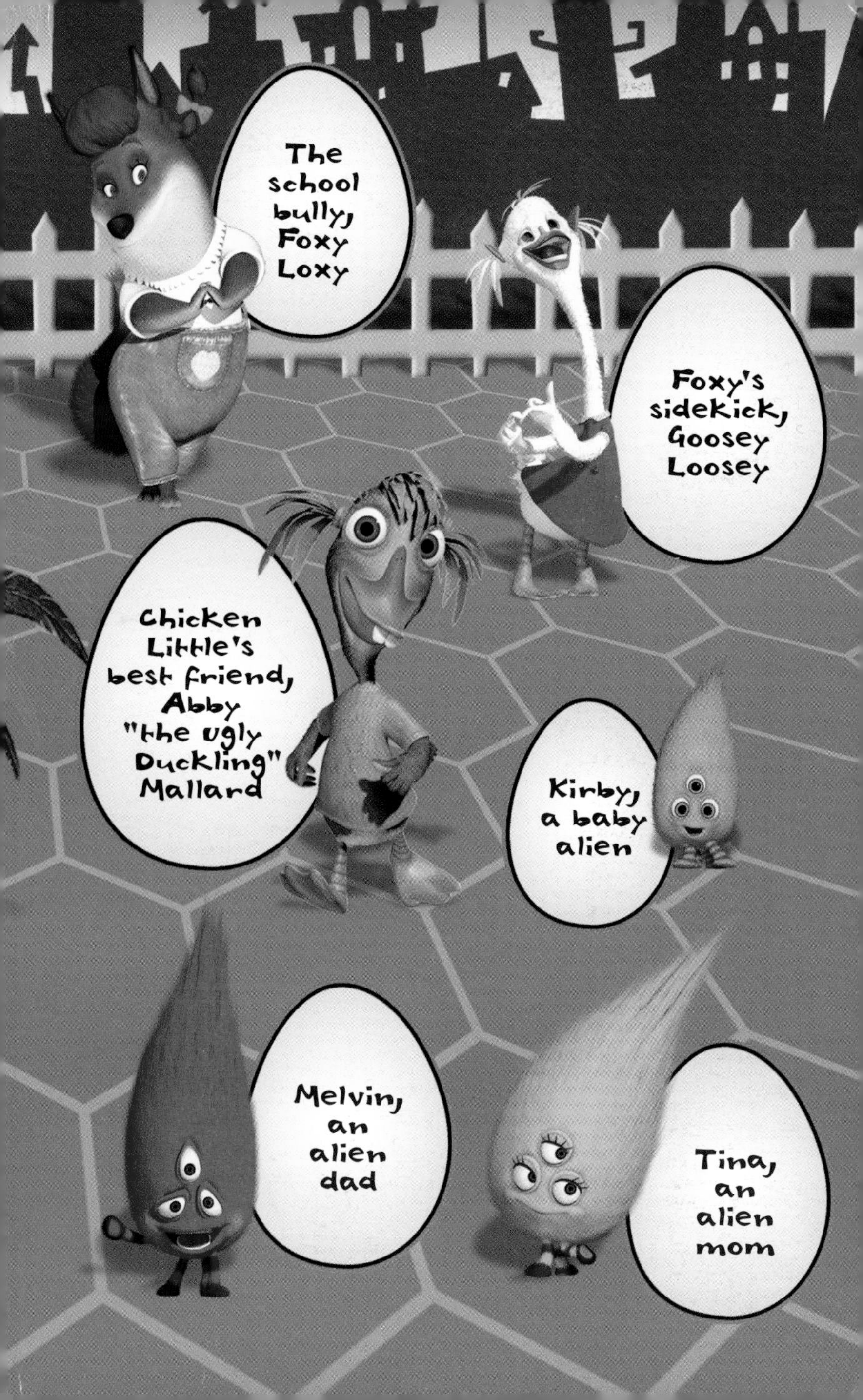
The school bully, Foxy Loxy
Foxy's sidekick, Goosey Loosey
Chicken Little's best friend, Abby "the ugly Duckling" Mallard
Kirby, a baby alien
Melvin, an alien dad
Tina, an alien mom

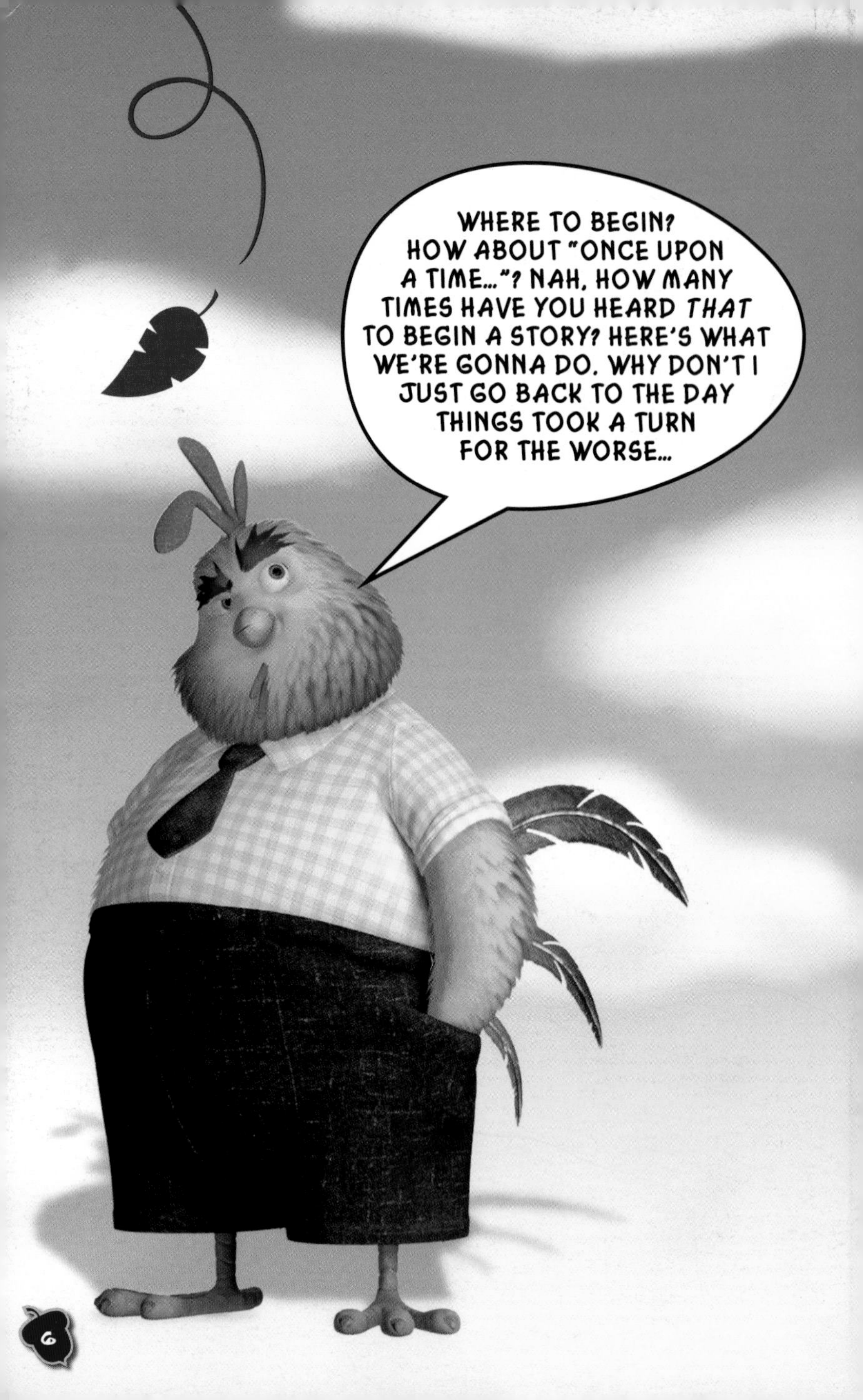
WHERE TO BEGIN? HOW ABOUT "ONCE UPON A TIME..."? NAH, HOW MANY TIMES HAVE YOU HEARD *THAT* TO BEGIN A STORY? HERE'S WHAT WE'RE GONNA DO. WHY DON'T I JUST GO BACK TO THE DAY THINGS TOOK A TURN FOR THE WORSE...

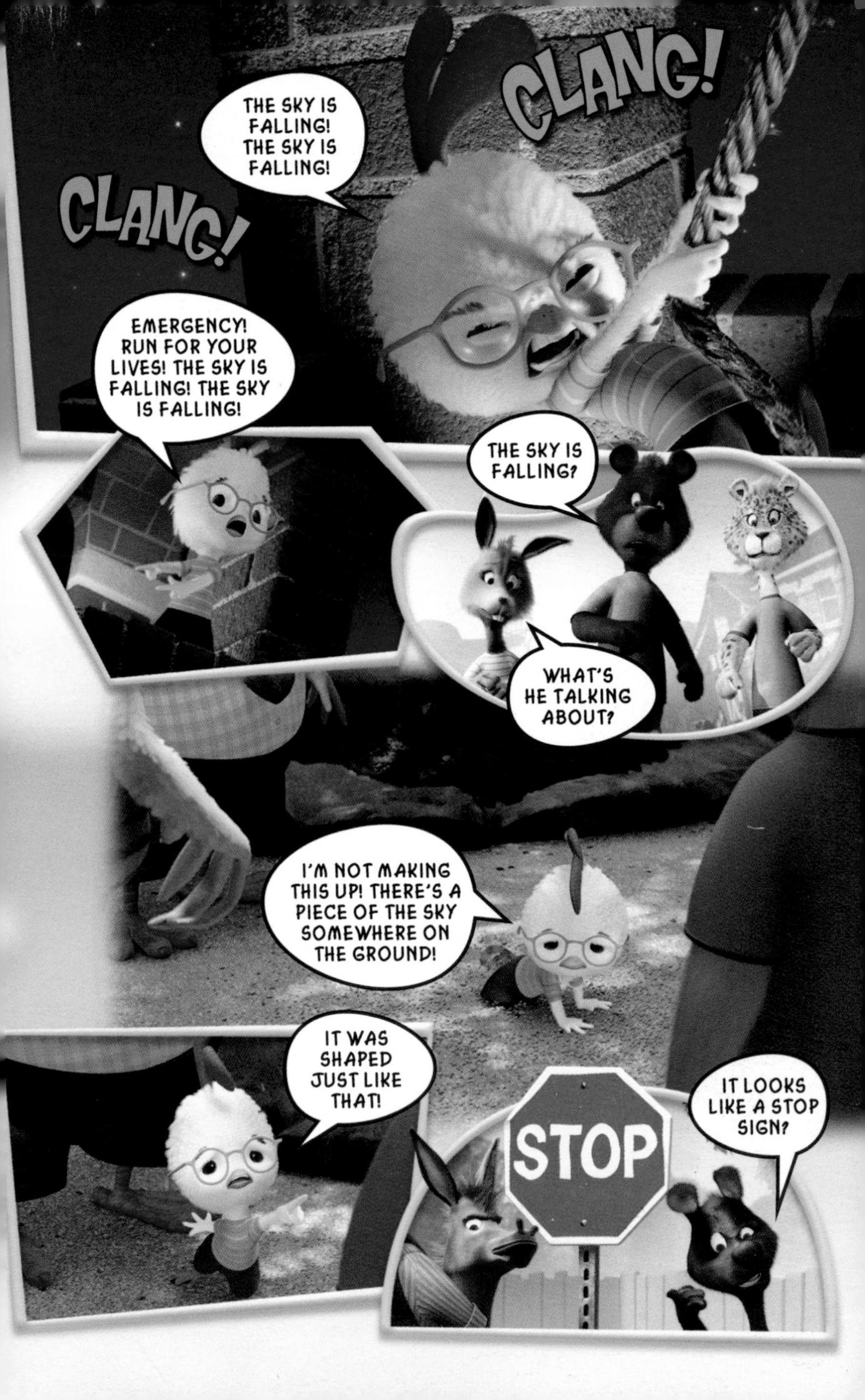
CLANG!
THE SKY IS FALLING! THE SKY IS FALLING!
CLANG!
EMERGENCY! RUN FOR YOUR LIVES! THE SKY IS FALLING! THE SKY IS FALLING!
THE SKY IS FALLING?
WHAT'S HE TALKING ABOUT?
I'M NOT MAKING THIS UP! THERE'S A PIECE OF THE SKY SOMEWHERE ON THE GROUND!
IT WAS SHAPED JUST LIKE THAT!
STOP
IT LOOKS LIKE A STOP SIGN?

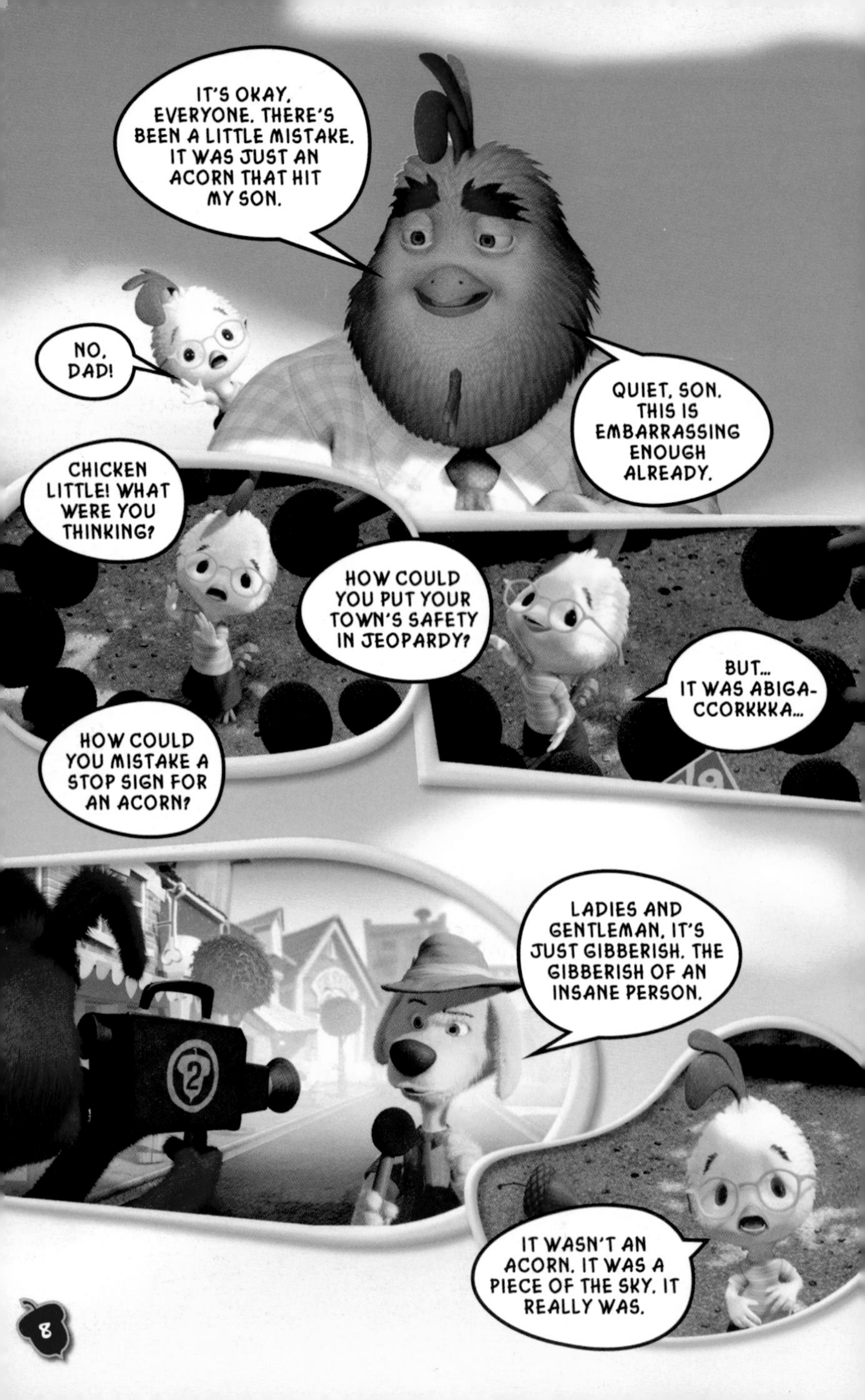
IT'S OKAY, EVERYONE. THERE'S BEEN A LITTLE MISTAKE. IT WAS JUST AN ACORN THAT HIT MY SON.
NO, DAD!
QUIET, SON. THIS IS EMBARRASSING ENOUGH ALREADY.
CHICKEN LITTLE! WHAT WERE YOU THINKING?
HOW COULD YOU PUT YOUR TOWN'S SAFETY IN JEOPARDY?
HOW COULD YOU MISTAKE A STOP SIGN FOR AN ACORN?
BUT... IT WAS ABIGA-CCORKKKA...
LADIES AND GENTLEMAN, IT'S JUST GIBBERISH. THE GIBBERISH OF AN INSANE PERSON.
IT WASN'T AN ACORN. IT WAS A PIECE OF THE SKY. IT REALLY WAS.

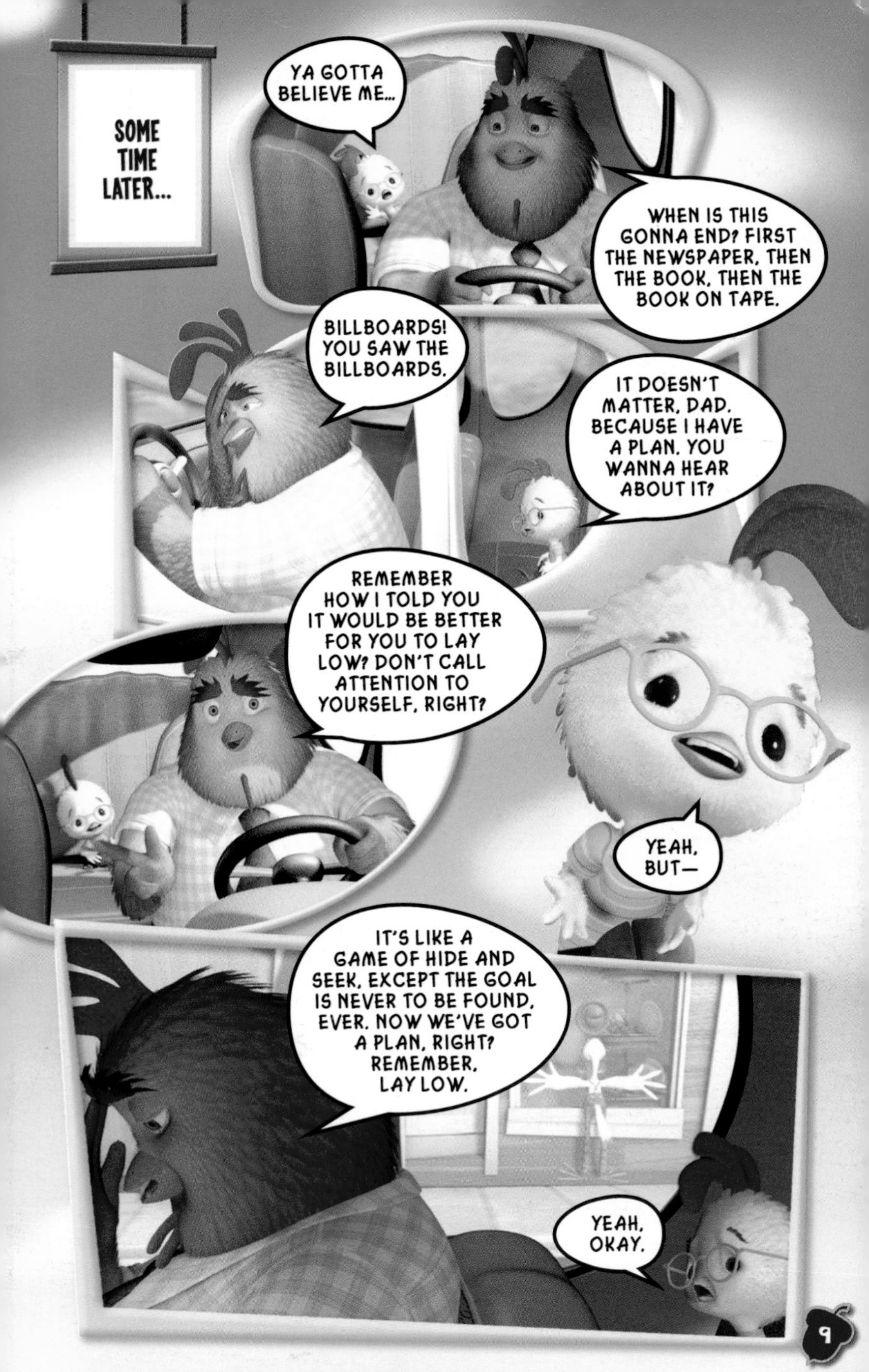
SOME TIME LATER...
YA GOTTA BELIEVE ME...
WHEN IS THIS GONNA END? FIRST THE NEWSPAPER, THEN THE BOOK, THEN THE BOOK ON TAPE.
BILLBOARDS! YOU SAW THE BILLBOARDS.
IT DOESN'T MATTER, DAD. BECAUSE I HAVE A PLAN. YOU WANNA HEAR ABOUT IT?
REMEMBER HOW I TOLD YOU IT WOULD BE BETTER FOR YOU TO LAY LOW? DON'T CALL ATTENTION TO YOURSELF, RIGHT?
YEAH, BUT—
IT'S LIKE A GAME OF HIDE AND SEEK, EXCEPT THE GOAL IS NEVER TO BE FOUND, EVER. NOW WE'VE GOT A PLAN, RIGHT? REMEMBER, LAY LOW.
YEAH, OKAY.

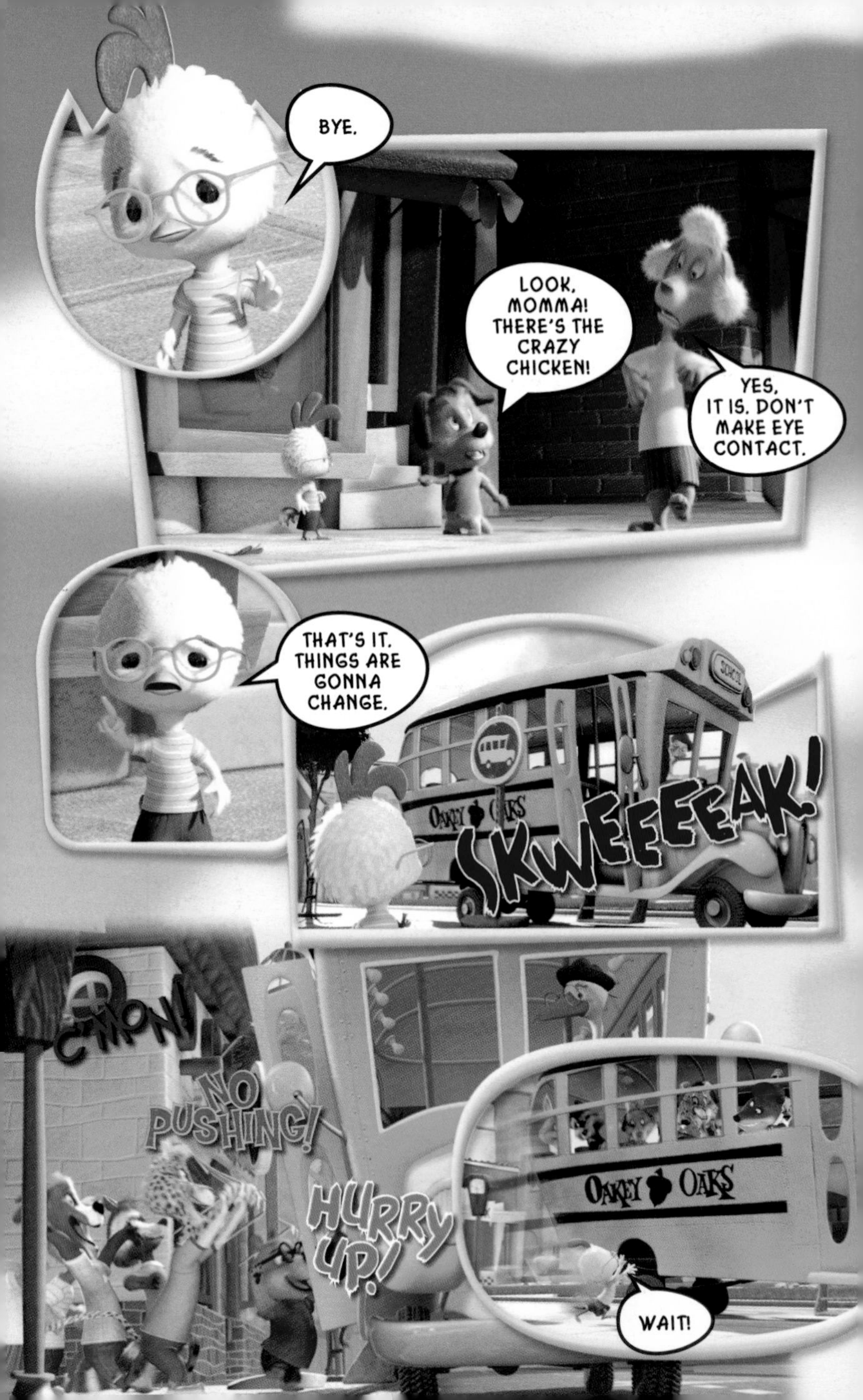
BYE.
LOOK, MOMMA! THERE'S THE CRAZY CHICKEN!
YES, IT IS. DON'T MAKE EYE CONTACT.
THAT'S IT. THINGS ARE GONNA CHANGE.
SCHOOL
OAKEY OAKS
SKWEEEEAK!
C'MON!
NO PUSHING!
HURRY UP!
OAKEY OAKS
WAIT!

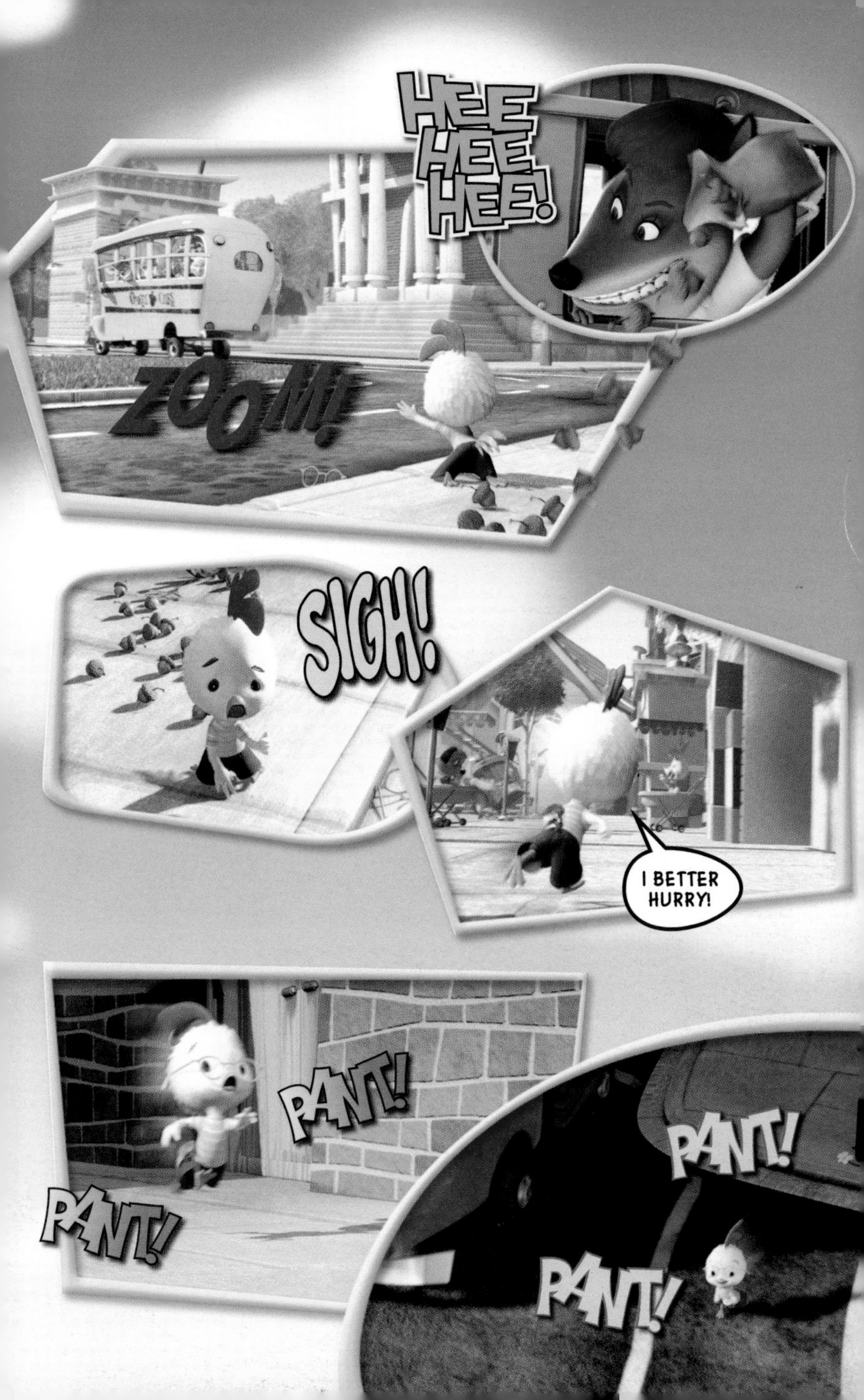
ZOOM!
HEE HEE HEE!
SIGH!
I BETTER HURRY!
PANT!
PANT!
PANT!
PANT!

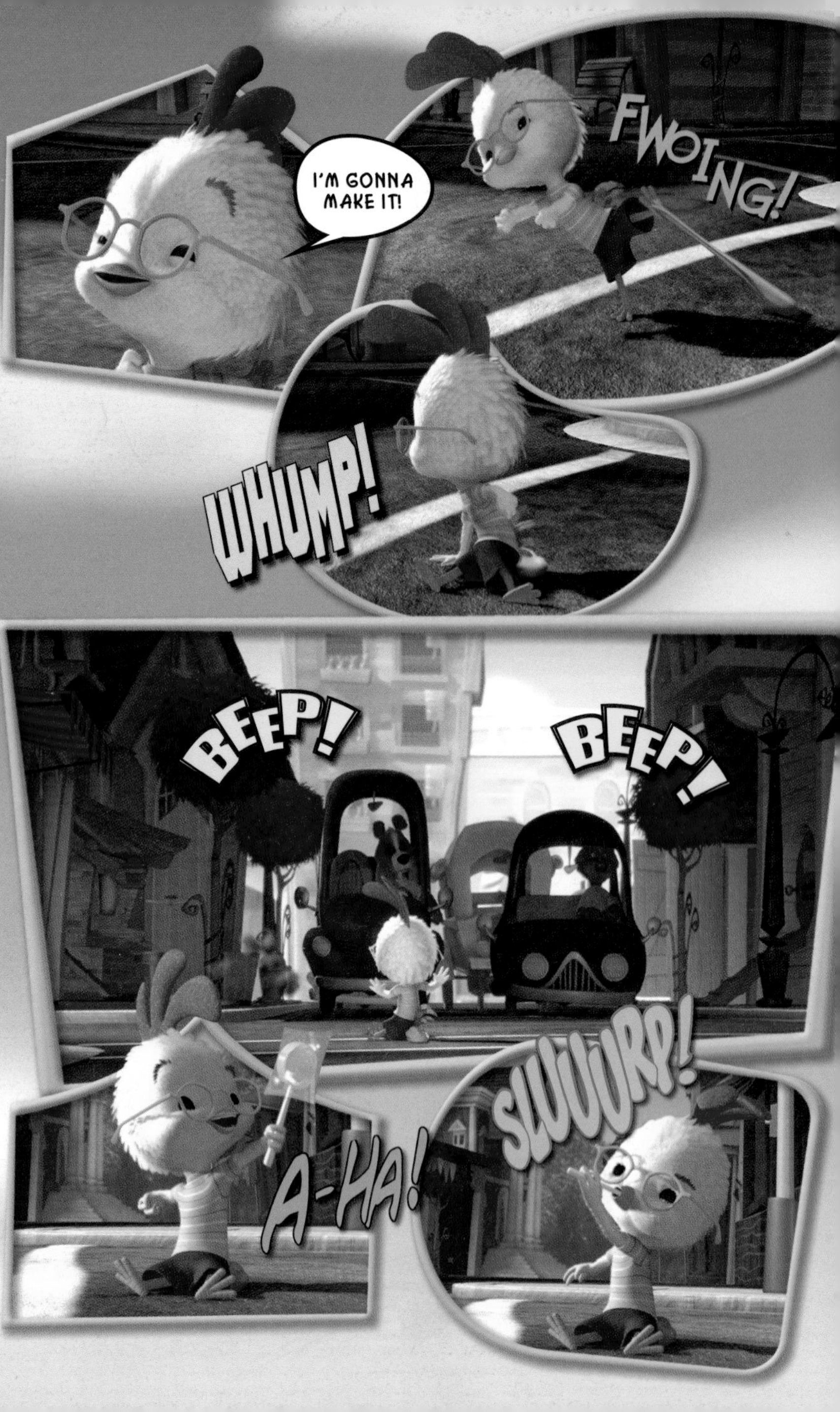
I'M GONNA MAKE IT!
FWOING!
WHUMP!
BEEP!
BEEP!
A-HA!
SLUUURP!

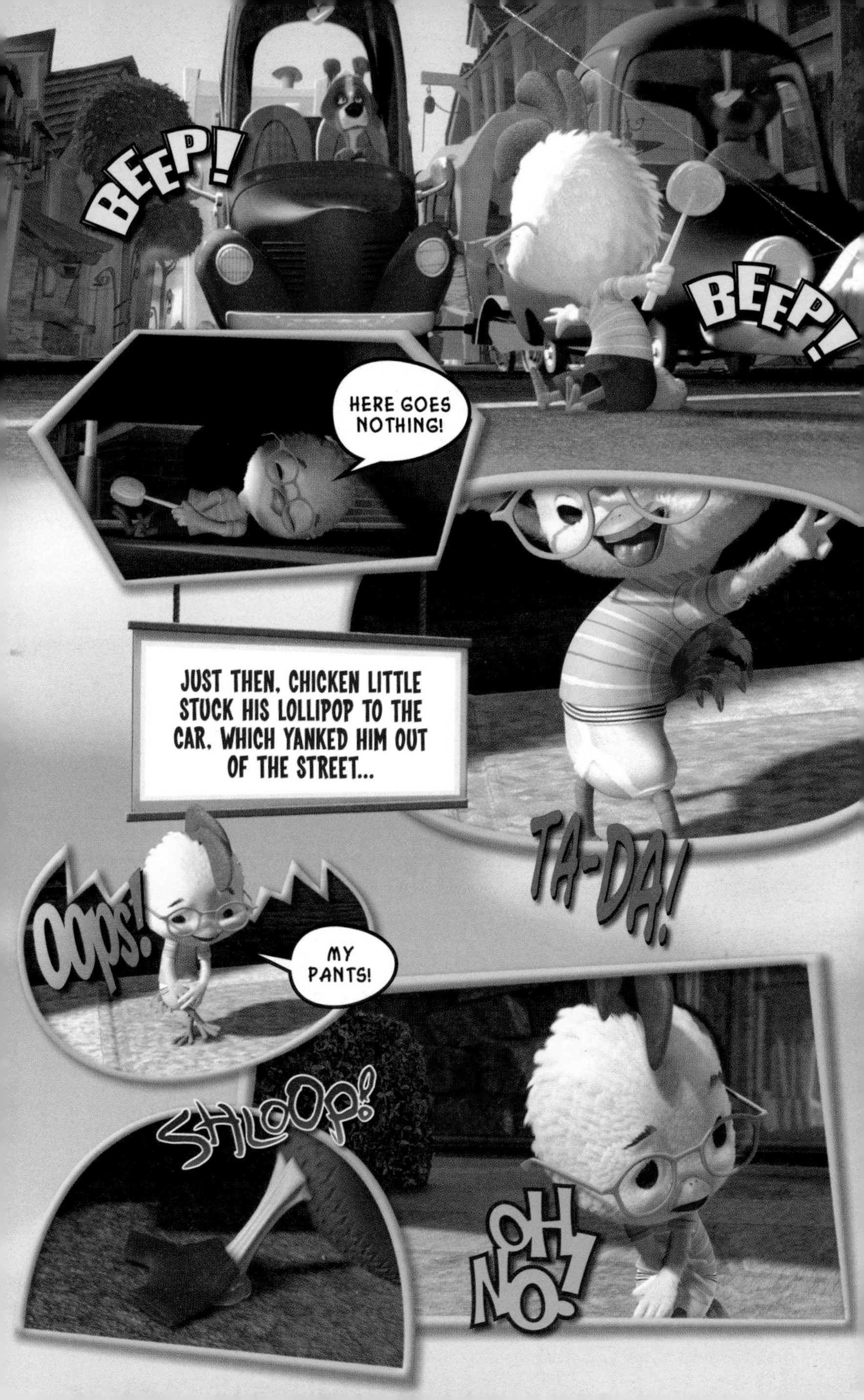
BEEP!
BEEP!
HERE GOES NOTHING!
JUST THEN, CHICKEN LITTLE STUCK HIS LOLLIPOP TO THE CAR, WHICH YANKED HIM OUT OF THE STREET...
TA-DA!
OOPS!
MY PANTS!
SHLOOP!
OH NO!

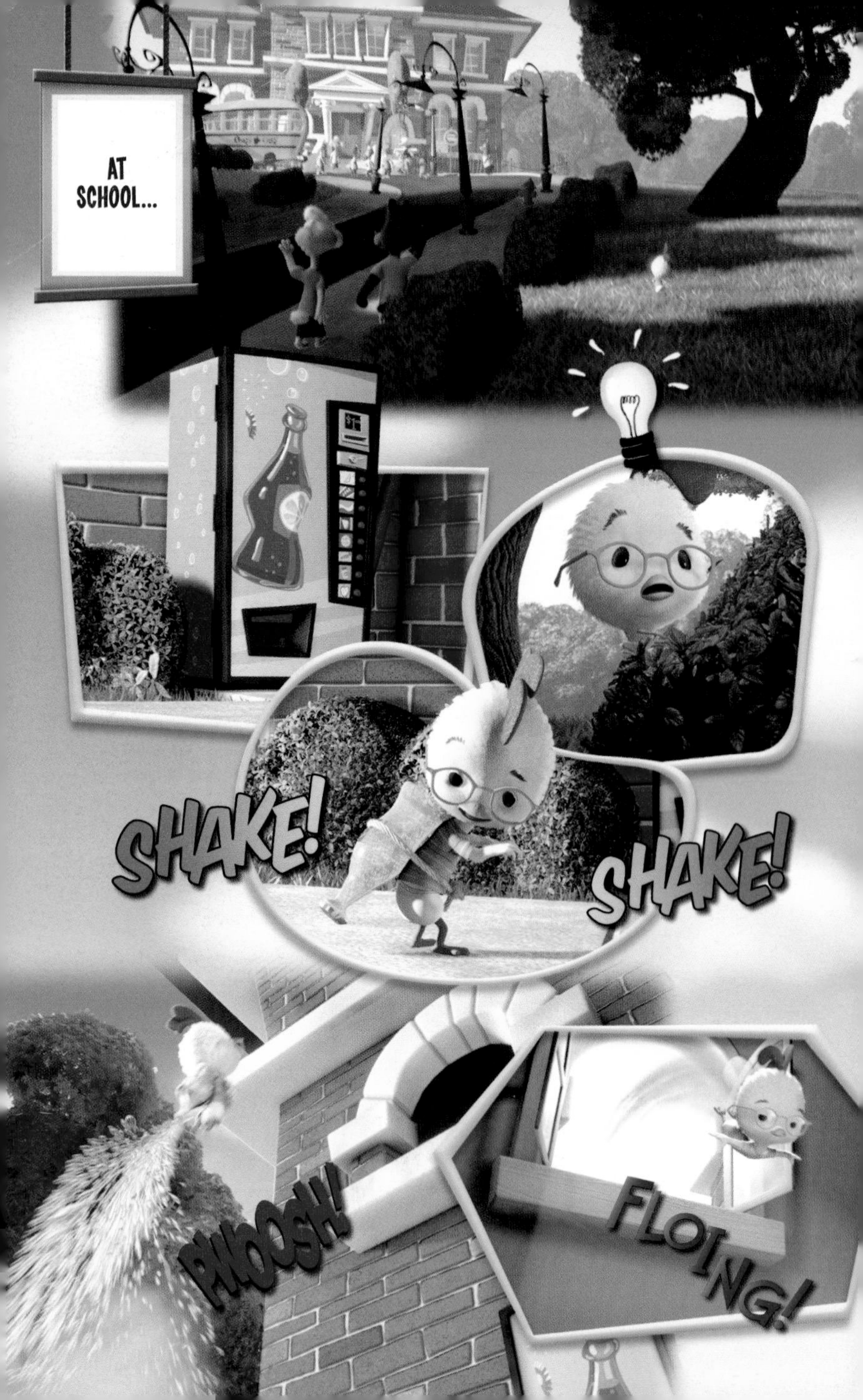
AT SCHOOL...
SHAKE!
SHAKE!
PHOOSH!
FLOING!

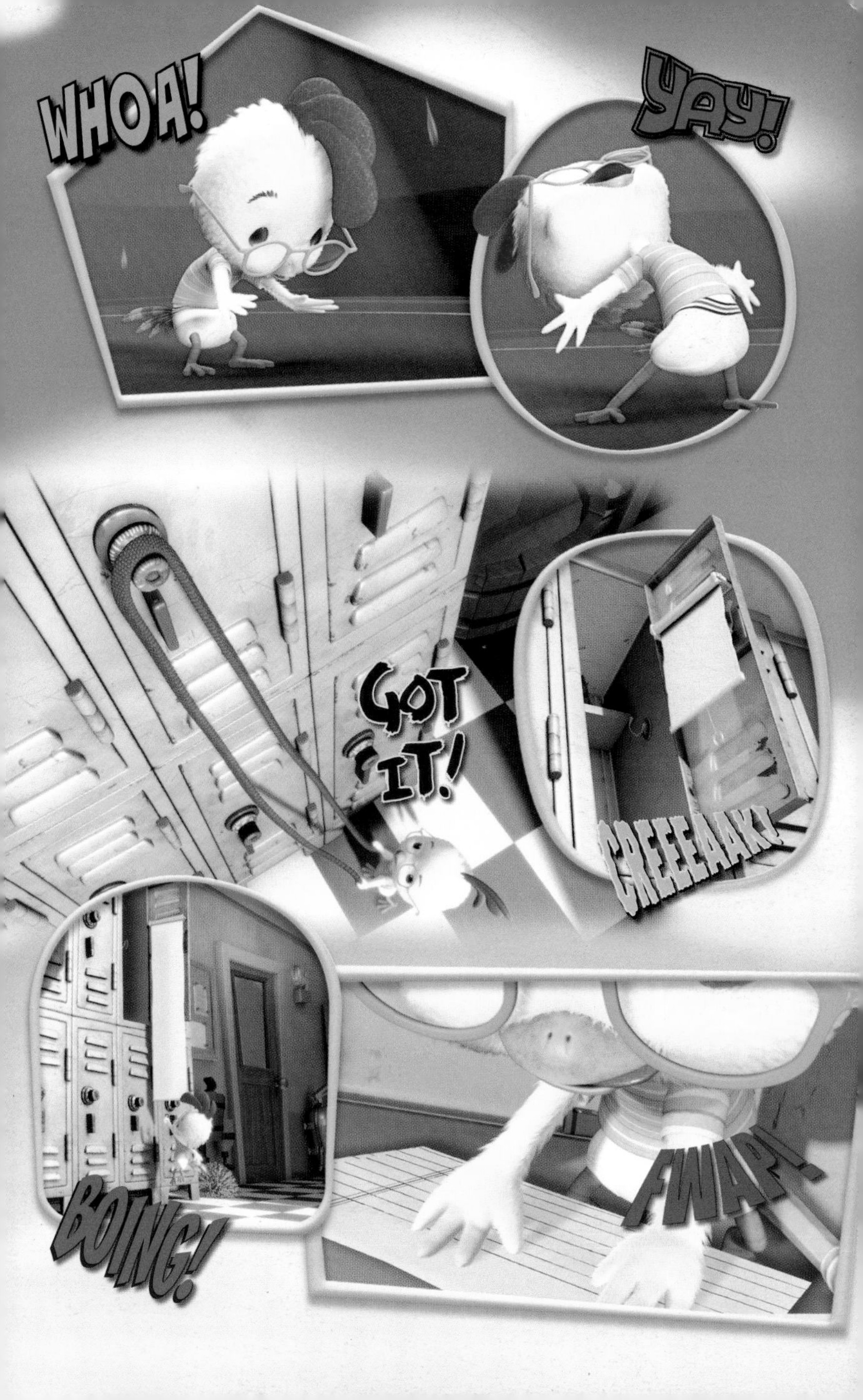
WHOA!
YAY!
GOT IT!
CREEEAAK!
BOING!
FWAP!

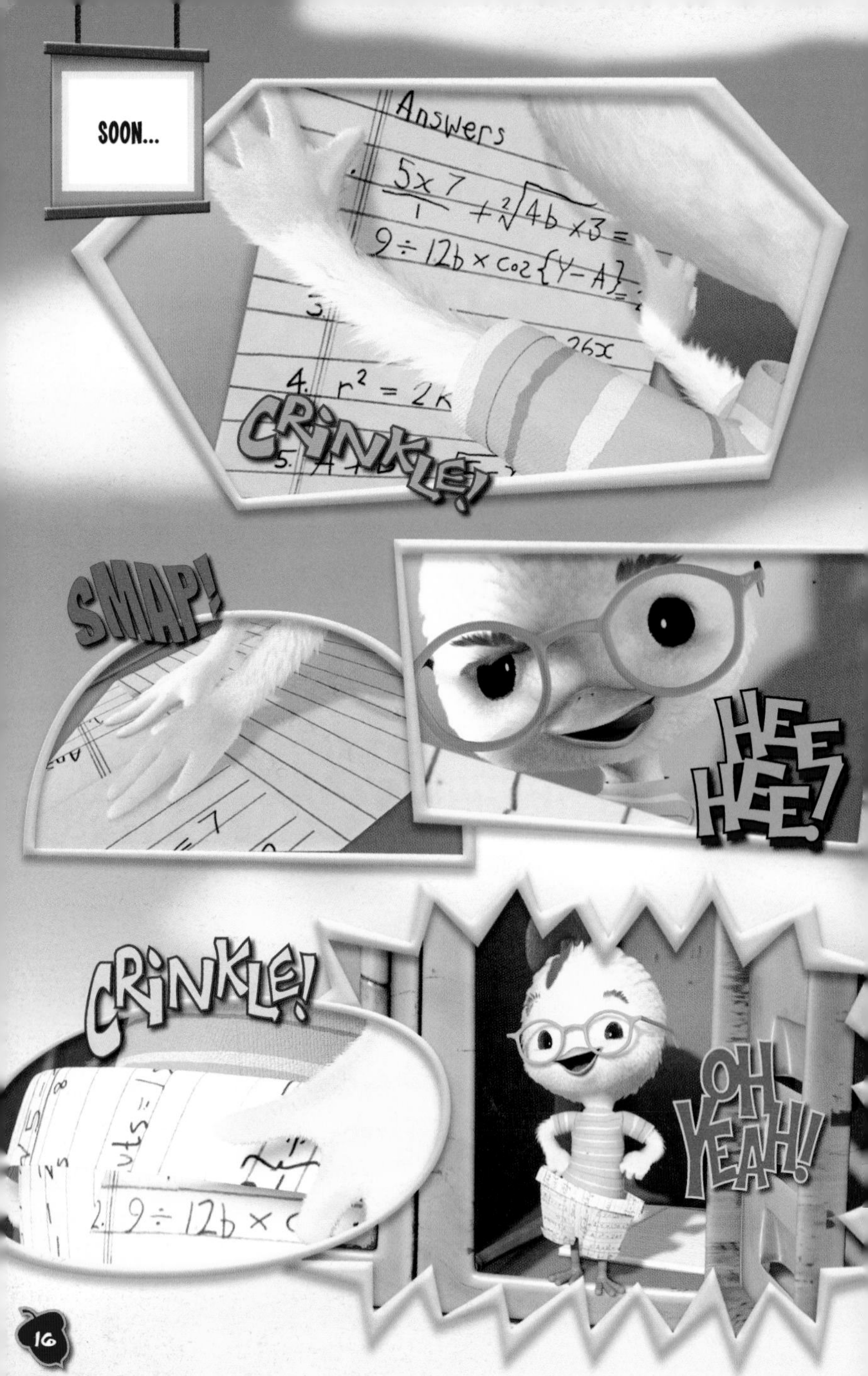
SOON...
Answers
CRINKLE!
SNAP!
HEE HEE!
CRINKLE!
OH YEAH!

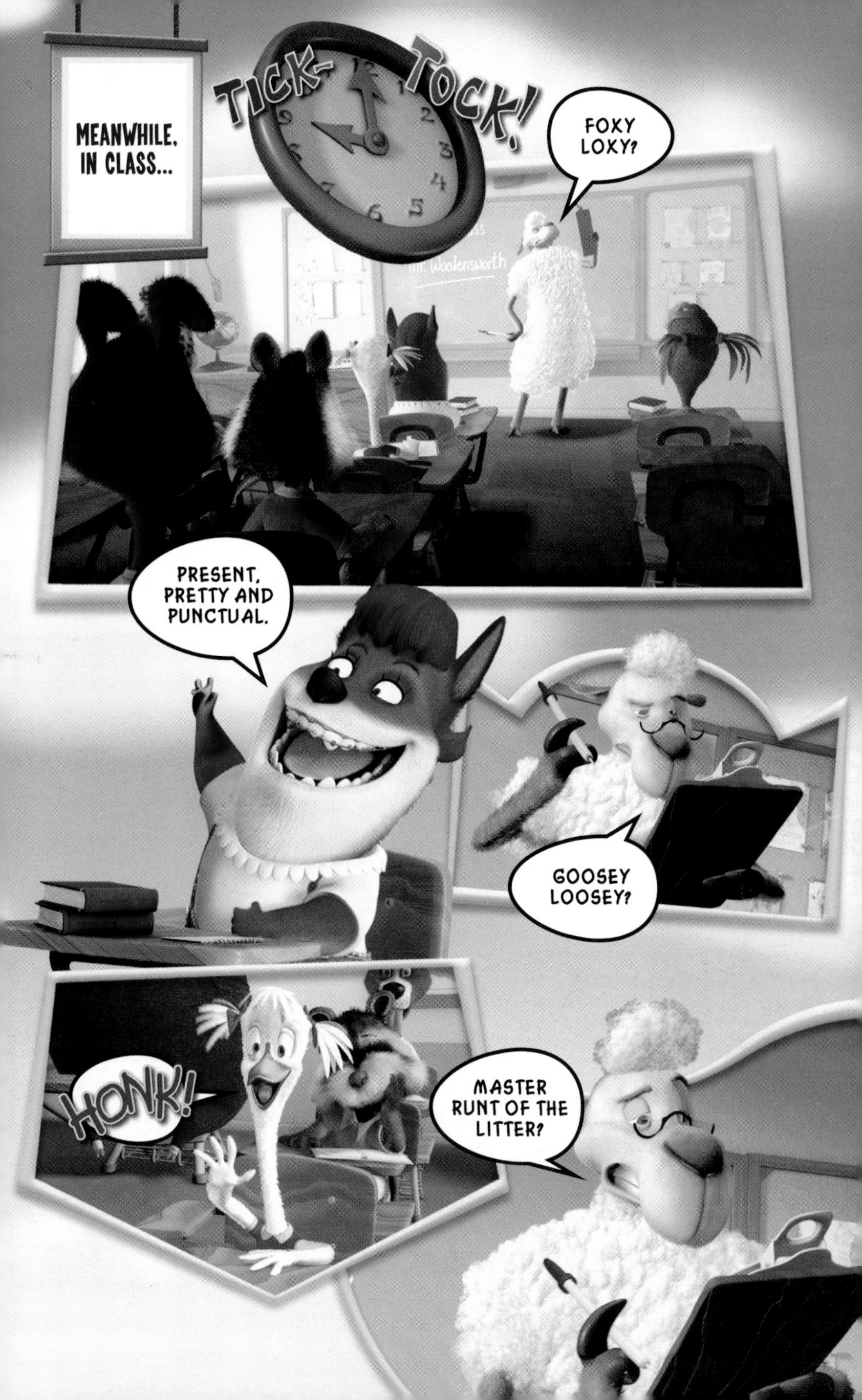
MEANWHILE, IN CLASS...
TICK-TOCK!
FOXY LOXY?
Mr. Woolensworth
PRESENT, PRETTY AND PUNCTUAL.
GOOSEY LOOSEY?
HONK!
MASTER RUNT OF THE LITTER?

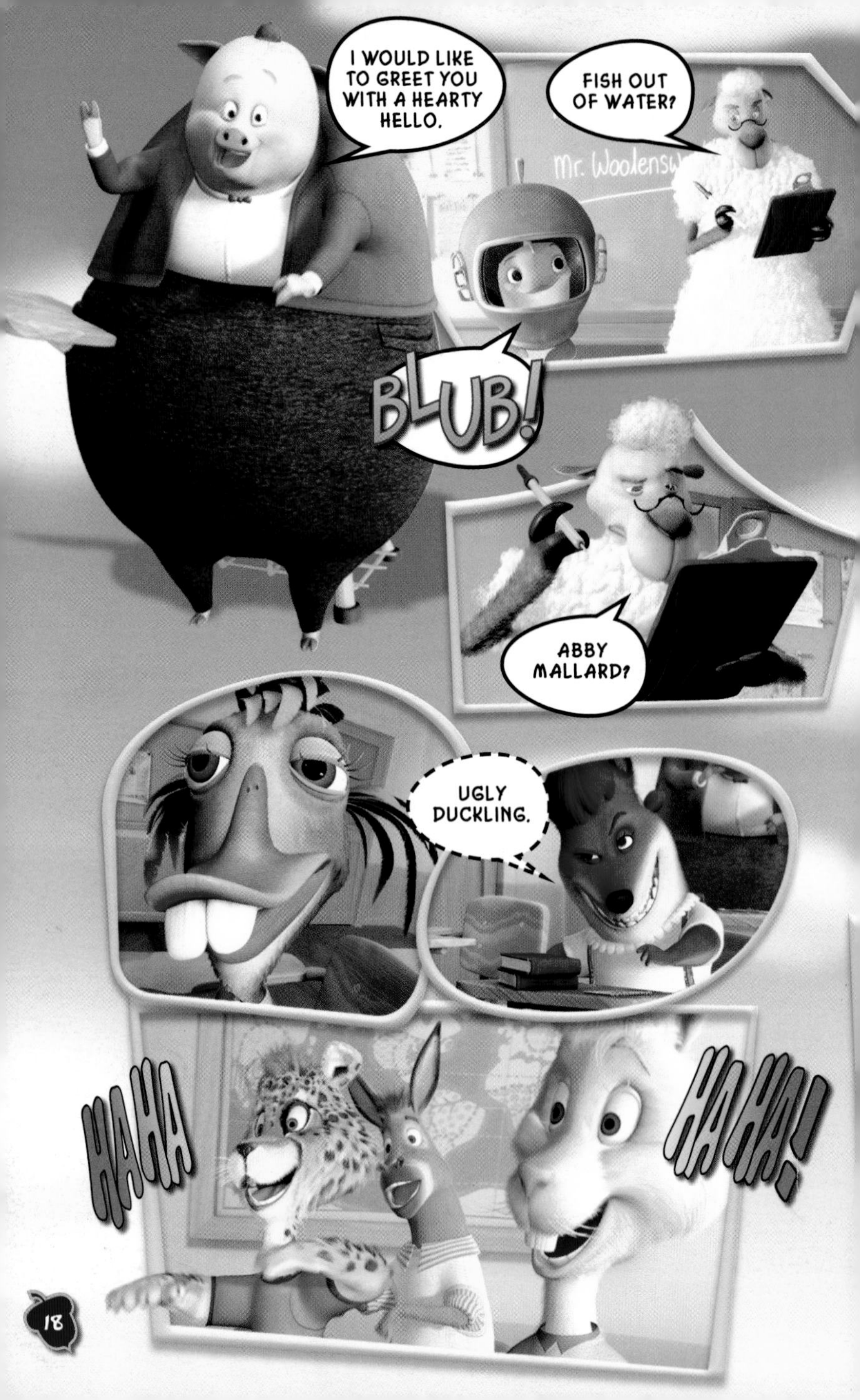
I WOULD LIKE TO GREET YOU WITH A HEARTY HELLO.
FISH OUT OF WATER?
Mr. Woolensw
BLUB!
ABBY MALLARD?
UGLY DUCKLING.
HAHA
HA HA HA!

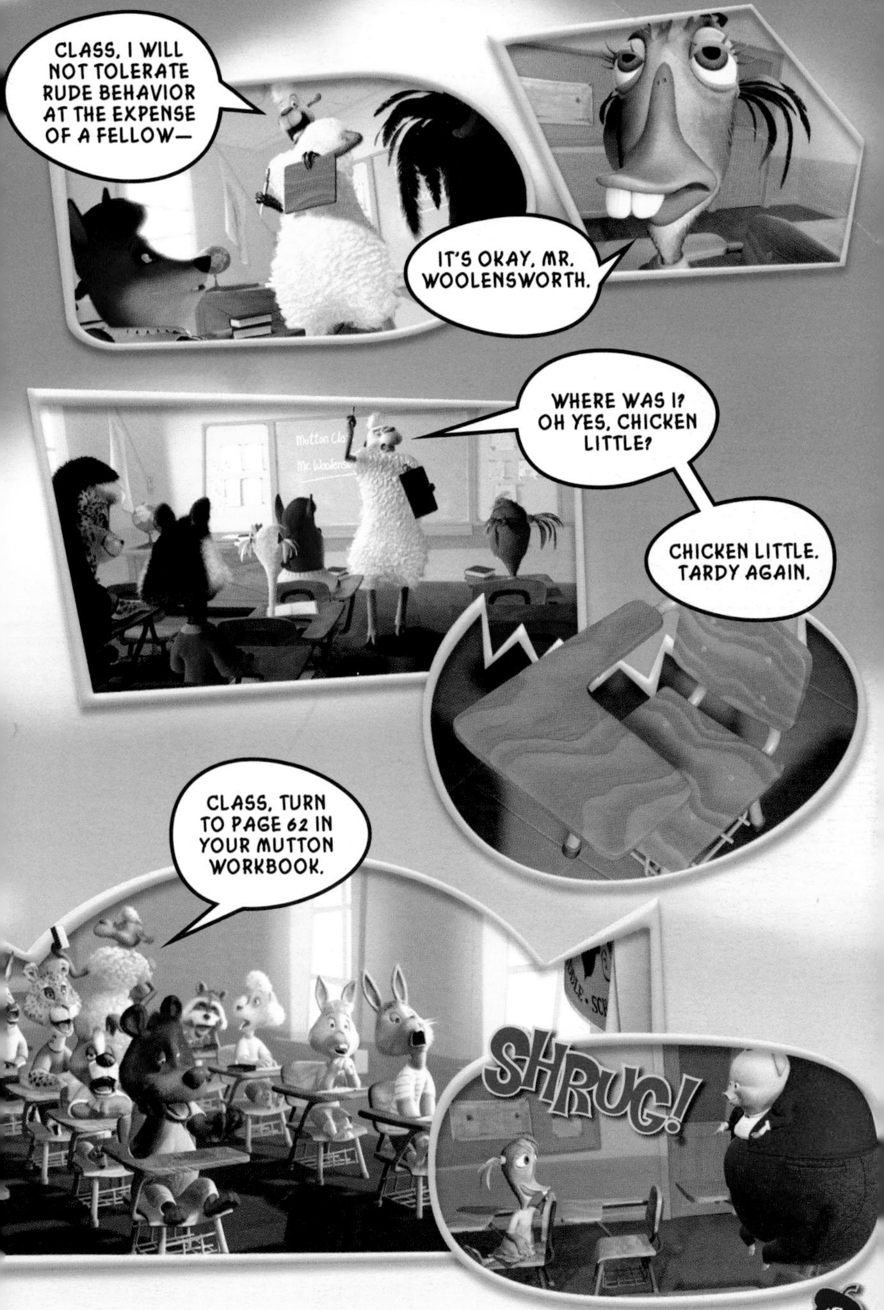
CLASS, I WILL NOT TOLERATE RUDE BEHAVIOR AT THE EXPENSE OF A FELLOW—
IT'S OKAY, MR. WOOLENSWORTH.
WHERE WAS I? OH YES, CHICKEN LITTLE?
CHICKEN LITTLE. TARDY AGAIN.
CLASS, TURN TO PAGE 62 IN YOUR MUTTON WORKBOOK.
SHRUG!

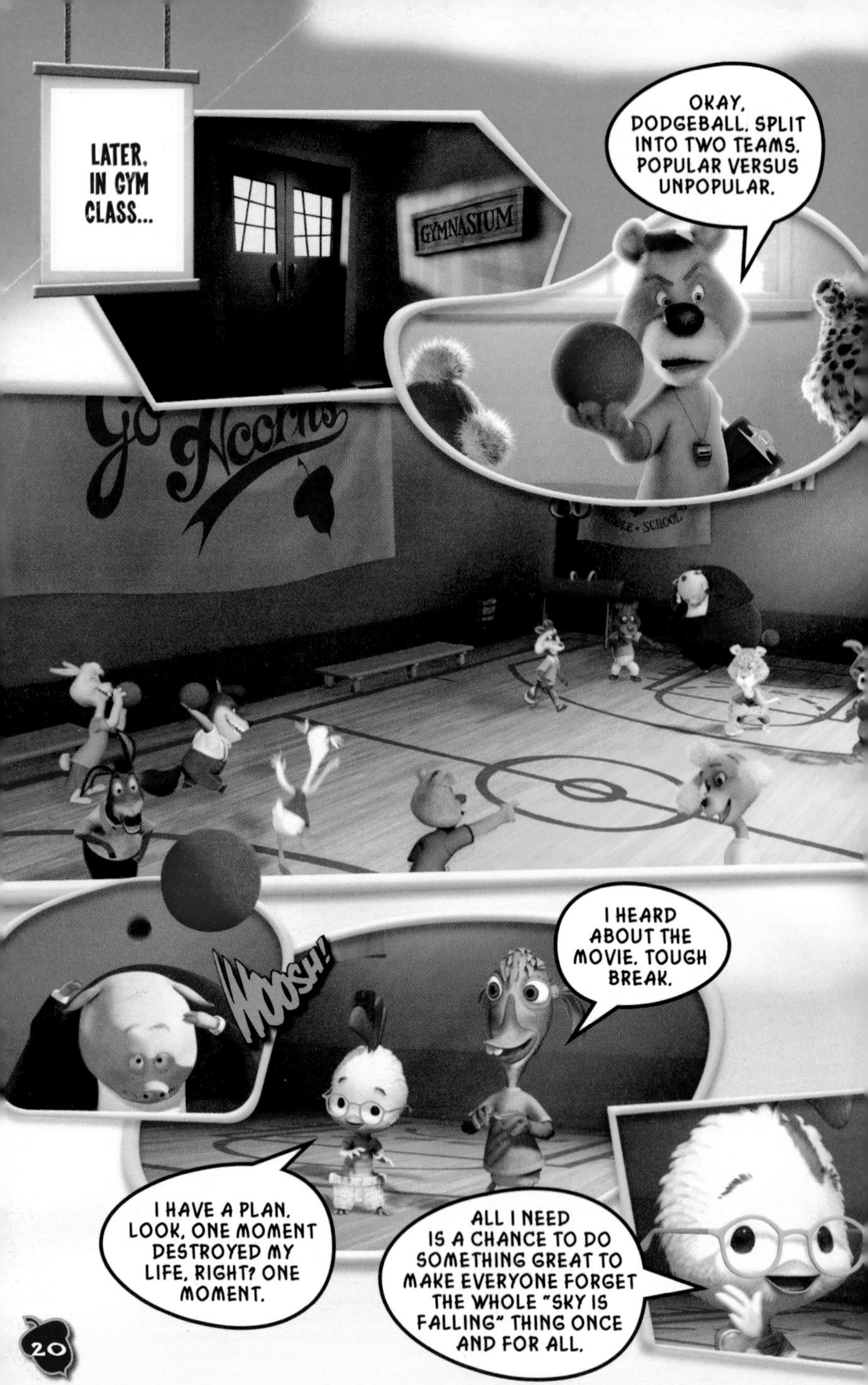
LATER, IN GYM CLASS...
GYMNASIUM
OKAY, DODGEBALL. SPLIT INTO TWO TEAMS. POPULAR VERSUS UNPOPULAR.
Go Acorns
WOOSH!
I HEARD ABOUT THE MOVIE. TOUGH BREAK.
I HAVE A PLAN. LOOK, ONE MOMENT DESTROYED MY LIFE, RIGHT? ONE MOMENT.
ALL I NEED IS A CHANCE TO DO SOMETHING GREAT TO MAKE EVERYONE FORGET THE WHOLE "SKY IS FALLING" THING ONCE AND FOR ALL.

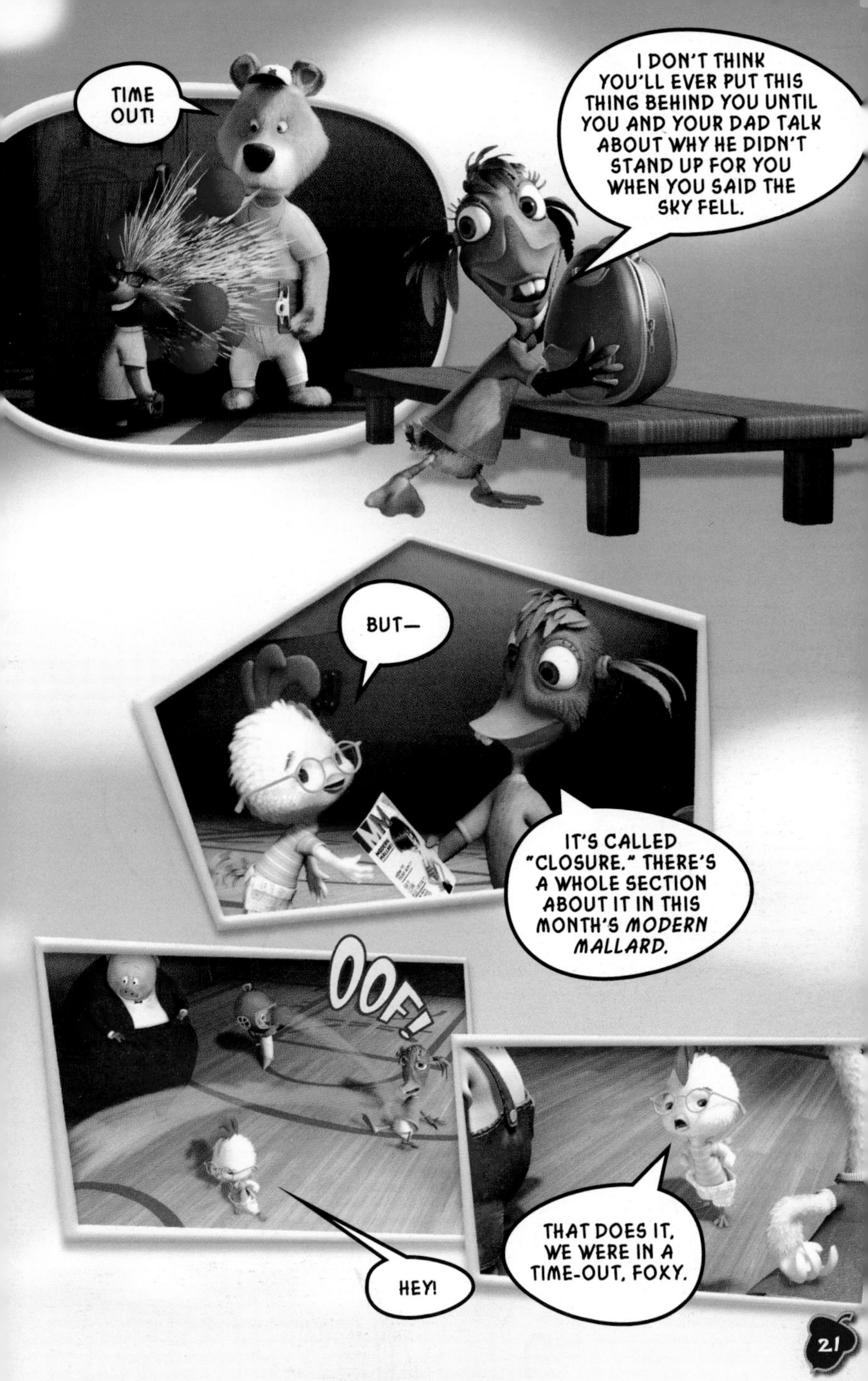
TIME OUT!
I DON'T THINK YOU'LL EVER PUT THIS THING BEHIND YOU UNTIL YOU AND YOUR DAD TALK ABOUT WHY HE DIDN'T STAND UP FOR YOU WHEN YOU SAID THE SKY FELL.
BUT—
IT'S CALLED "CLOSURE." THERE'S A WHOLE SECTION ABOUT IT IN THIS MONTH'S *MODERN MALLARD.*
OOF!
HEY!
THAT DOES IT. WE WERE IN A TIME-OUT, FOXY.

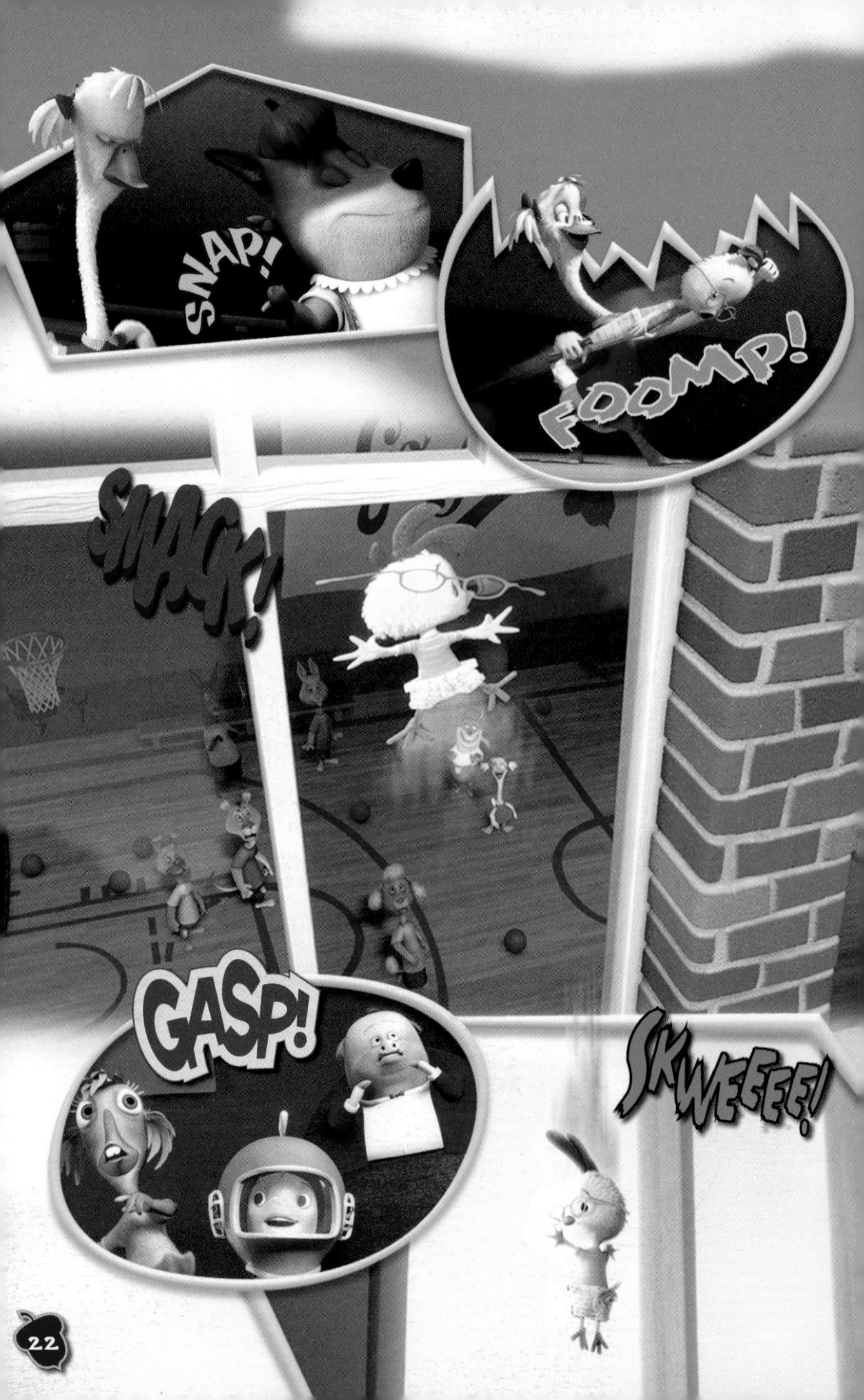
SNAP!
FOOMP!
SMACK!
GASP!
SKWEEEE!

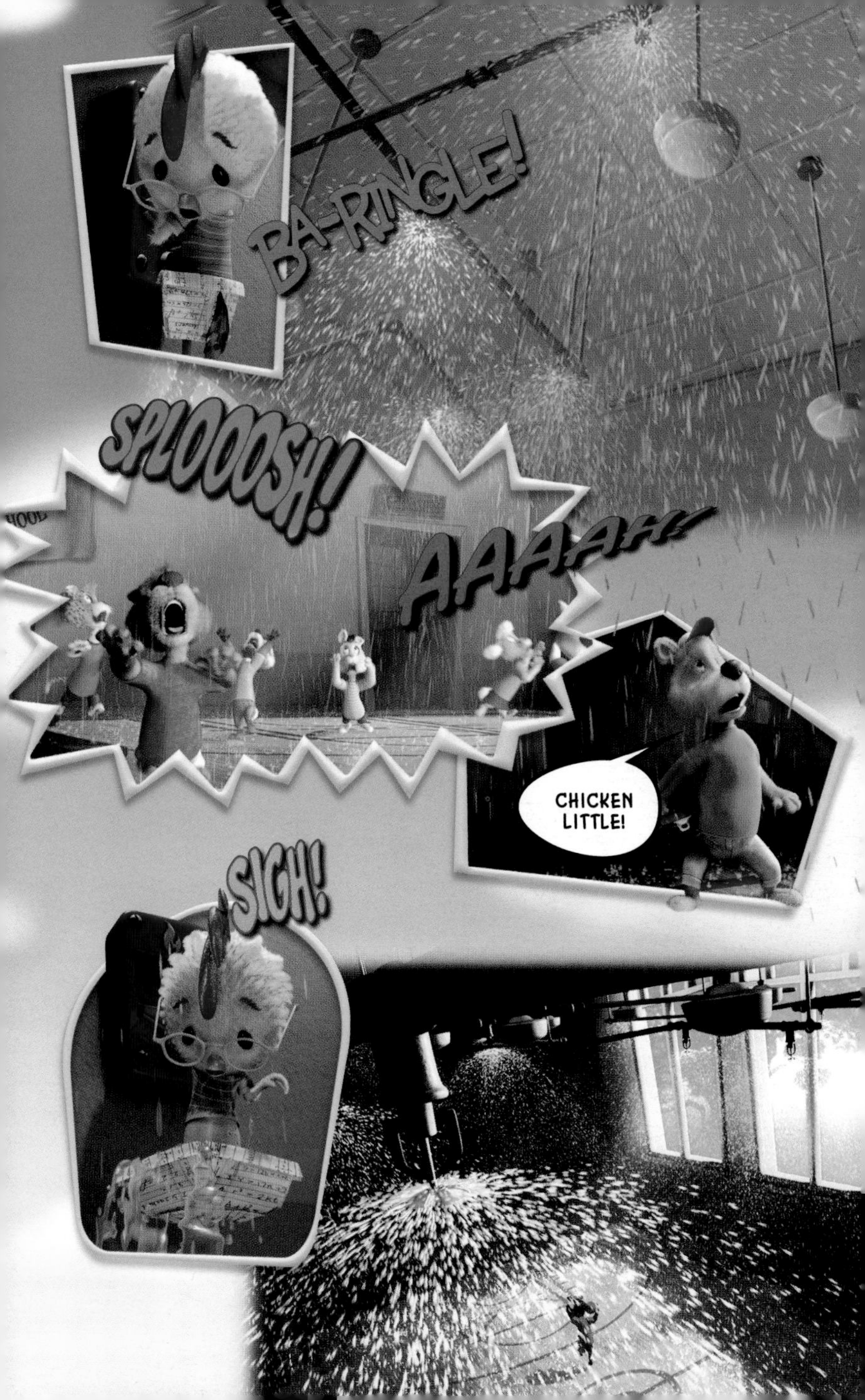
BA-RINGLE!
SPLOOOSH!
AAAAH!
CHICKEN LITTLE!
SIGH!

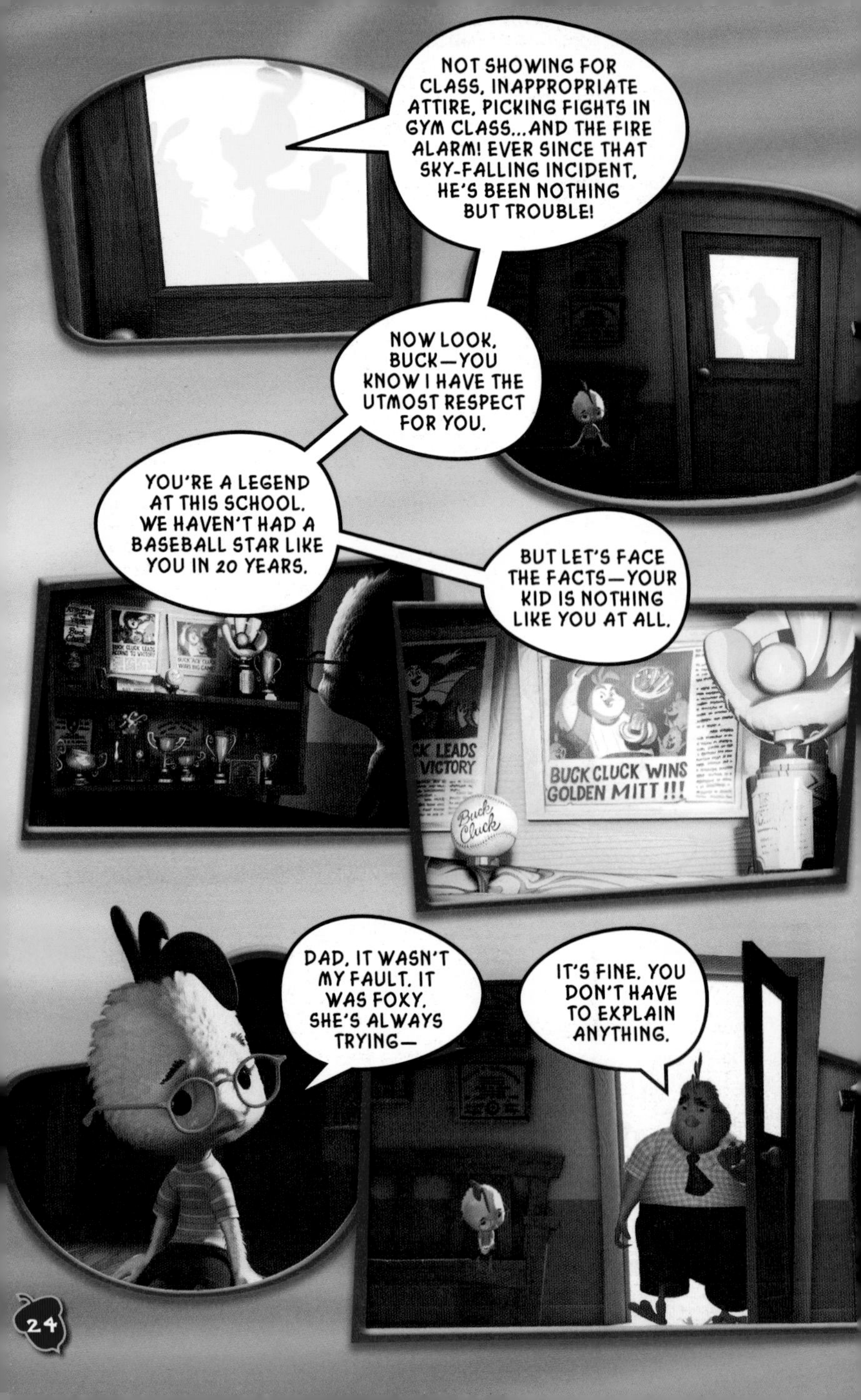
NOT SHOWING FOR CLASS, INAPPROPRIATE ATTIRE, PICKING FIGHTS IN GYM CLASS...AND THE FIRE ALARM! EVER SINCE THAT SKY-FALLING INCIDENT, HE'S BEEN NOTHING BUT TROUBLE!
NOW LOOK, BUCK—YOU KNOW I HAVE THE UTMOST RESPECT FOR YOU.
YOU'RE A LEGEND AT THIS SCHOOL. WE HAVEN'T HAD A BASEBALL STAR LIKE YOU IN 20 YEARS.
BUT LET'S FACE THE FACTS—YOUR KID IS NOTHING LIKE YOU AT ALL.
CK LEADS VICTORY
BUCK CLUCK WINS GOLDEN MITT !!!
Buck Cluck
DAD, IT WASN'T MY FAULT. IT WAS FOXY. SHE'S ALWAYS TRYING—
IT'S FINE. YOU DON'T HAVE TO EXPLAIN ANYTHING.

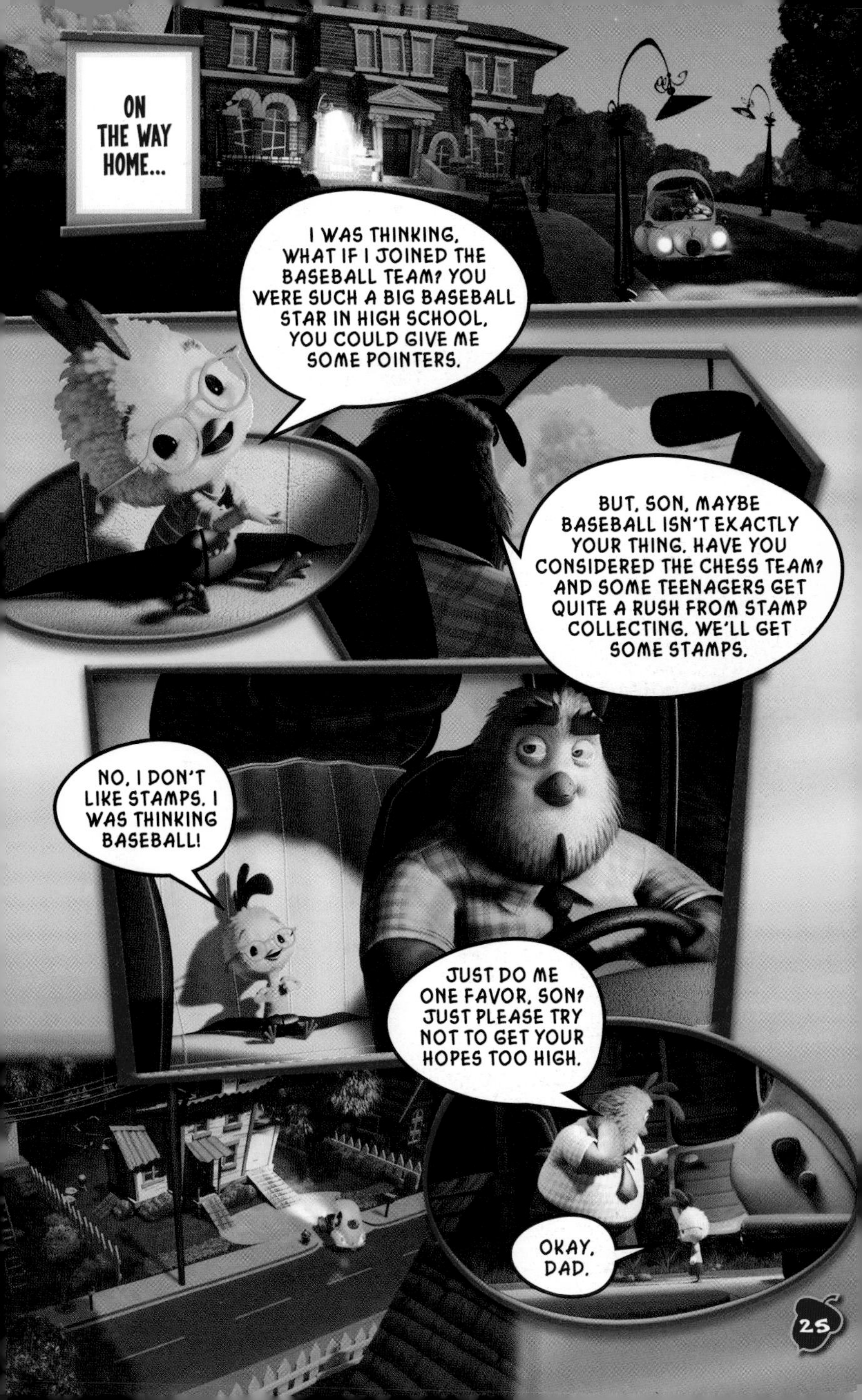

ON THE WAY HOME...
I WAS THINKING, WHAT IF I JOINED THE BASEBALL TEAM? YOU WERE SUCH A BIG BASEBALL STAR IN HIGH SCHOOL, YOU COULD GIVE ME SOME POINTERS.
BUT, SON, MAYBE BASEBALL ISN'T EXACTLY YOUR THING. HAVE YOU CONSIDERED THE CHESS TEAM? AND SOME TEENAGERS GET QUITE A RUSH FROM STAMP COLLECTING. WE'LL GET SOME STAMPS.
NO, I DON'T LIKE STAMPS. I WAS THINKING BASEBALL!
JUST DO ME ONE FAVOR, SON? JUST PLEASE TRY NOT TO GET YOUR HOPES TOO HIGH.
OKAY, DAD.

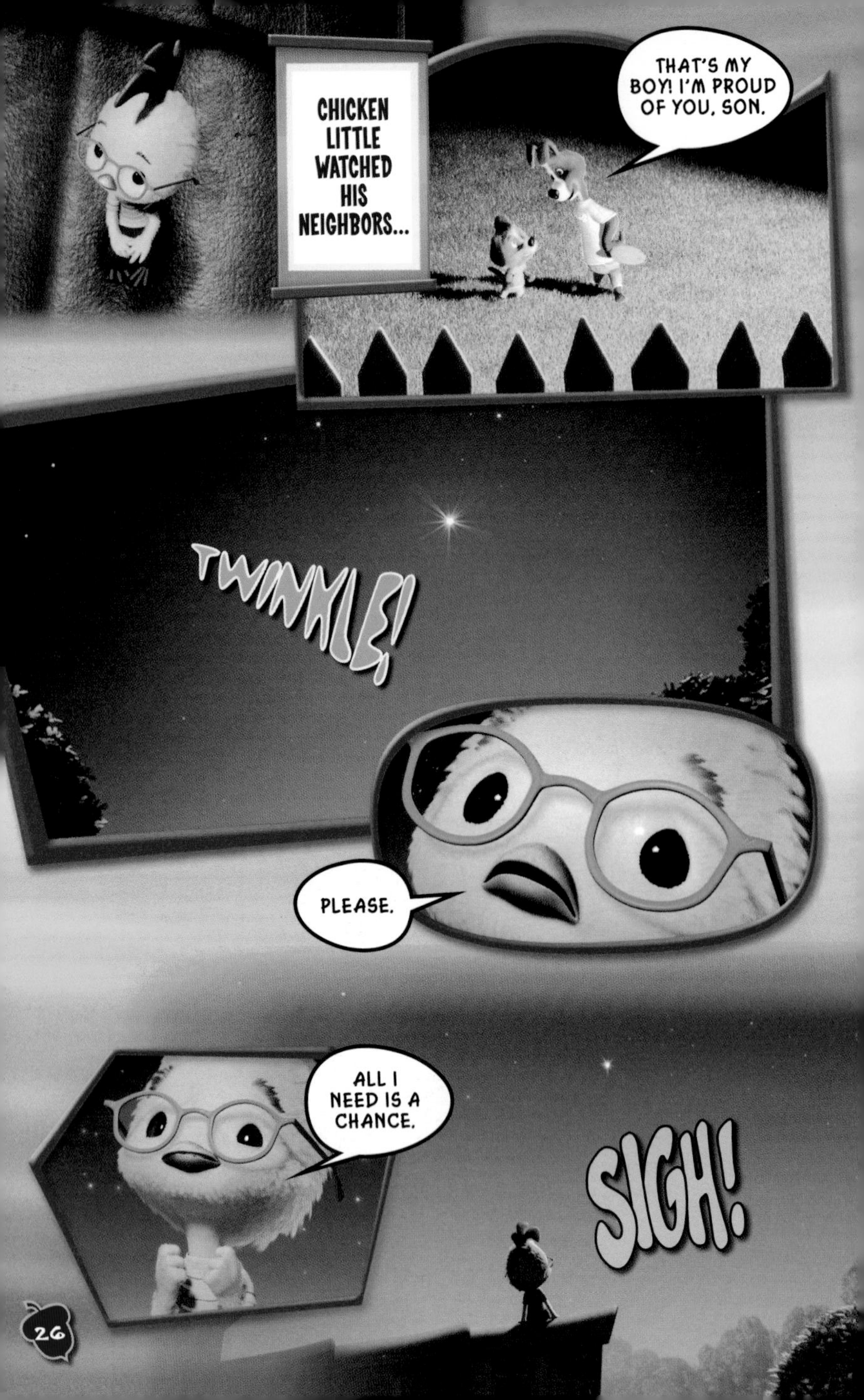
CHICKEN LITTLE WATCHED HIS NEIGHBORS...
THAT'S MY BOY! I'M PROUD OF YOU, SON.
TWINKLE!
PLEASE.
ALL I NEED IS A CHANCE.
SIGH!

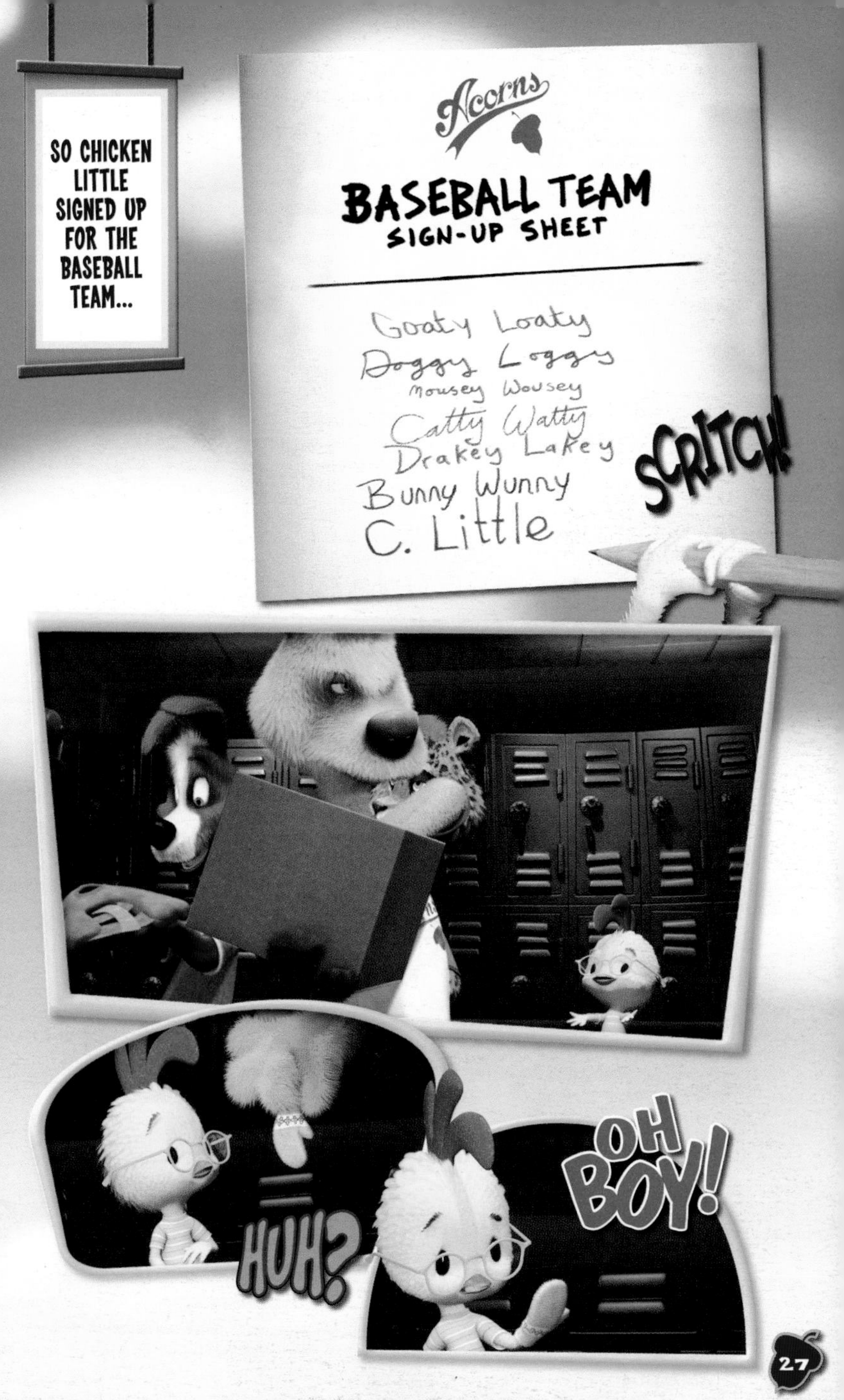
SO CHICKEN LITTLE SIGNED UP FOR THE BASEBALL TEAM...
Acorns
BASEBALL TEAM
SIGN-UP SHEET
Goaty Loaty
Doggy Loggy
Mousey Wousey
Catty Watty
Drakey Lakey
Bunny Wunny
C. Little
SCRITCH!
HUH?
OH BOY!

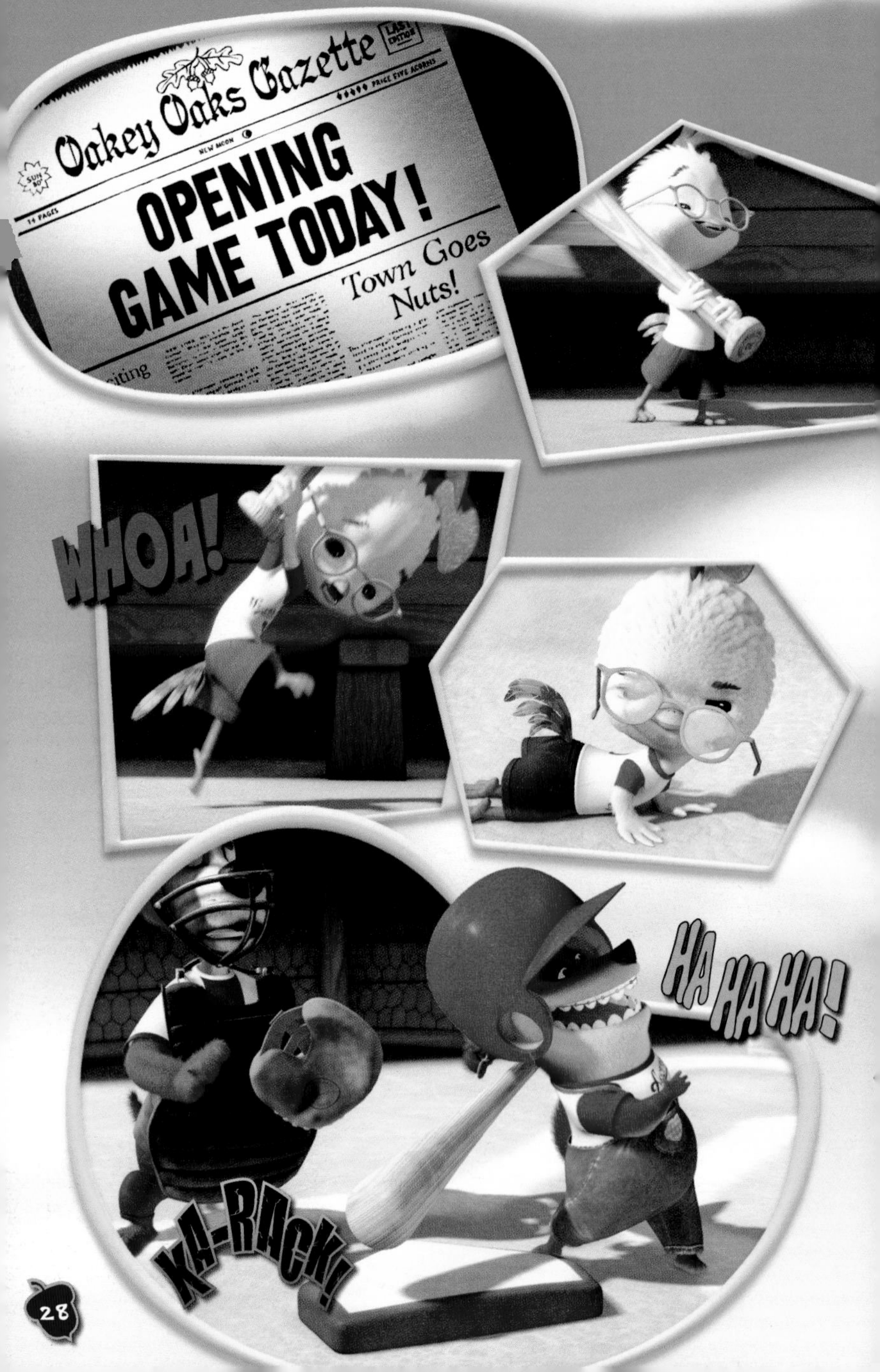
Oakey Oaks Gazette
LAST EDITION
PRICE FIVE ACORNS
NEW MOON
OPENING GAME TODAY!
Town Goes Nuts!
WHOA!
HA HA HA!
KA-RACK!

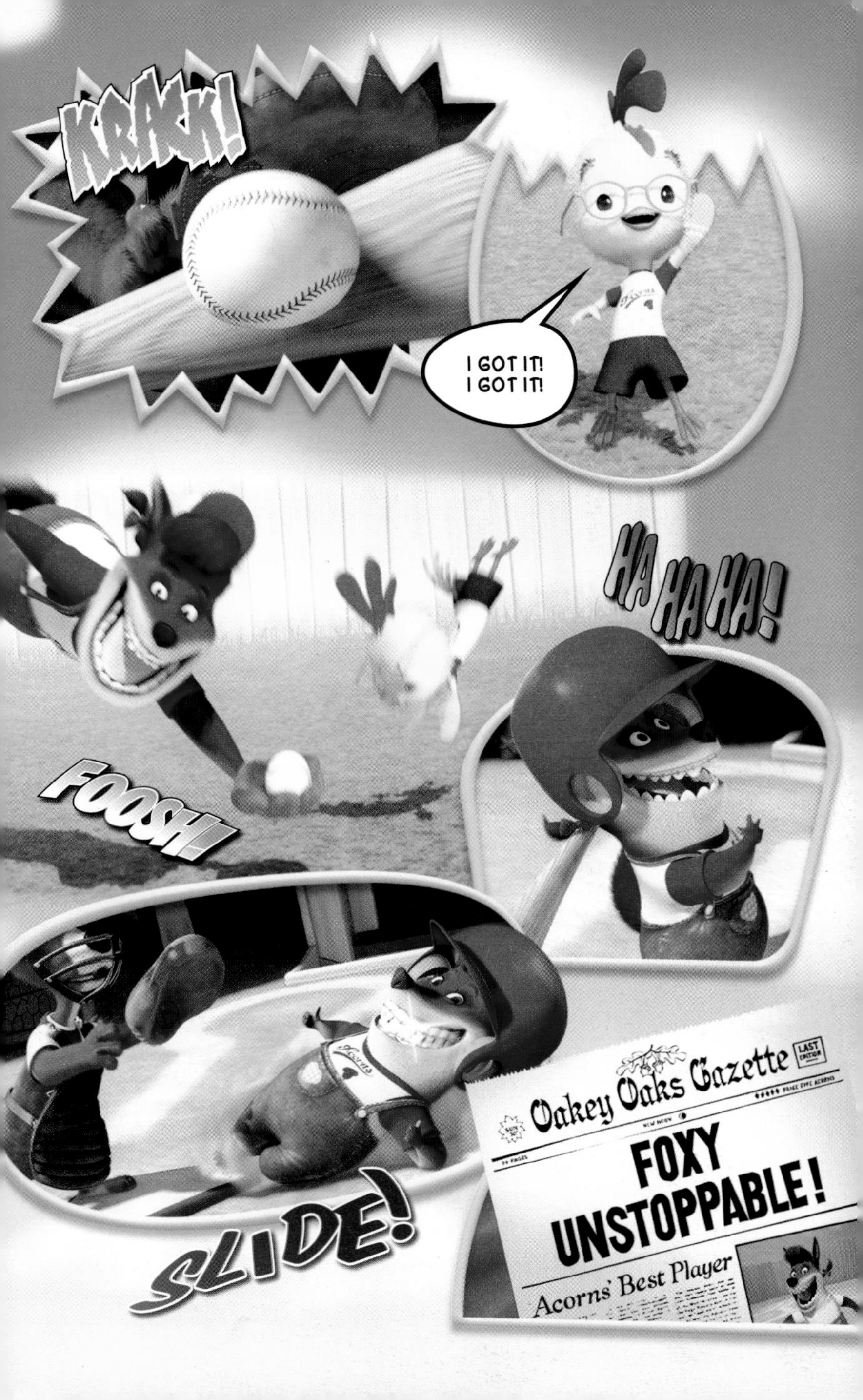
KRACK!
I GOT IT!
I GOT IT!
HA HA HA!
FOOSH!
SLIDE!
Oakey Oaks Gazette
LAST EDITION
FOXY UNSTOPPABLE!
Acorns' Best Player

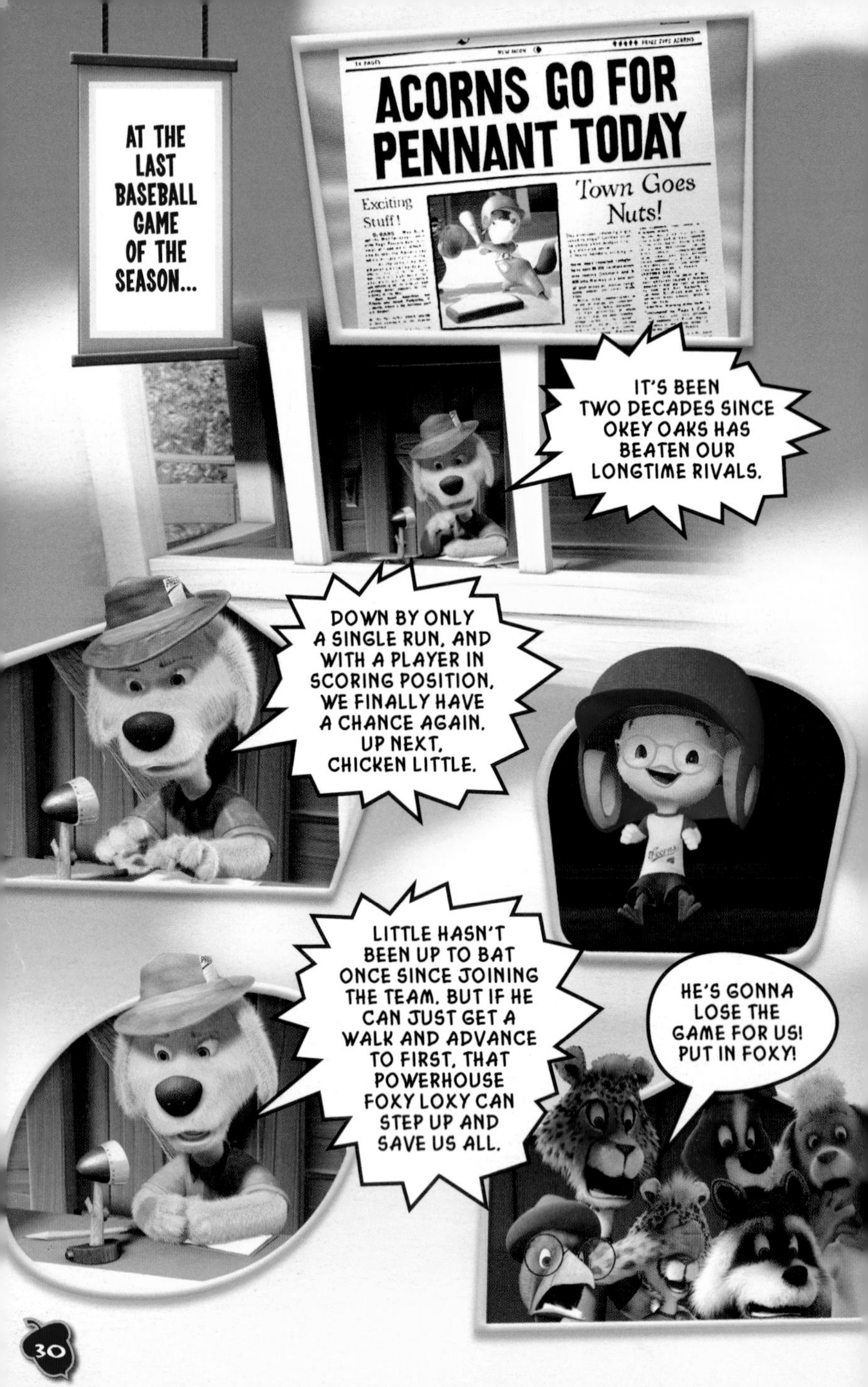
AT THE LAST BASEBALL GAME OF THE SEASON...
ACORNS GO FOR PENNANT TODAY
Exciting Stuff!
Town Goes Nuts!
IT'S BEEN TWO DECADES SINCE OKEY OAKS HAS BEATEN OUR LONGTIME RIVALS.
DOWN BY ONLY A SINGLE RUN, AND WITH A PLAYER IN SCORING POSITION, WE FINALLY HAVE A CHANCE AGAIN. UP NEXT, CHICKEN LITTLE.
LITTLE HASN'T BEEN UP TO BAT ONCE SINCE JOINING THE TEAM. BUT IF HE CAN JUST GET A WALK AND ADVANCE TO FIRST, THAT POWERHOUSE FOXY LOXY CAN STEP UP AND SAVE US ALL.
HE'S GONNA LOSE THE GAME FOR US! PUT IN FOXY!

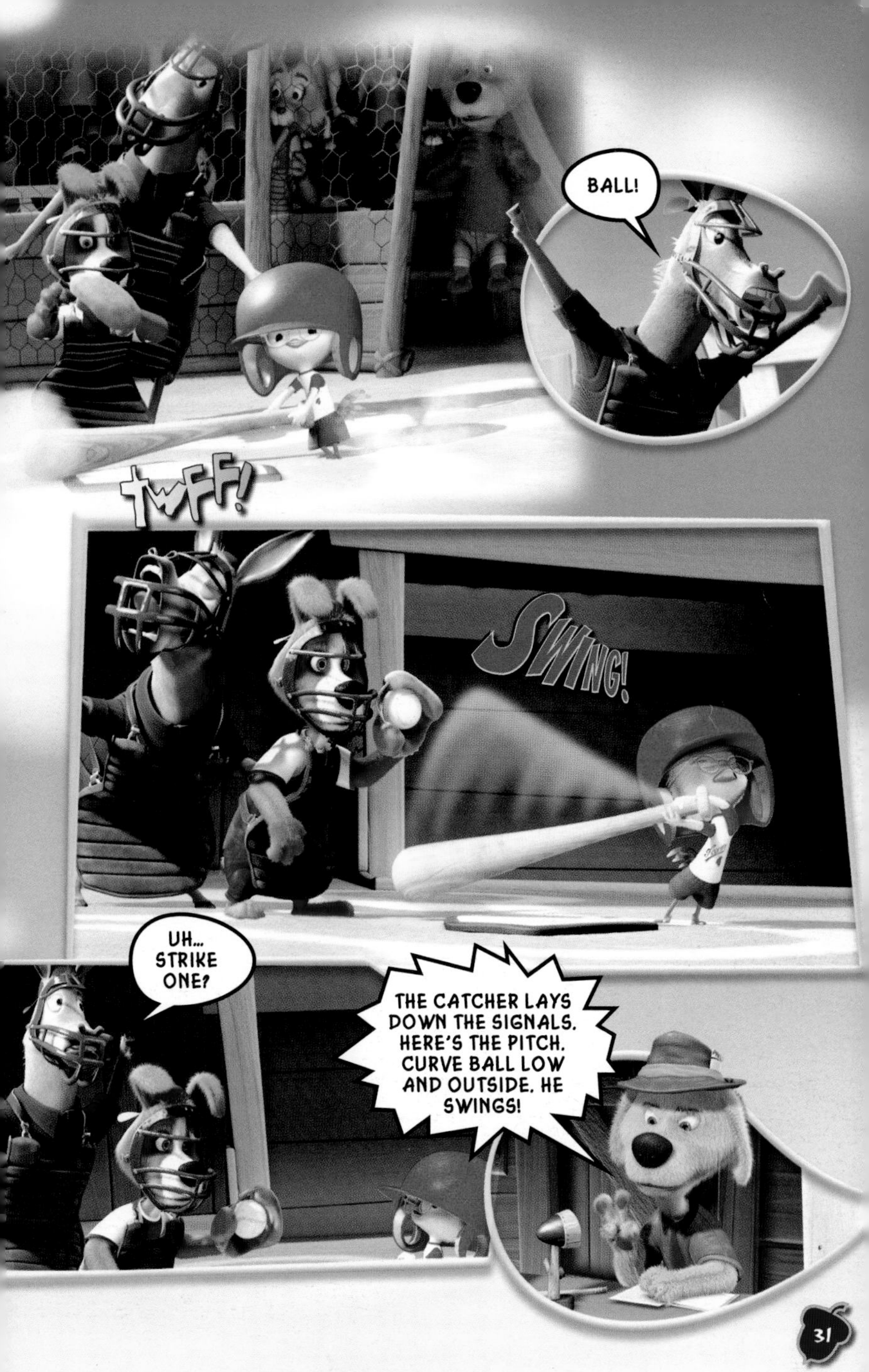
BALL!
TWFF!
SWING!
UH... STRIKE ONE?
THE CATCHER LAYS DOWN THE SIGNALS. HERE'S THE PITCH. CURVE BALL LOW AND OUTSIDE. HE SWINGS!

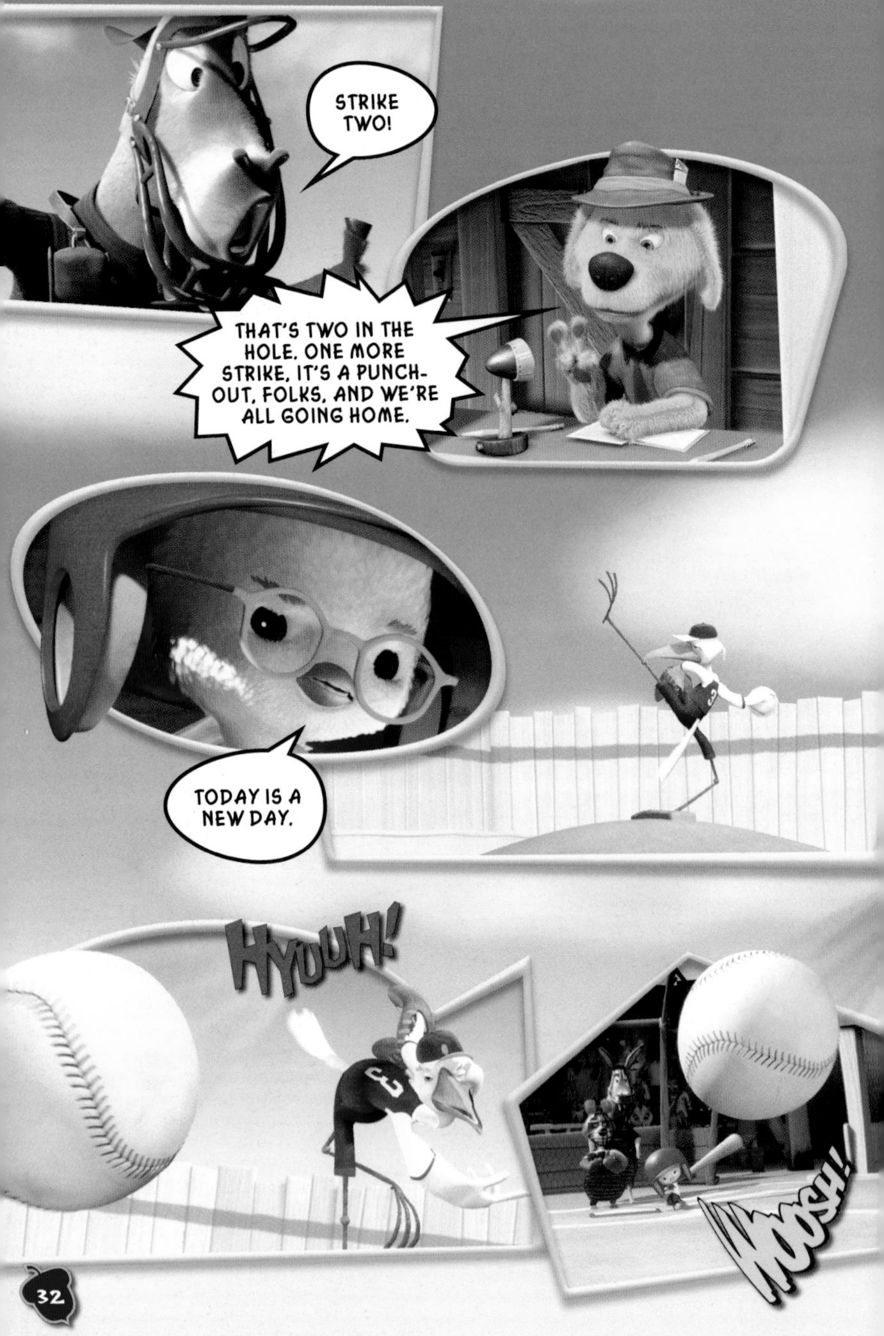
STRIKE TWO!
THAT'S TWO IN THE HOLE. ONE MORE STRIKE, IT'S A PUNCH-OUT, FOLKS, AND WE'RE ALL GOING HOME.
TODAY IS A NEW DAY.
HYUUH!
WHOOSH!

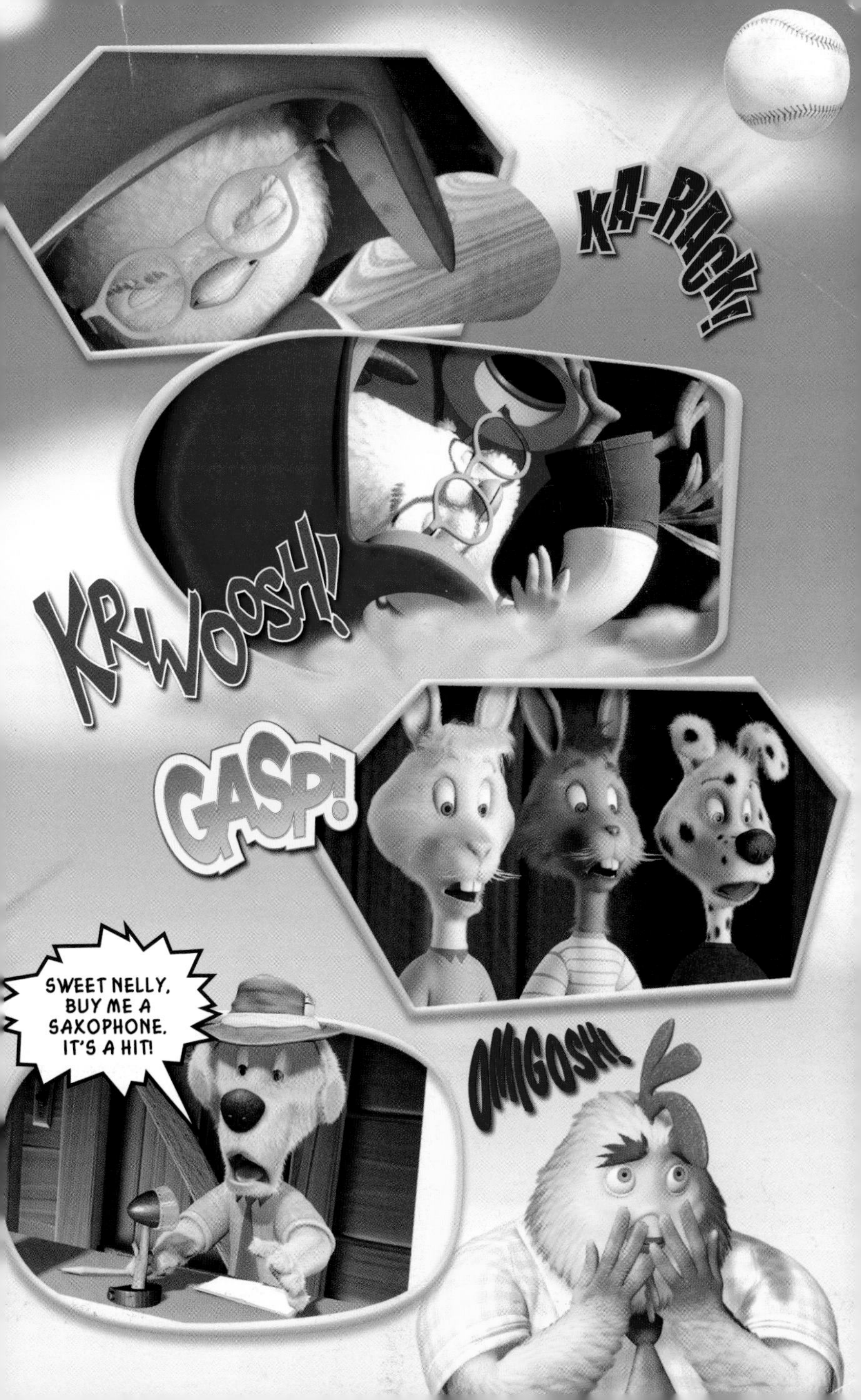
KA-RACK!
KRWOOSH!
GASP!
SWEET NELLY, BUY ME A SAXOPHONE. IT'S A HIT!
OMIGOSH!

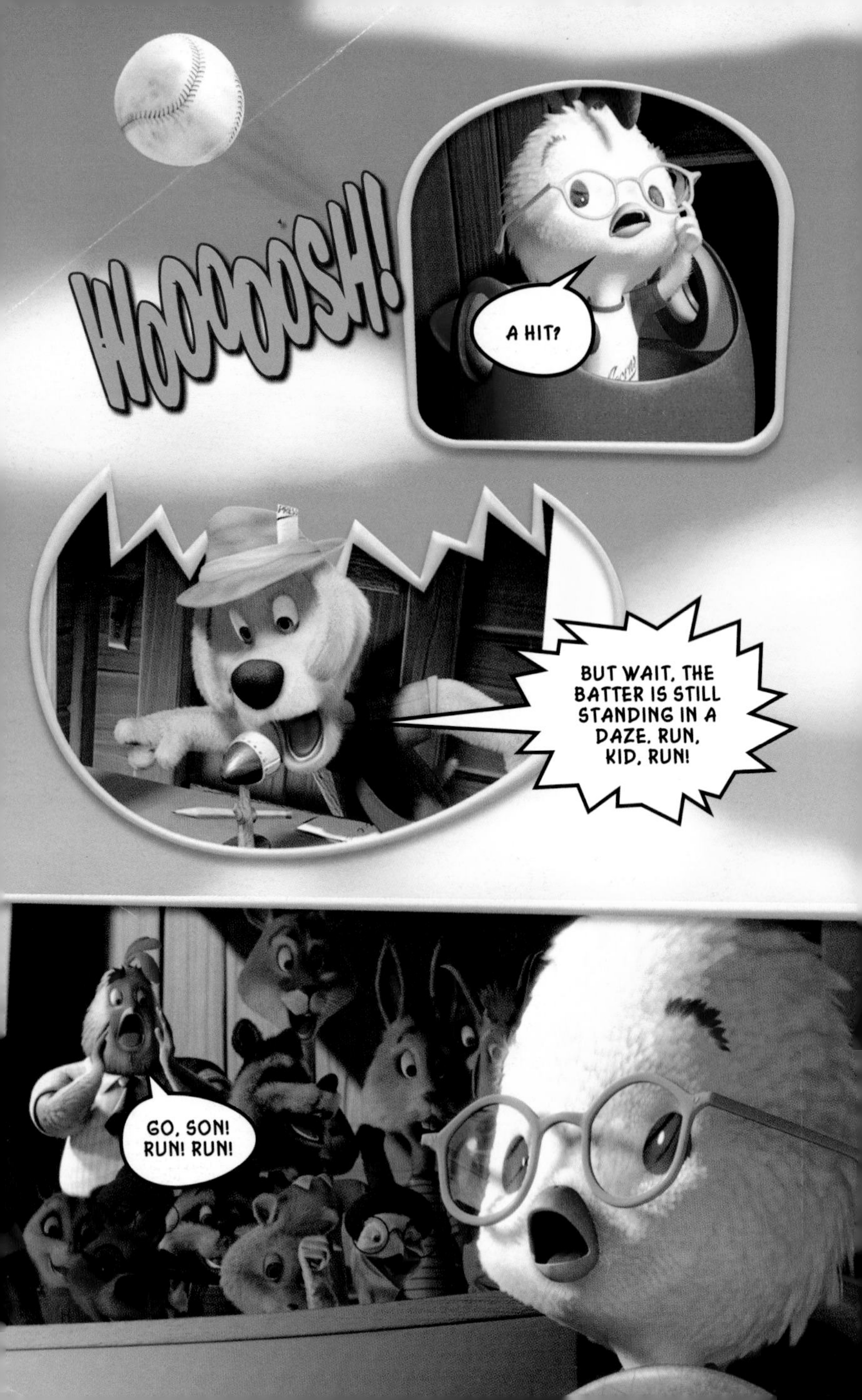
WHOOOOSH!
A HIT?
BUT WAIT, THE BATTER IS STILL STANDING IN A DAZE. RUN, KID, RUN!
GO, SON! RUN! RUN!

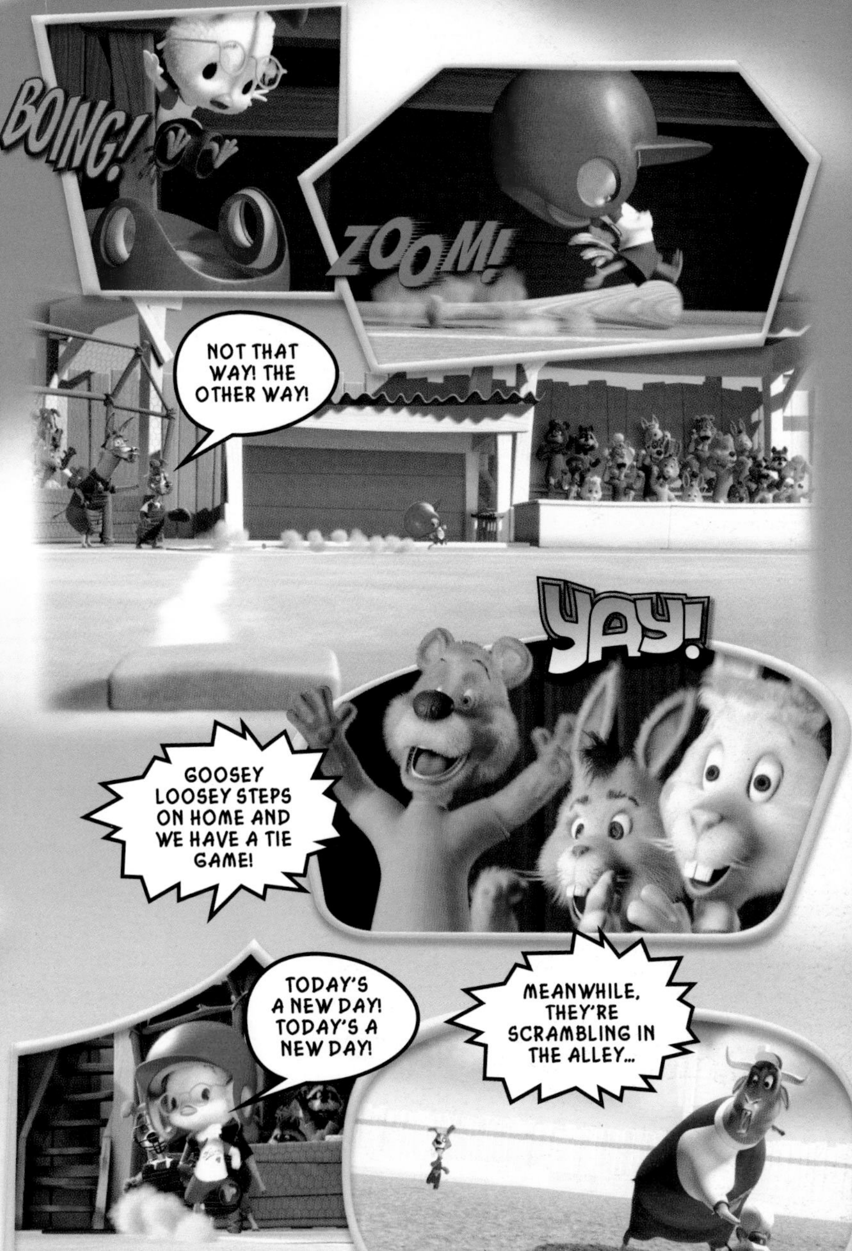
BOING!
ZOOM!
NOT THAT WAY! THE OTHER WAY!
YAY!
GOOSEY LOOSEY STEPS ON HOME AND WE HAVE A TIE GAME!
TODAY'S A NEW DAY! TODAY'S A NEW DAY!
MEANWHILE, THEY'RE SCRAMBLING IN THE ALLEY...

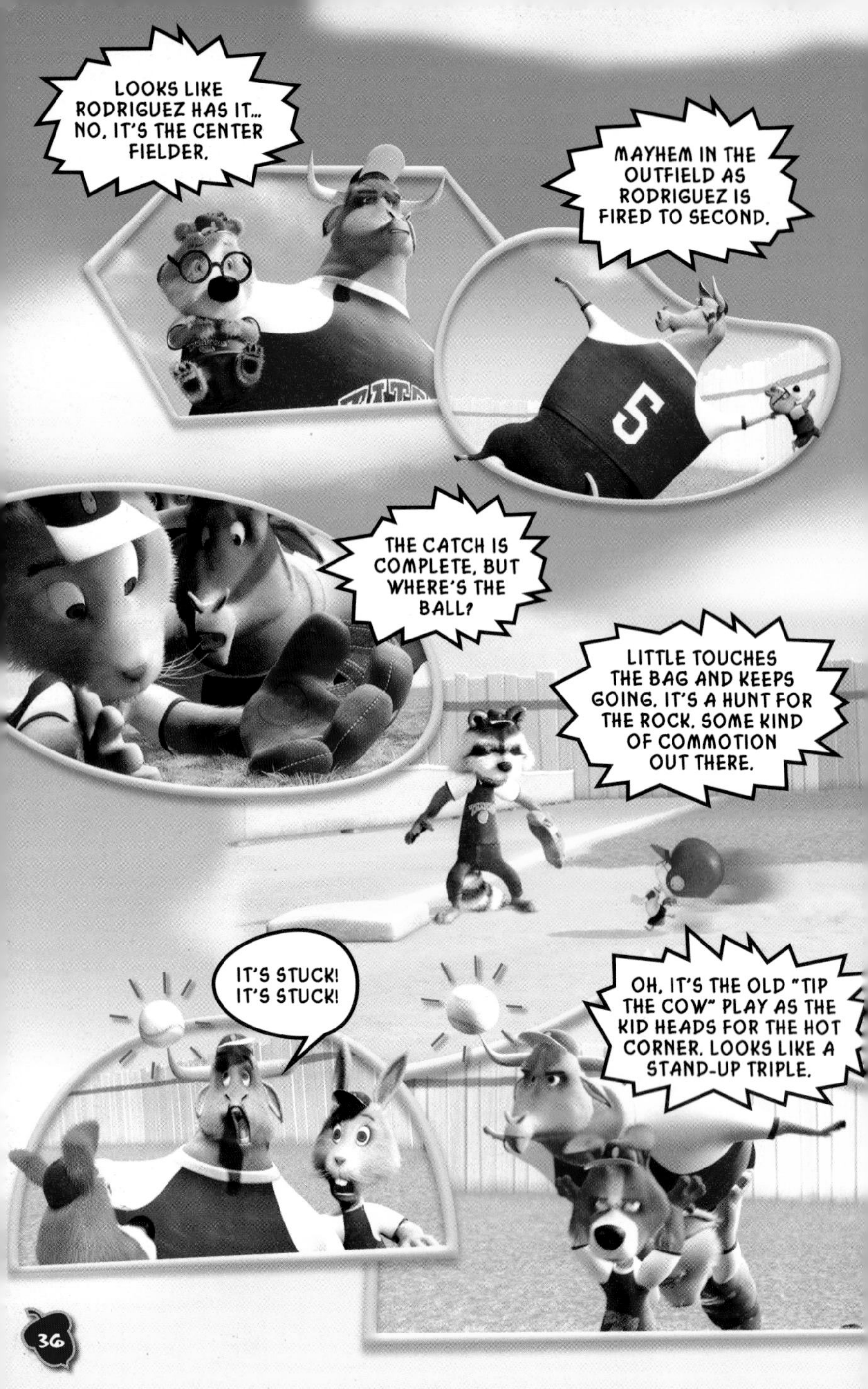
LOOKS LIKE RODRIGUEZ HAS IT... NO, IT'S THE CENTER FIELDER.
MAYHEM IN THE OUTFIELD AS RODRIGUEZ IS FIRED TO SECOND.
THE CATCH IS COMPLETE, BUT WHERE'S THE BALL?
LITTLE TOUCHES THE BAG AND KEEPS GOING. IT'S A HUNT FOR THE ROCK. SOME KIND OF COMMOTION OUT THERE.
IT'S STUCK! IT'S STUCK!
OH, IT'S THE OLD "TIP THE COW" PLAY AS THE KID HEADS FOR THE HOT CORNER. LOOKS LIKE A STAND-UP TRIPLE.

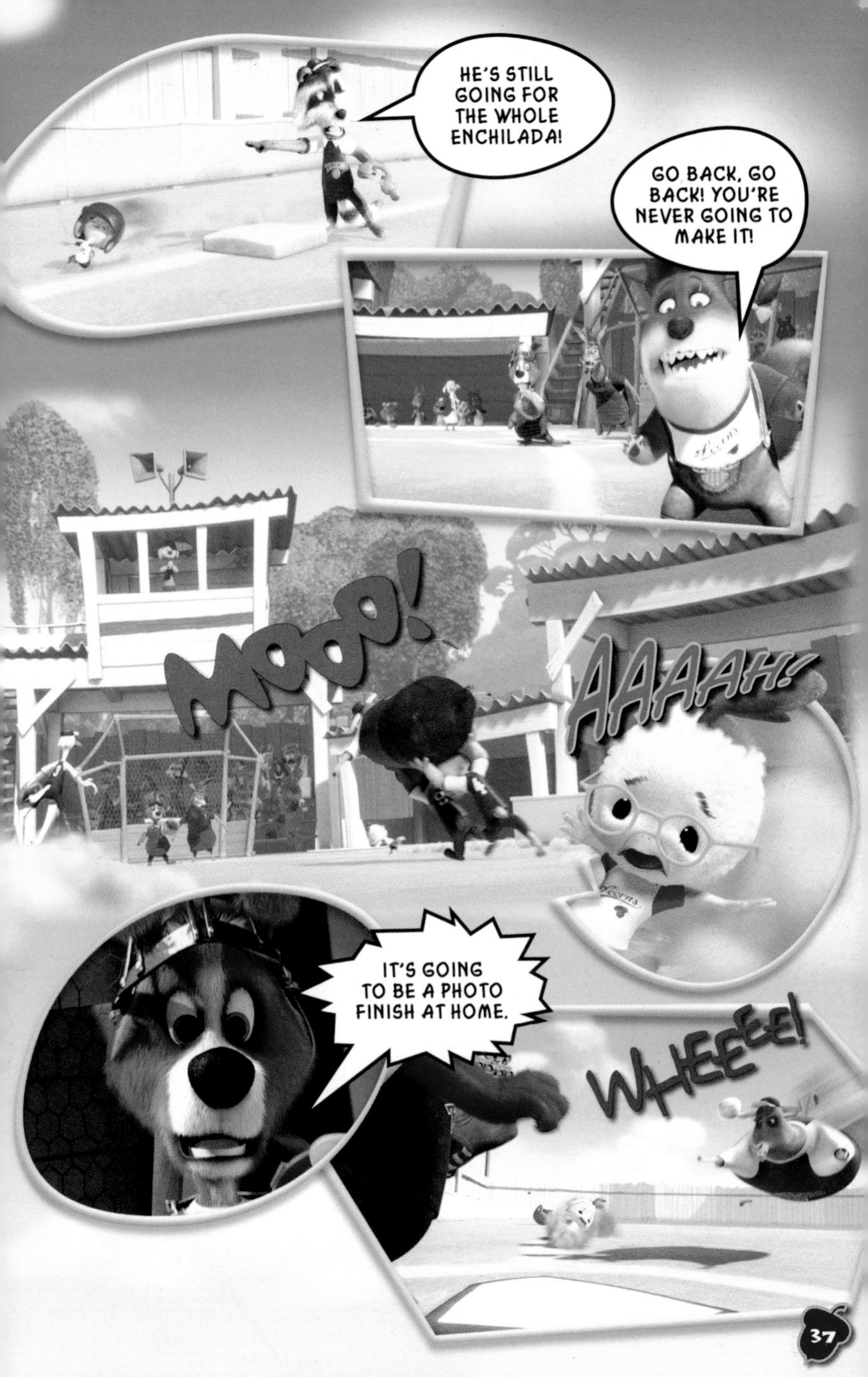
HE'S STILL GOING FOR THE WHOLE ENCHILADA!
GO BACK, GO BACK! YOU'RE NEVER GOING TO MAKE IT!
MOOO!
AAAAH!
IT'S GOING TO BE A PHOTO FINISH AT HOME.
WHEEEE!

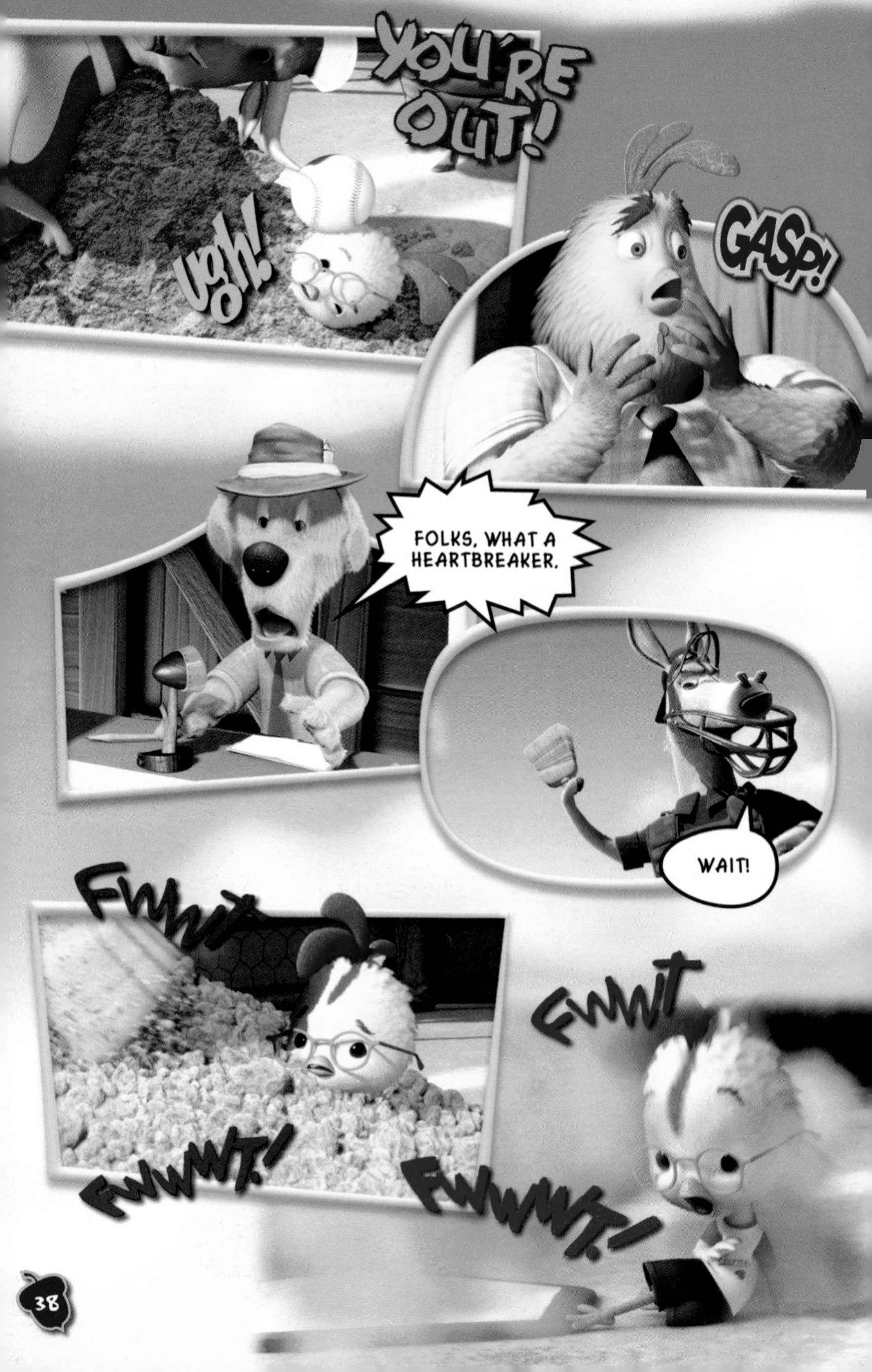
YOU'RE OUT!
UGH!
GASP!
FOLKS, WHAT A HEARTBREAKER.
WAIT!
FWWT
FWWWT!
FWWT
FWWWT!

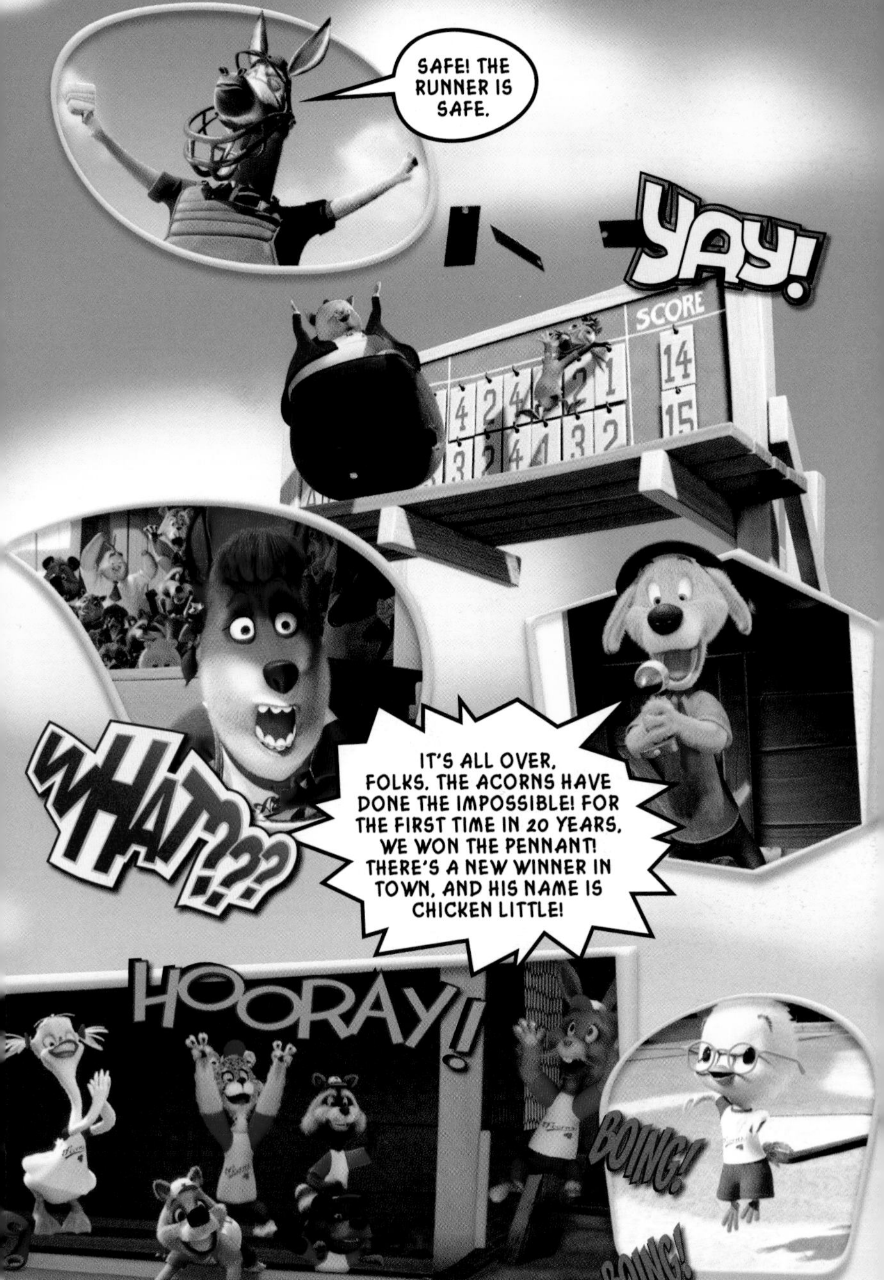
SAFE! THE RUNNER IS SAFE.
YAY!
SCORE
WHAT?!??
IT'S ALL OVER, FOLKS. THE ACORNS HAVE DONE THE IMPOSSIBLE! FOR THE FIRST TIME IN 20 YEARS, WE WON THE PENNANT! THERE'S A NEW WINNER IN TOWN, AND HIS NAME IS CHICKEN LITTLE!
HOORAY!!
BOING!
BOING!

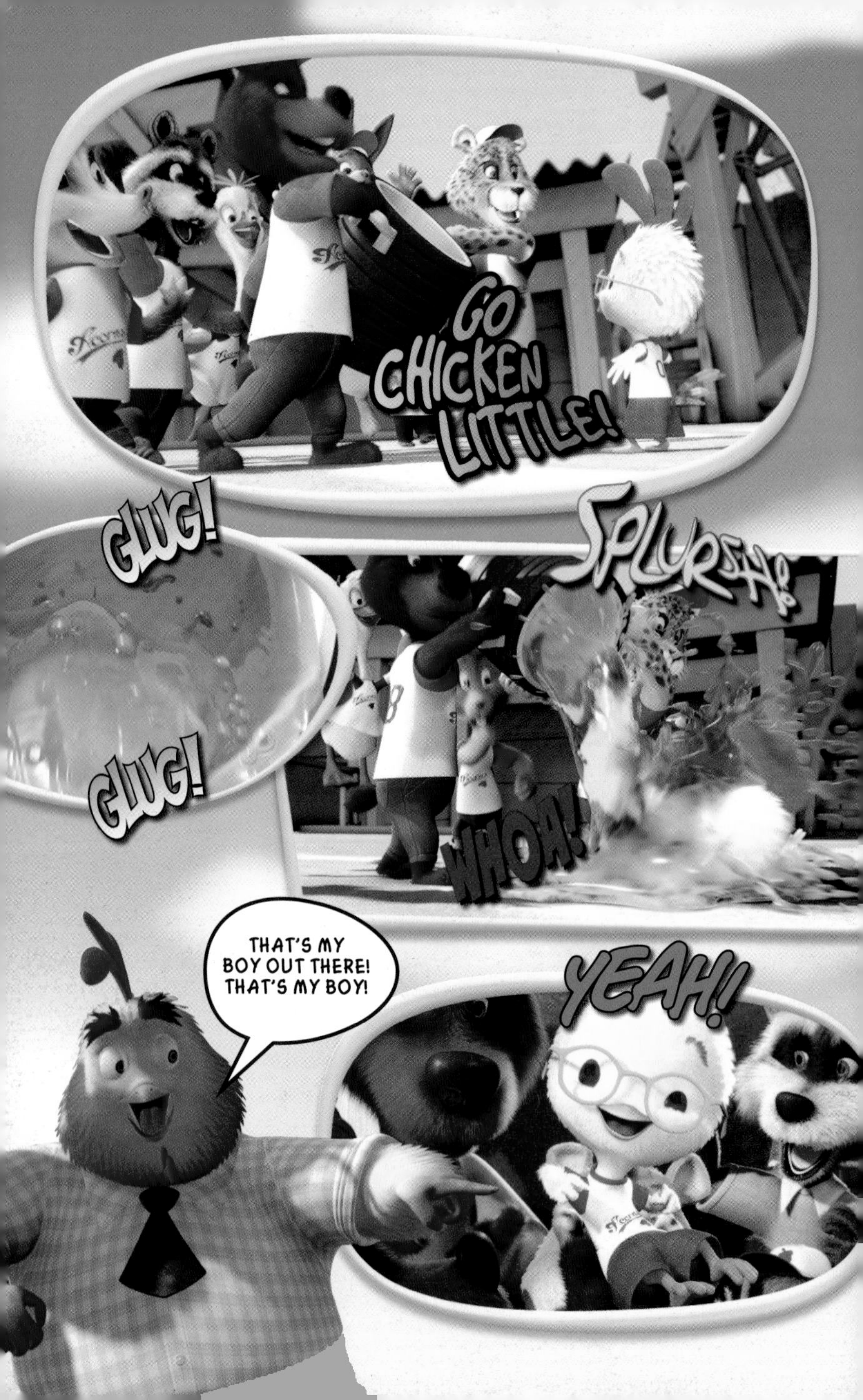
GO CHICKEN LITTLE!
GLUG!
GLUG!
SPLURSH!
WHOA!
THAT'S MY BOY OUT THERE! THAT'S MY BOY!
YEAH!

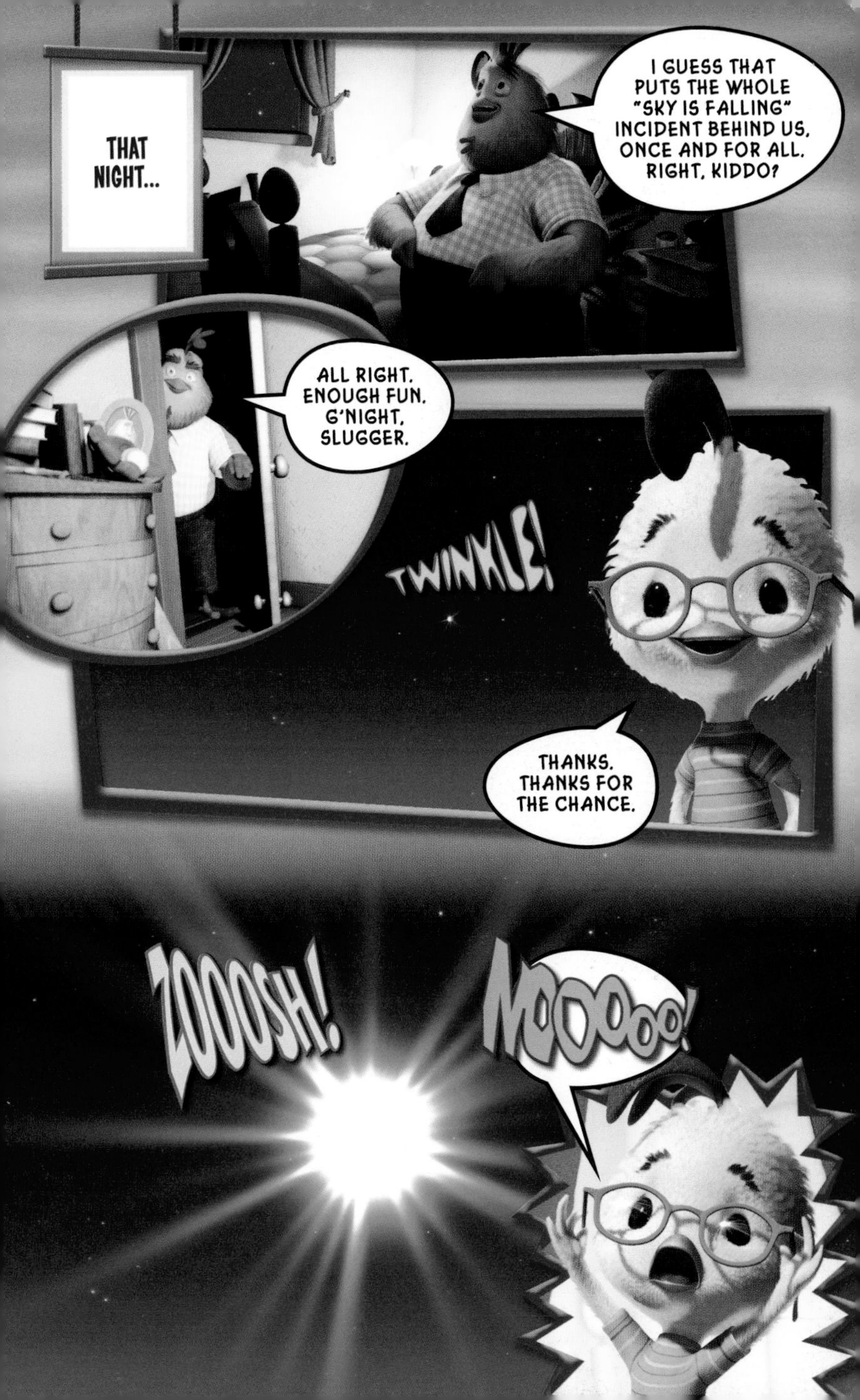
THAT NIGHT...
I GUESS THAT PUTS THE WHOLE "SKY IS FALLING" INCIDENT BEHIND US, ONCE AND FOR ALL, RIGHT, KIDDO?
ALL RIGHT. ENOUGH FUN. G'NIGHT, SLUGGER.
TWINKLE!
THANKS. THANKS FOR THE CHANCE.
ZOOOSH!
NOOOoo!

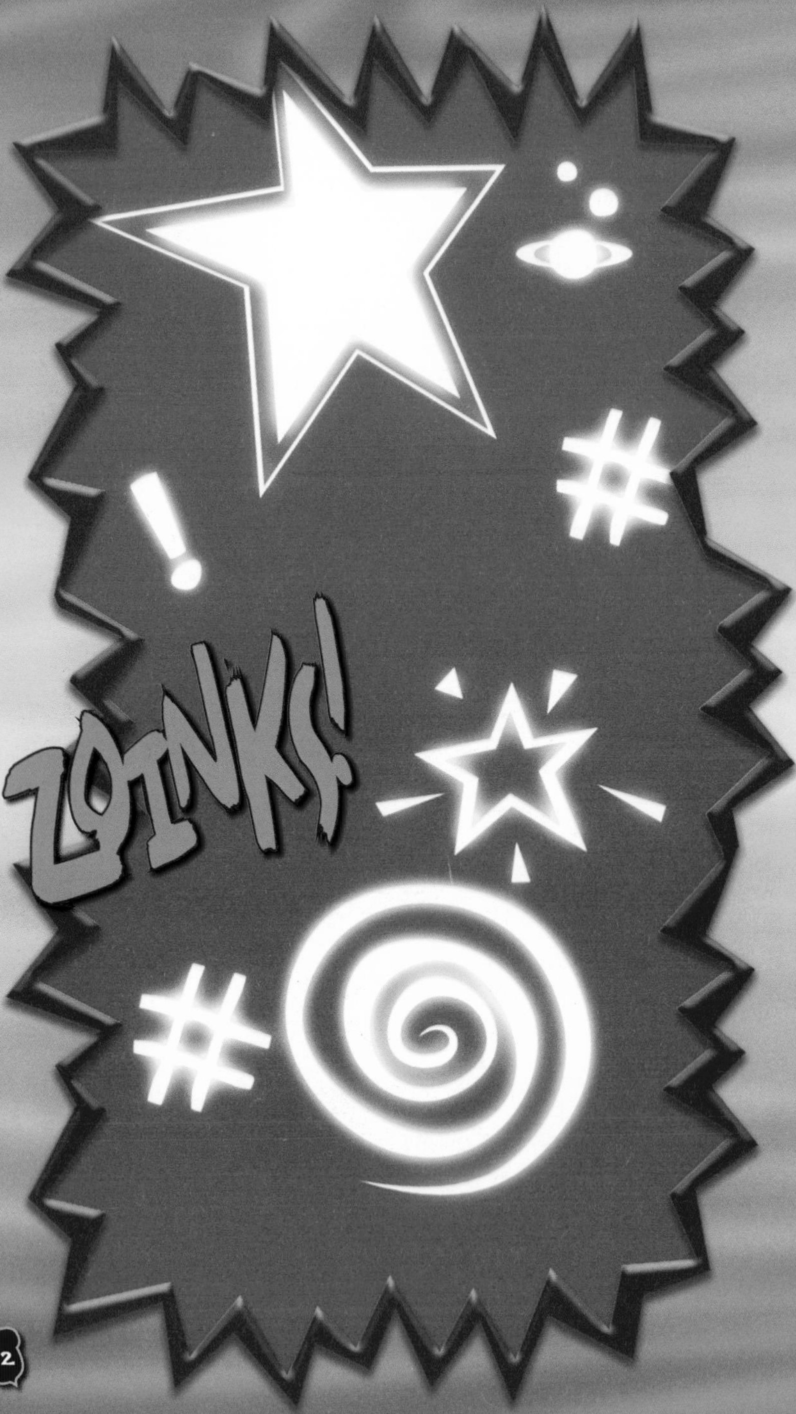
ZOINKS!

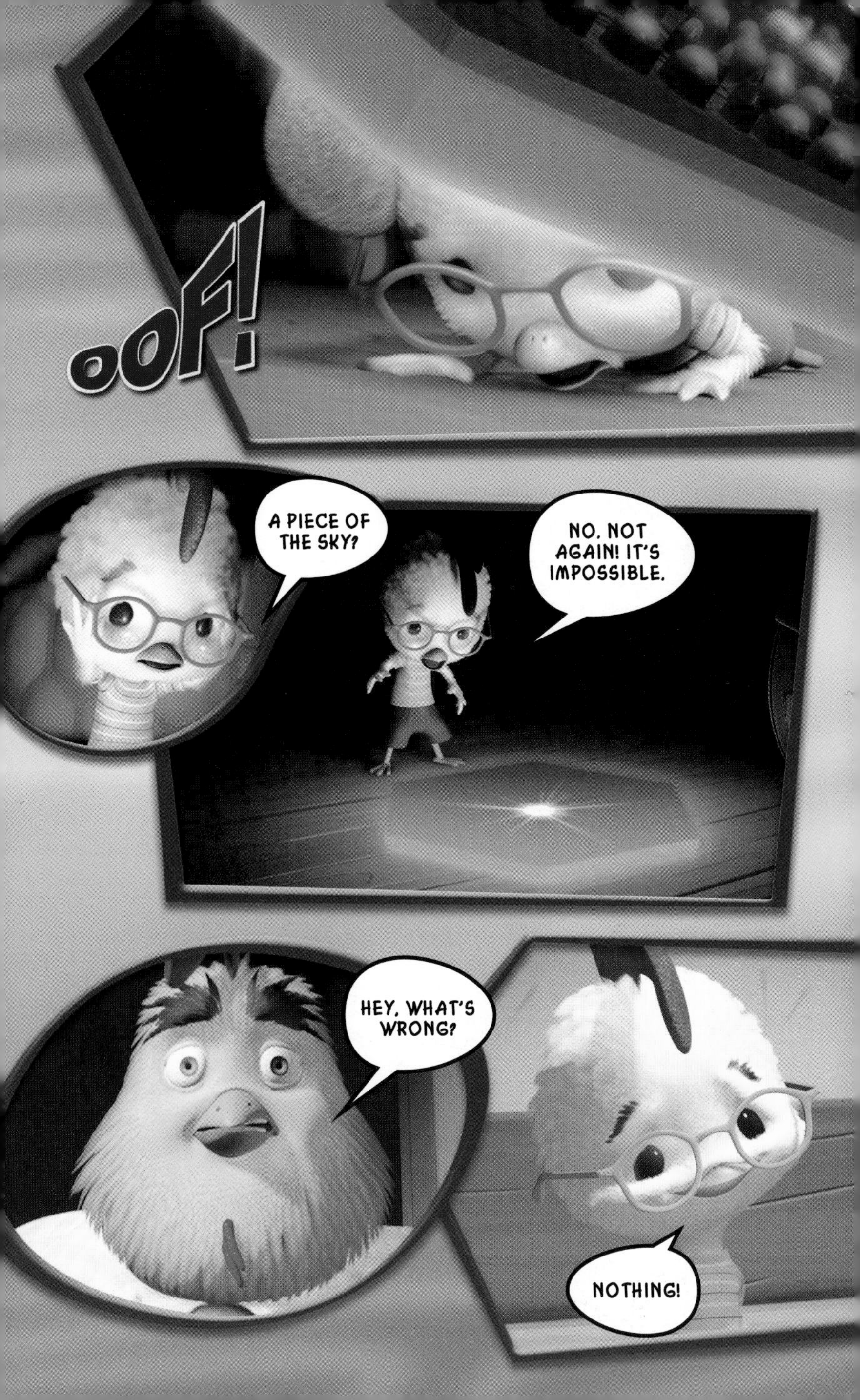
OOF!
A PIECE OF THE SKY?
NO. NOT AGAIN! IT'S IMPOSSIBLE.
HEY, WHAT'S WRONG?
NOTHING!

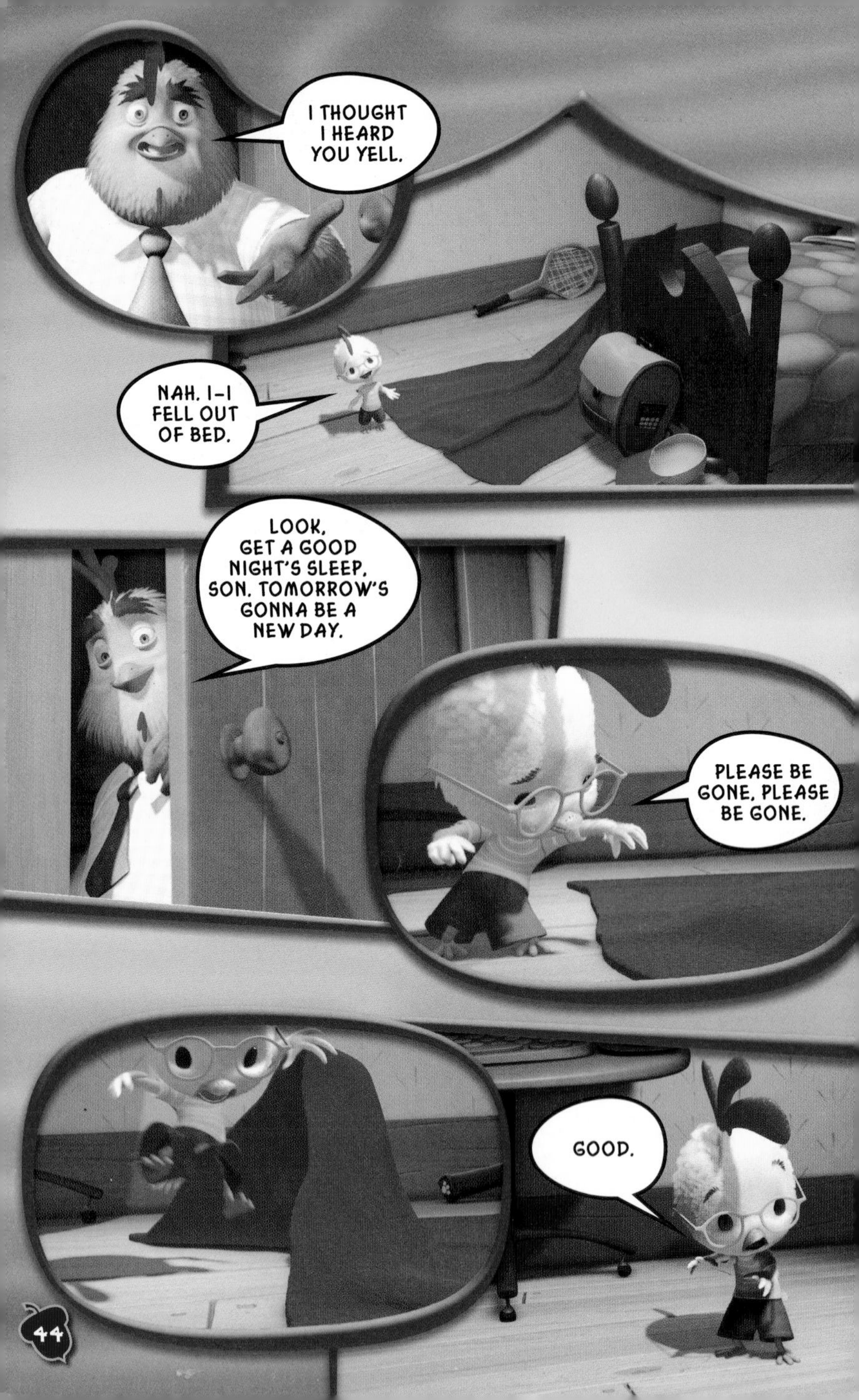
I THOUGHT I HEARD YOU YELL.
NAH. I-I FELL OUT OF BED.
LOOK, GET A GOOD NIGHT'S SLEEP, SON. TOMORROW'S GONNA BE A NEW DAY.
PLEASE BE GONE, PLEASE BE GONE.
GOOD.

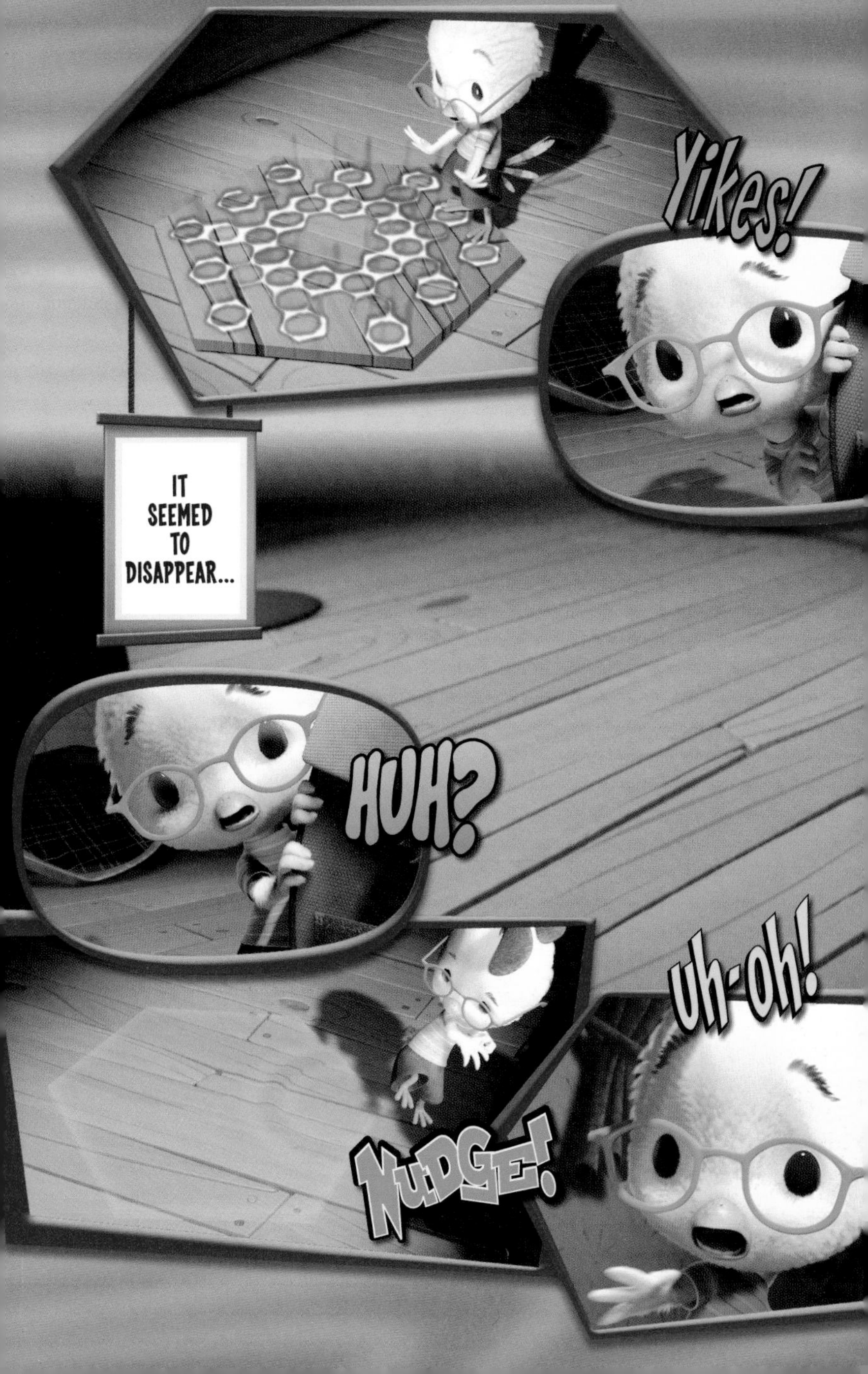
Yikes!
IT SEEMED TO DISAPPEAR...
HUH?
Uh-oh!
NUDGE!

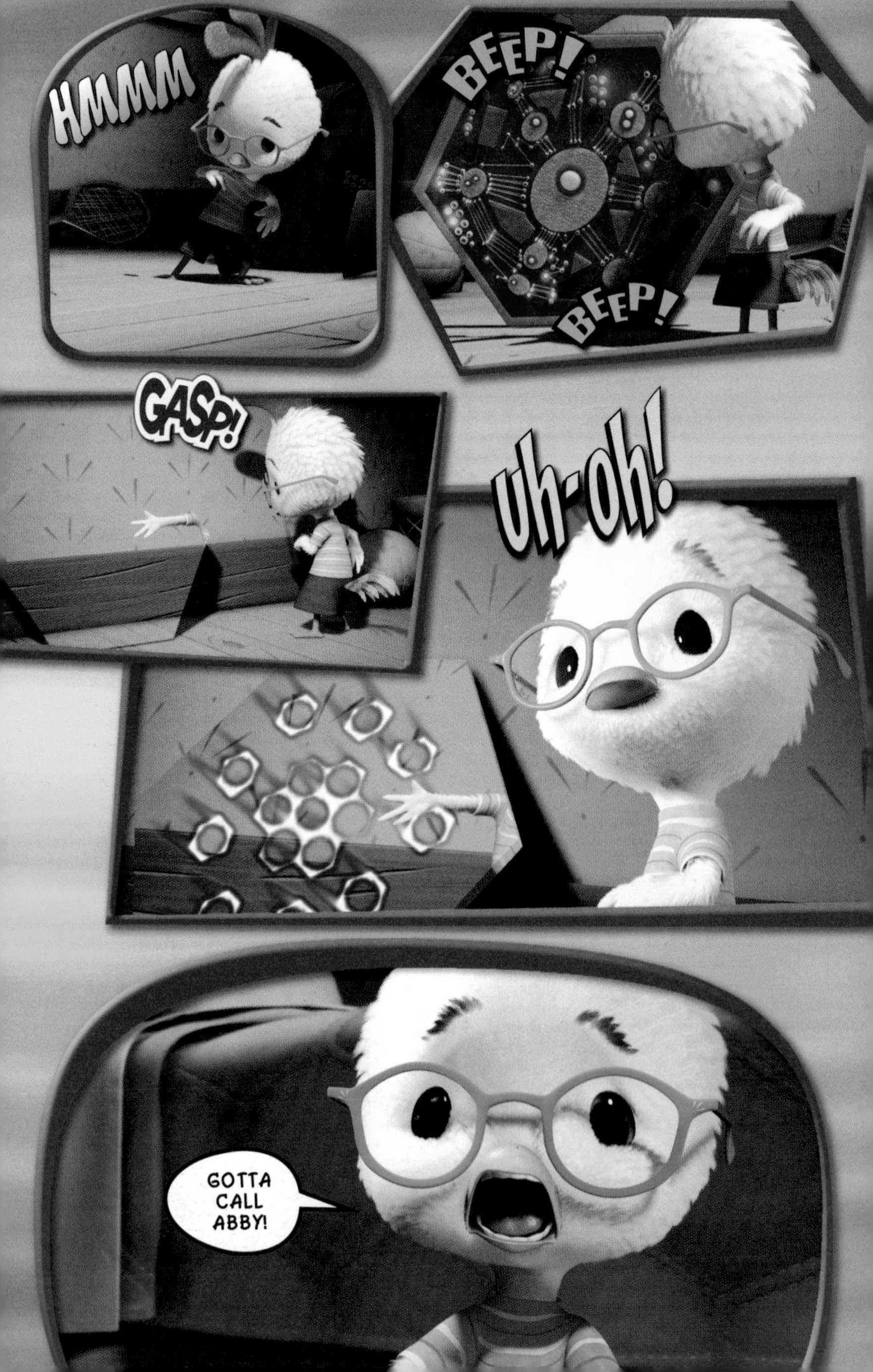
HMMM
BEEP!
BEEP!
GASP!
UH-OH!
GOTTA CALL ABBY!

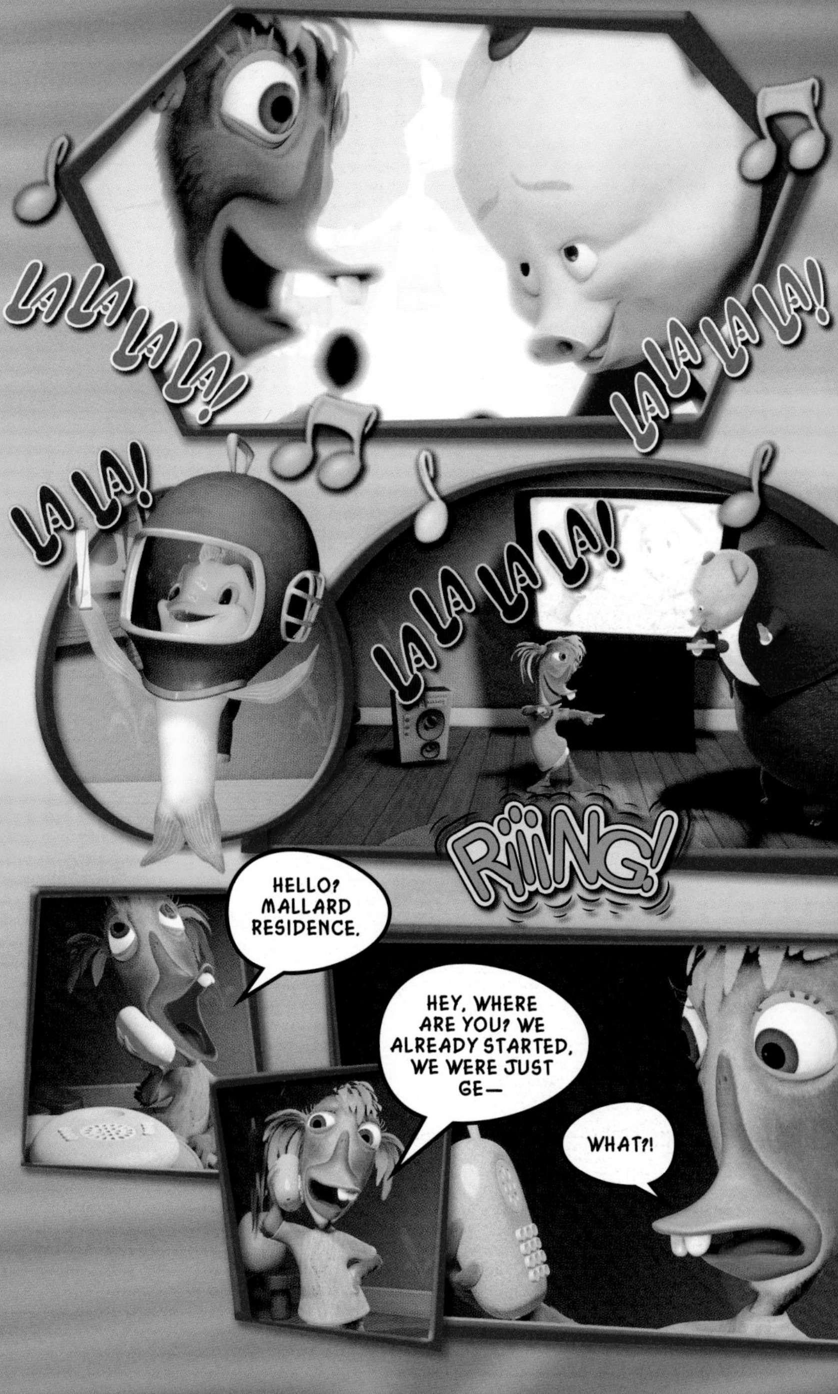
LA LA LA LA LA!
LA LA LA LA LA!
LA LA!
LA LA LA LA LA!
RIIING!
HELLO? MALLARD RESIDENCE.
HEY, WHERE ARE YOU? WE ALREADY STARTED, WE WERE JUST GE—
WHAT?!

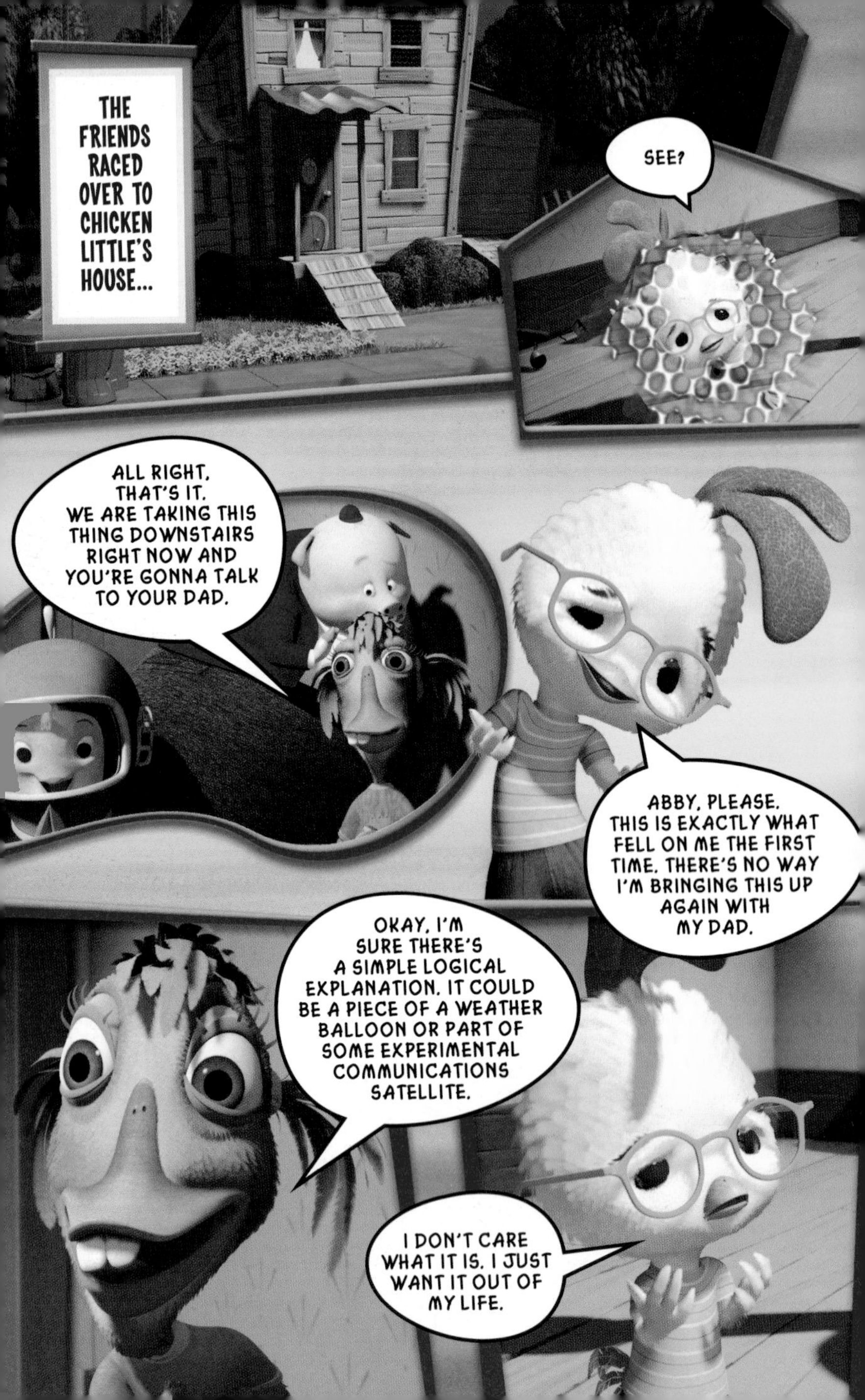
THE FRIENDS RACED OVER TO CHICKEN LITTLE'S HOUSE...
SEE?
ALL RIGHT, THAT'S IT. WE ARE TAKING THIS THING DOWNSTAIRS RIGHT NOW AND YOU'RE GONNA TALK TO YOUR DAD.
ABBY, PLEASE. THIS IS EXACTLY WHAT FELL ON ME THE FIRST TIME. THERE'S NO WAY I'M BRINGING THIS UP AGAIN WITH MY DAD.
OKAY, I'M SURE THERE'S A SIMPLE LOGICAL EXPLANATION. IT COULD BE A PIECE OF A WEATHER BALLOON OR PART OF SOME EXPERIMENTAL COMMUNICATIONS SATELLITE.
I DON'T CARE WHAT IT IS. I JUST WANT IT OUT OF MY LIFE.

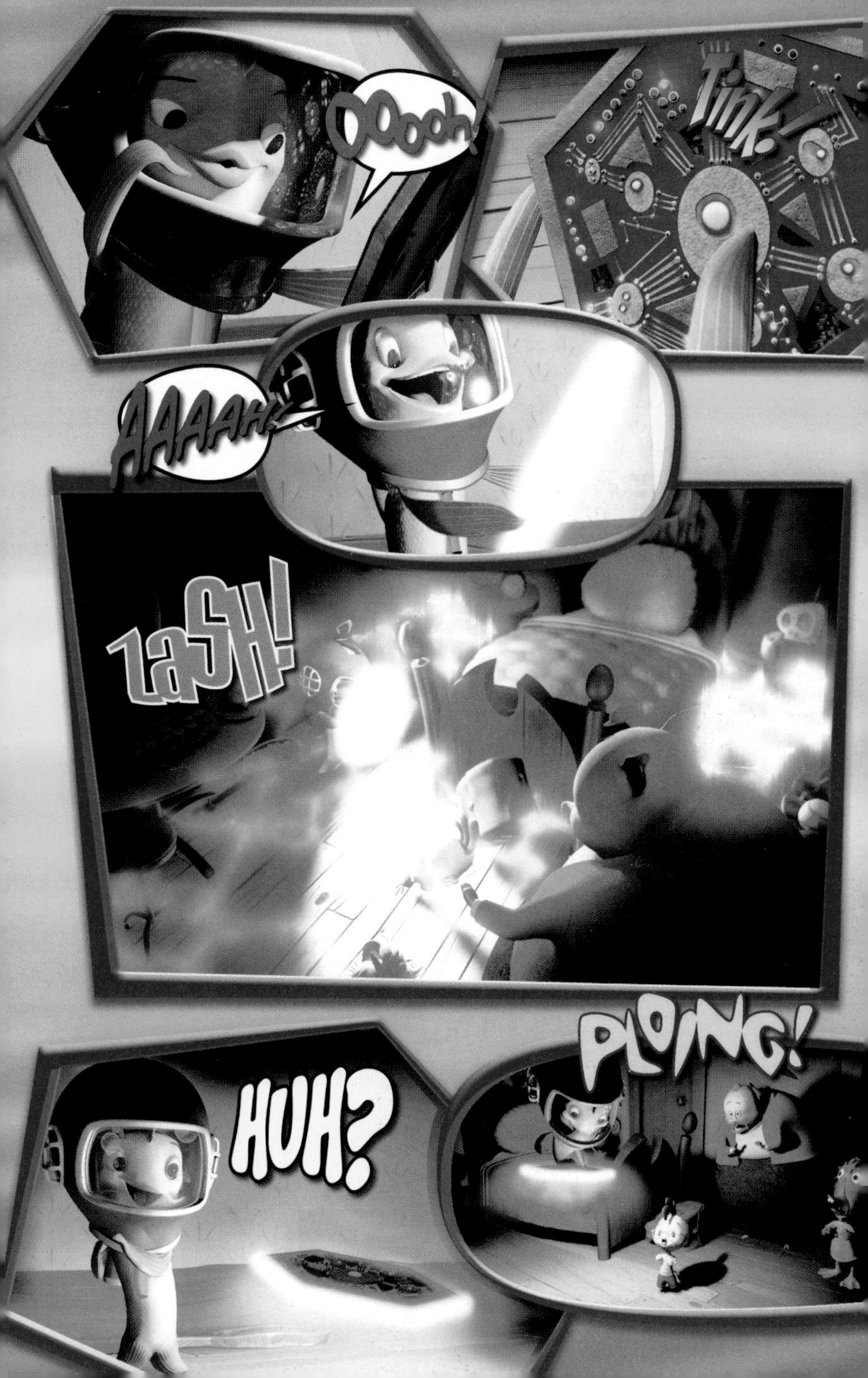
OOooh!
Tink!
AAAAH!
ZaSH!
HUH?
PLOING!

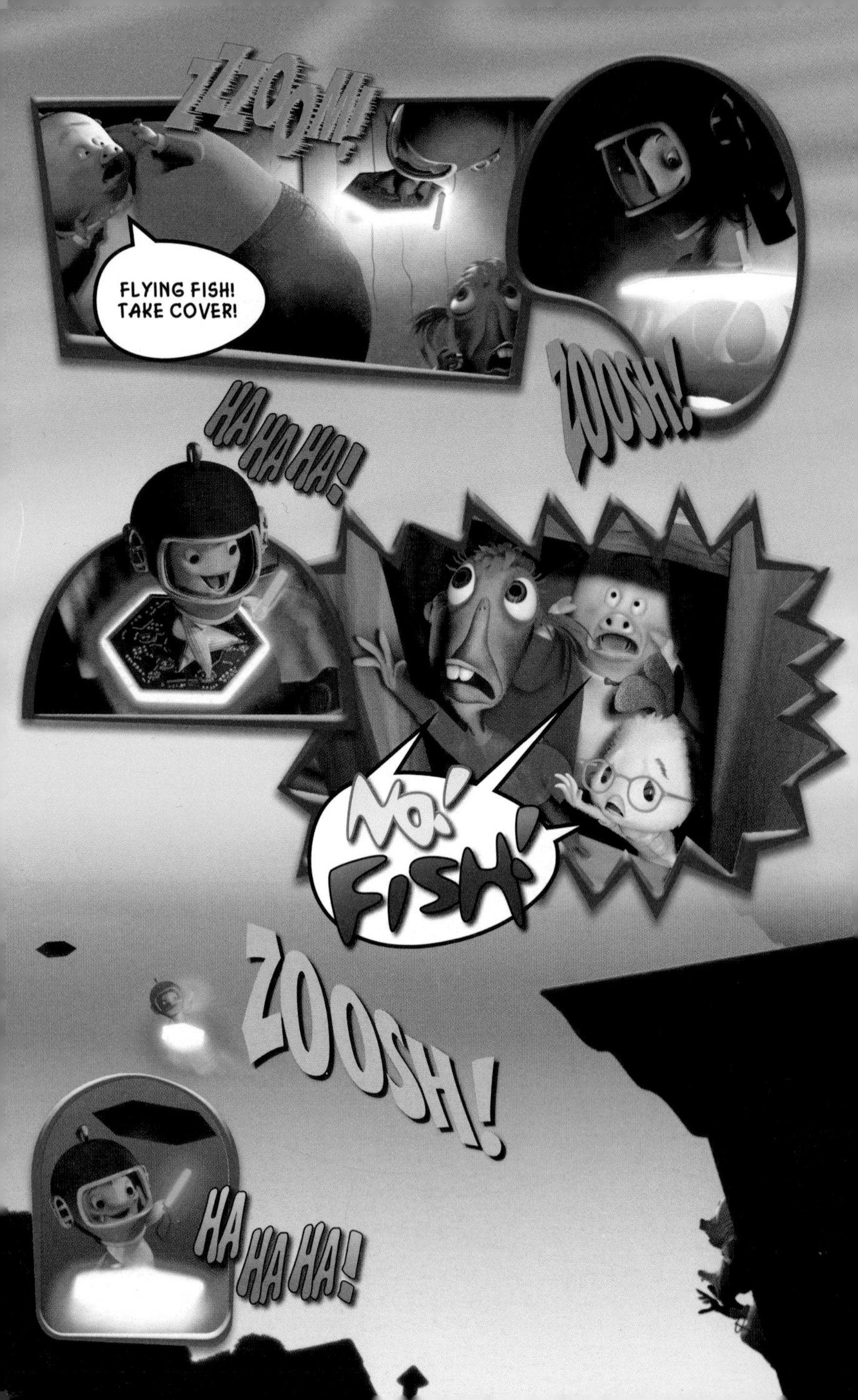
ZZZOOM!
FLYING FISH! TAKE COVER!
ZOOSH!
HA HA HA!
NO! FISH!
ZOOSH!
HA HA HA!

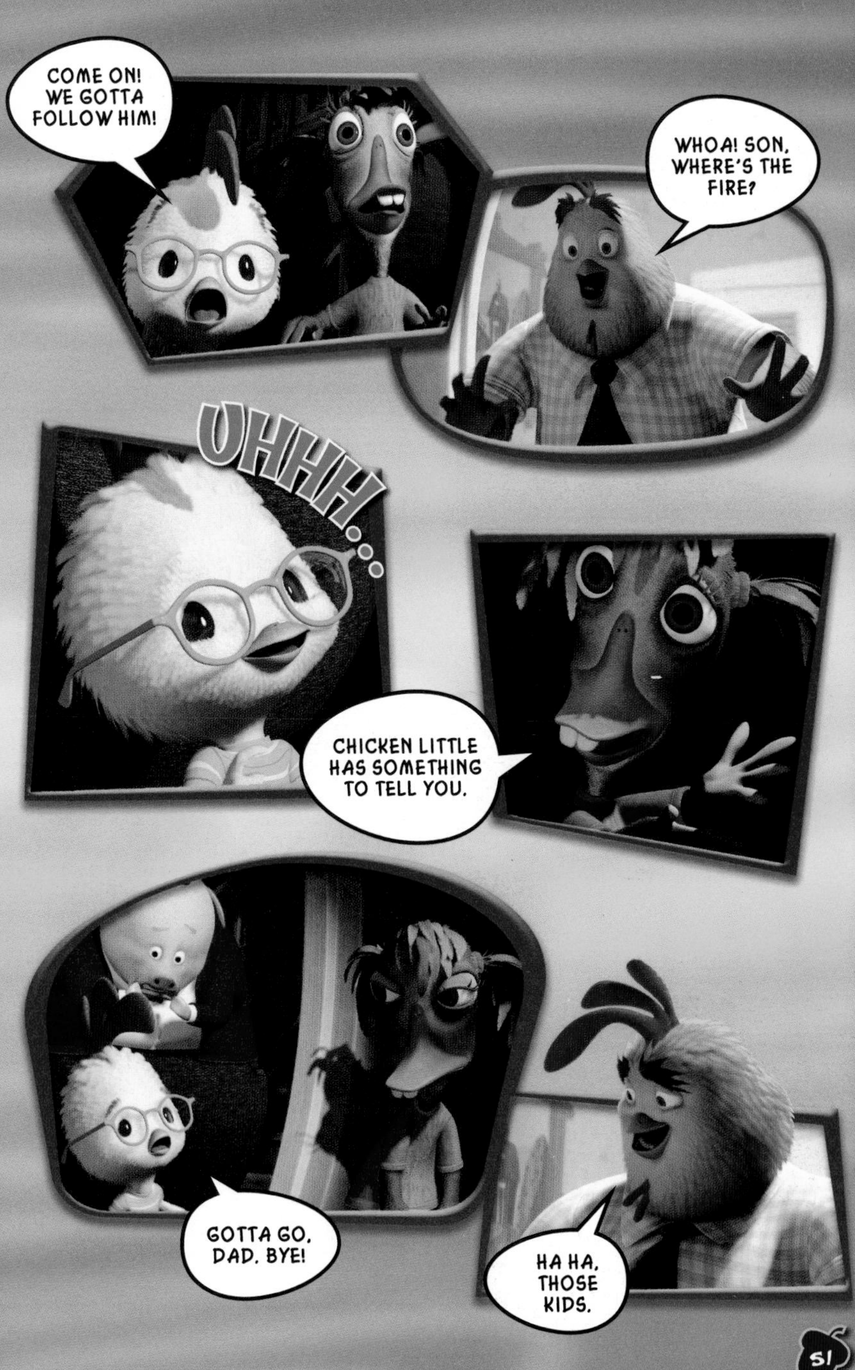
COME ON! WE GOTTA FOLLOW HIM!
WHOA! SON, WHERE'S THE FIRE?
UHHH...
CHICKEN LITTLE HAS SOMETHING TO TELL YOU.
GOTTA GO, DAD. BYE!
HA HA, THOSE KIDS.

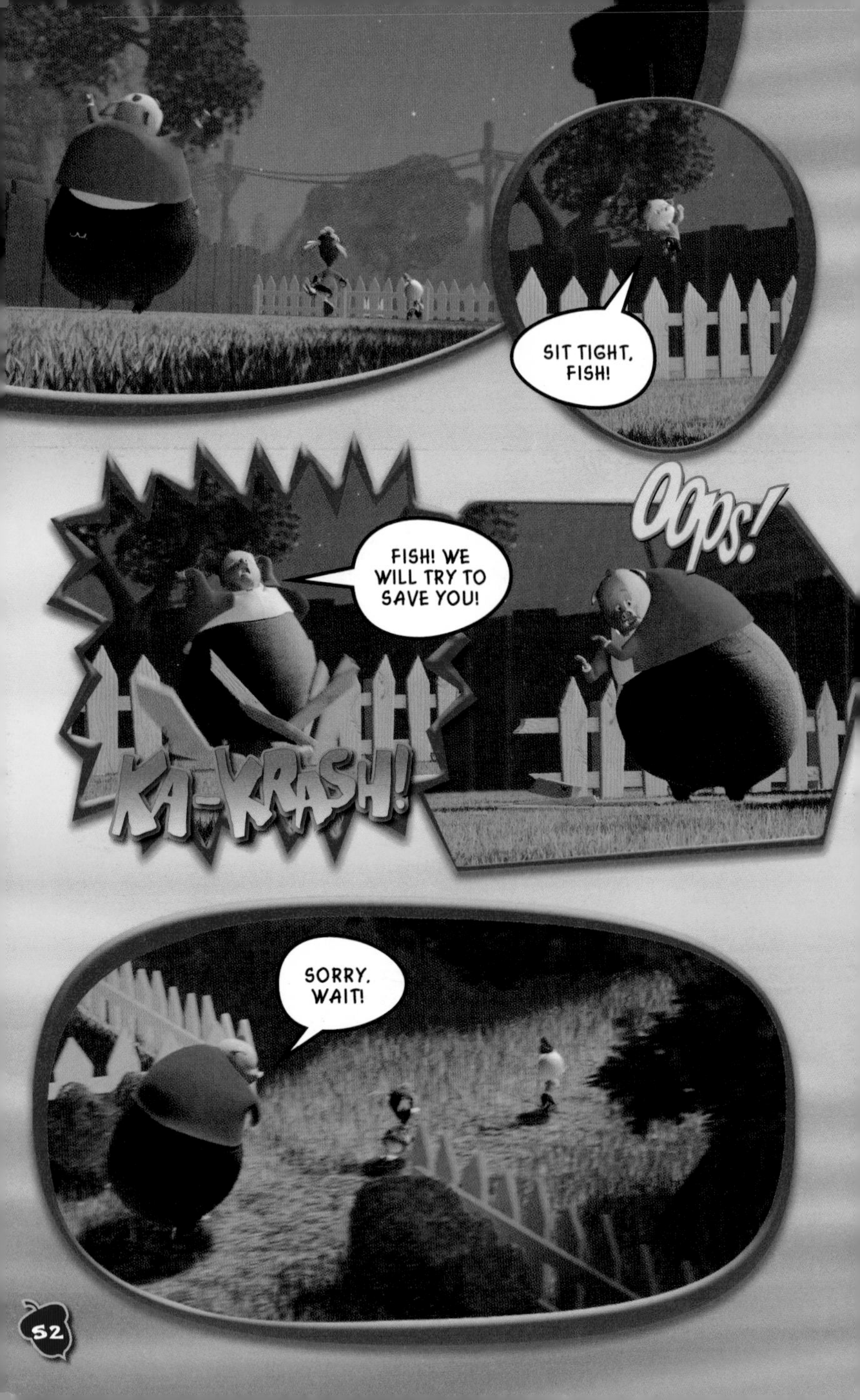
SIT TIGHT, FISH!
KA-KRASH!
FISH! WE WILL TRY TO SAVE YOU!
OOPS!
SORRY, WAIT!

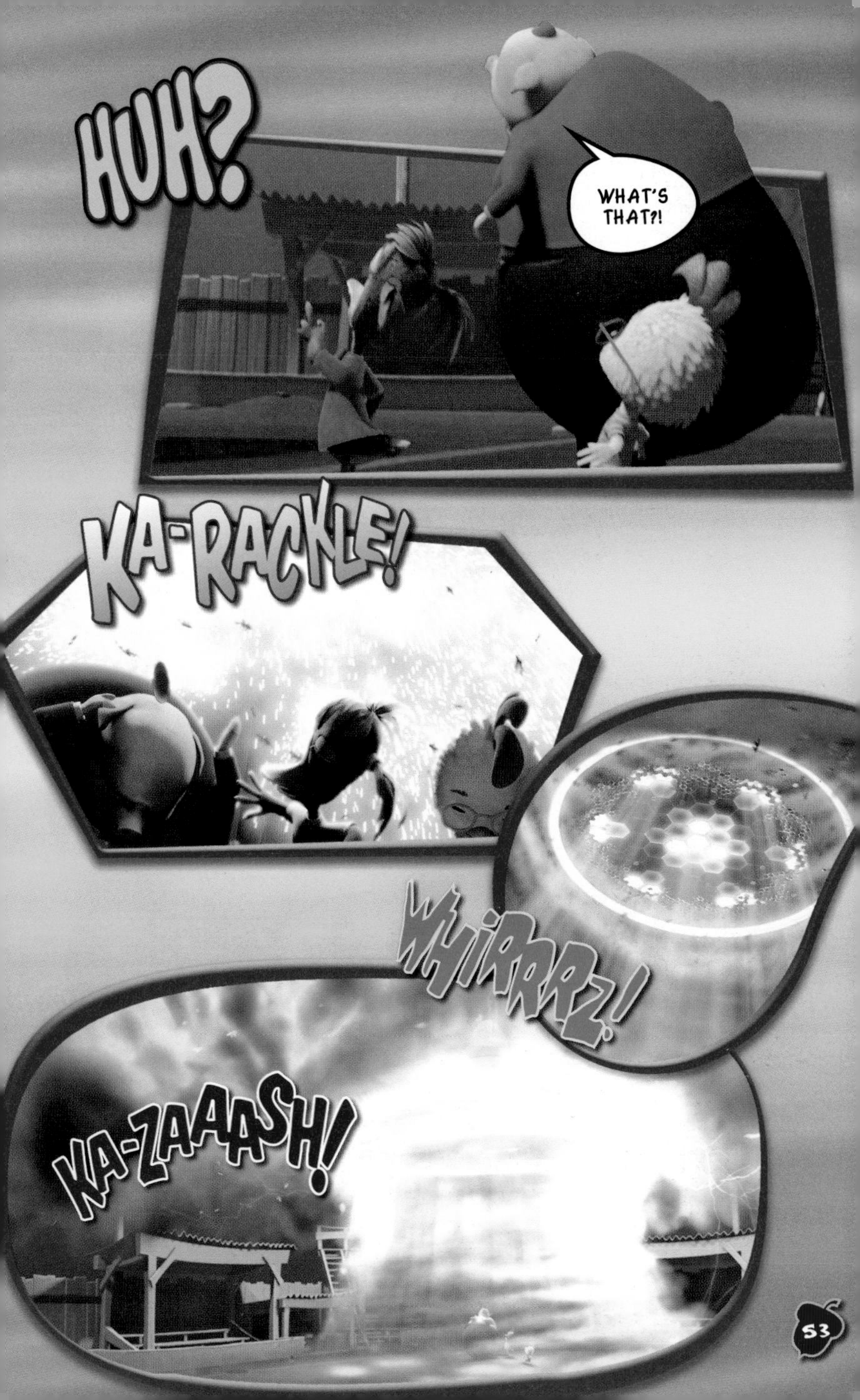
HUH?
WHAT'S THAT?!
KA-RACKLE!
WHIRRRZ!
KA-ZAAAASH!

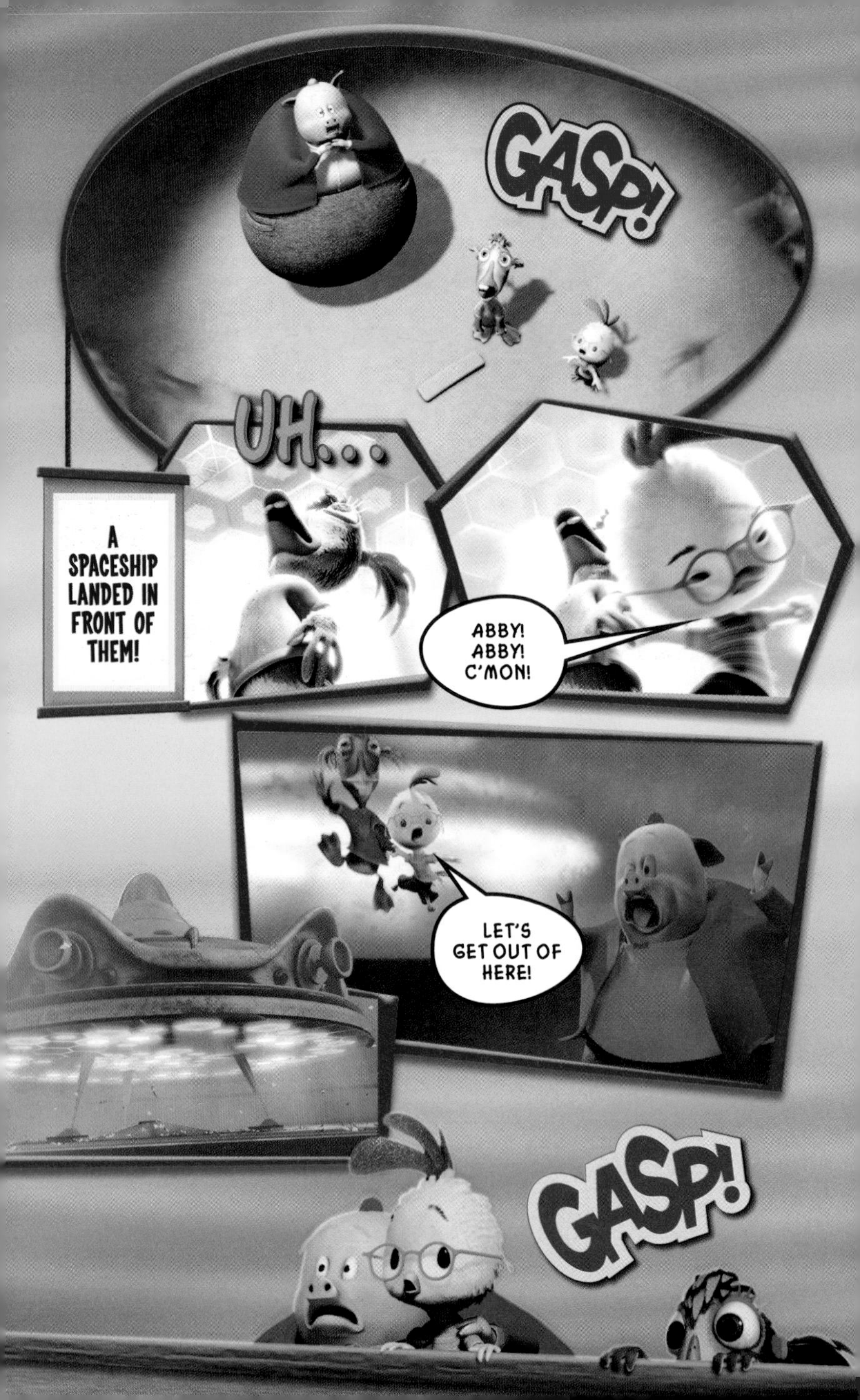
GASP!
UH...
A SPACESHIP LANDED IN FRONT OF THEM!
ABBY! ABBY! C'MON!
LET'S GET OUT OF HERE!
GASP!

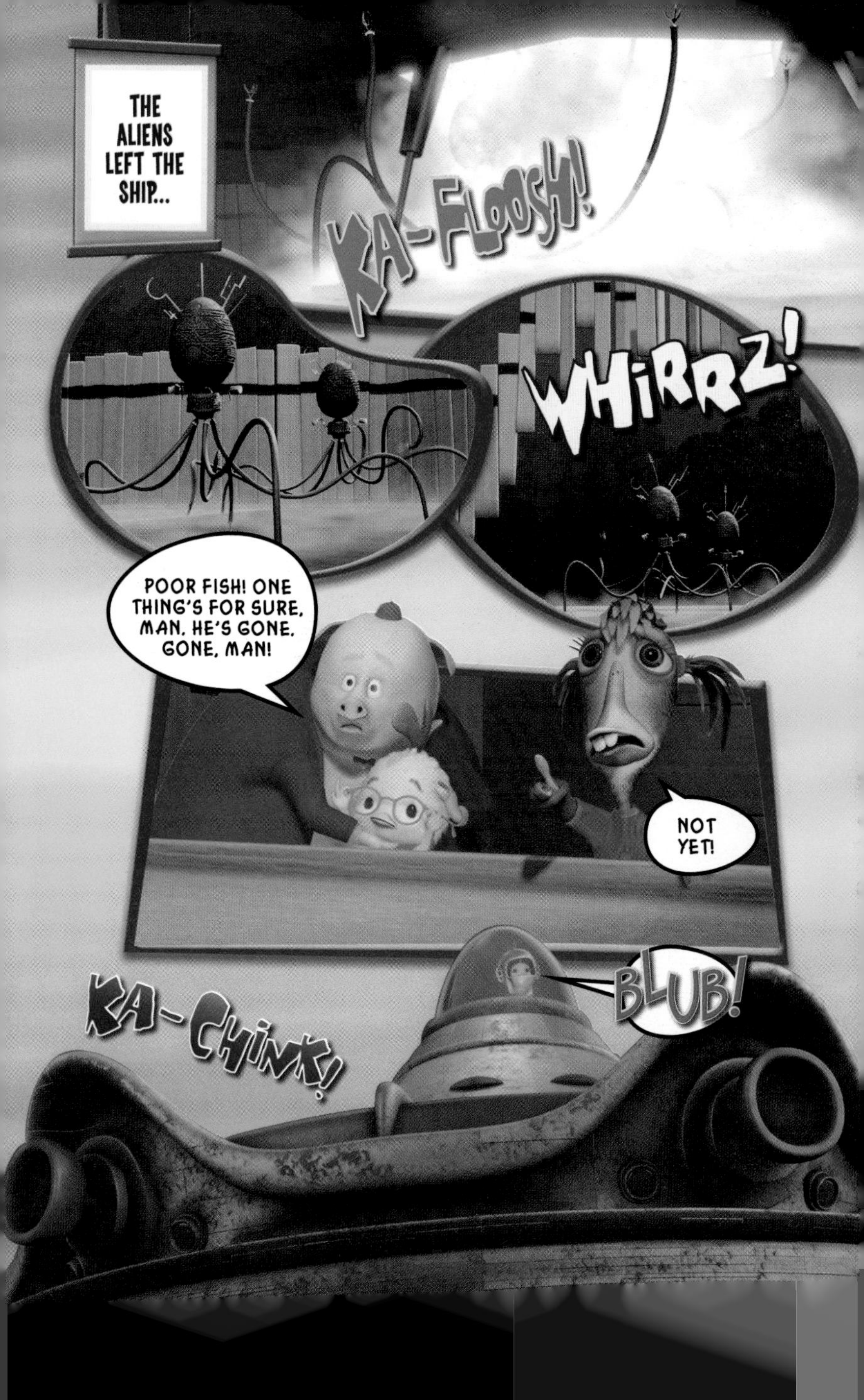
THE ALIENS LEFT THE SHIP...
KA-FLOOSH!
WHIRRZ!
POOR FISH! ONE THING'S FOR SURE, MAN. HE'S GONE. GONE, MAN!
NOT YET!
KA-CHINK!
BLUB!

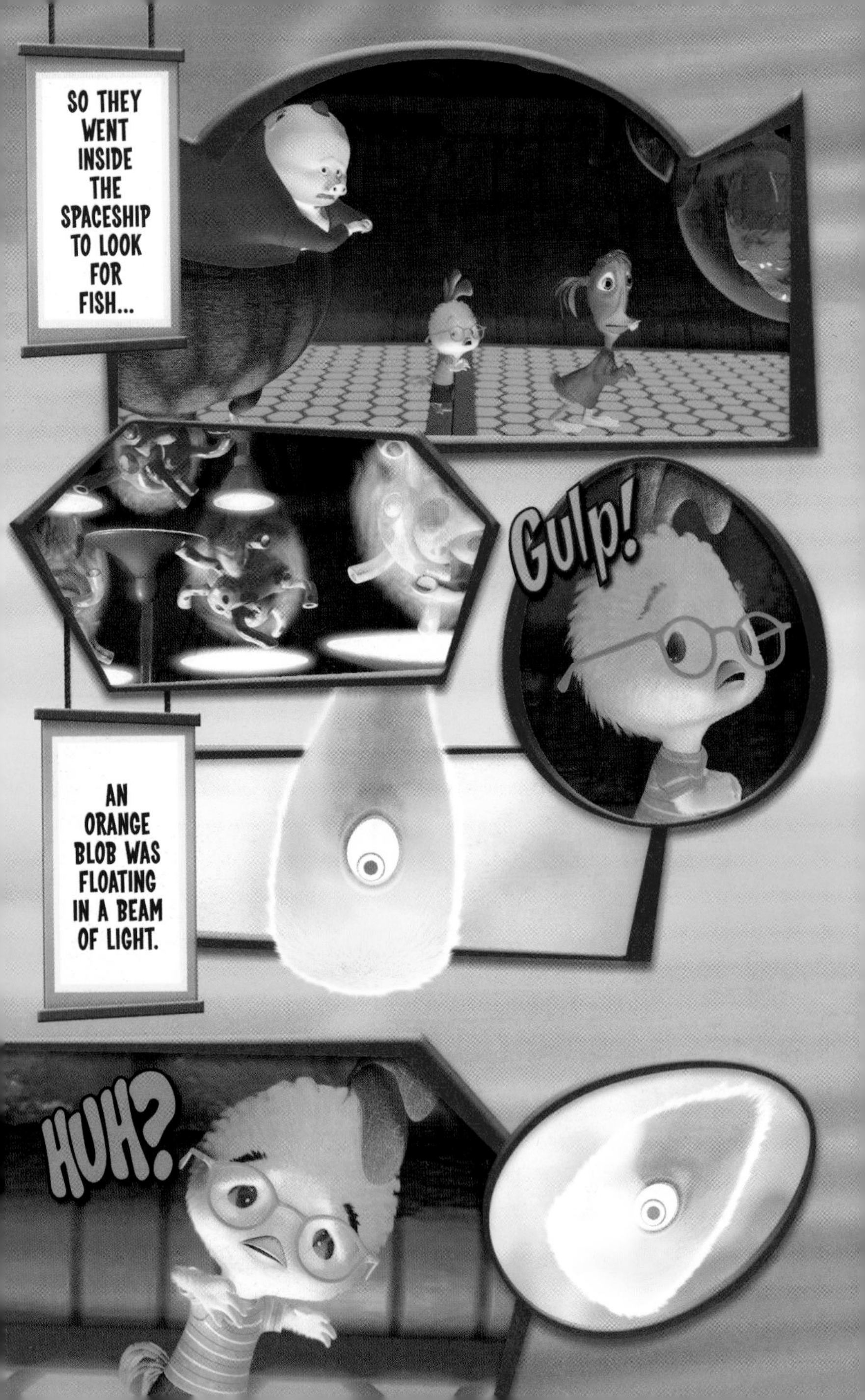
SO THEY WENT INSIDE THE SPACESHIP TO LOOK FOR FISH...
Gulp!
AN ORANGE BLOB WAS FLOATING IN A BEAM OF LIGHT.
HUH?

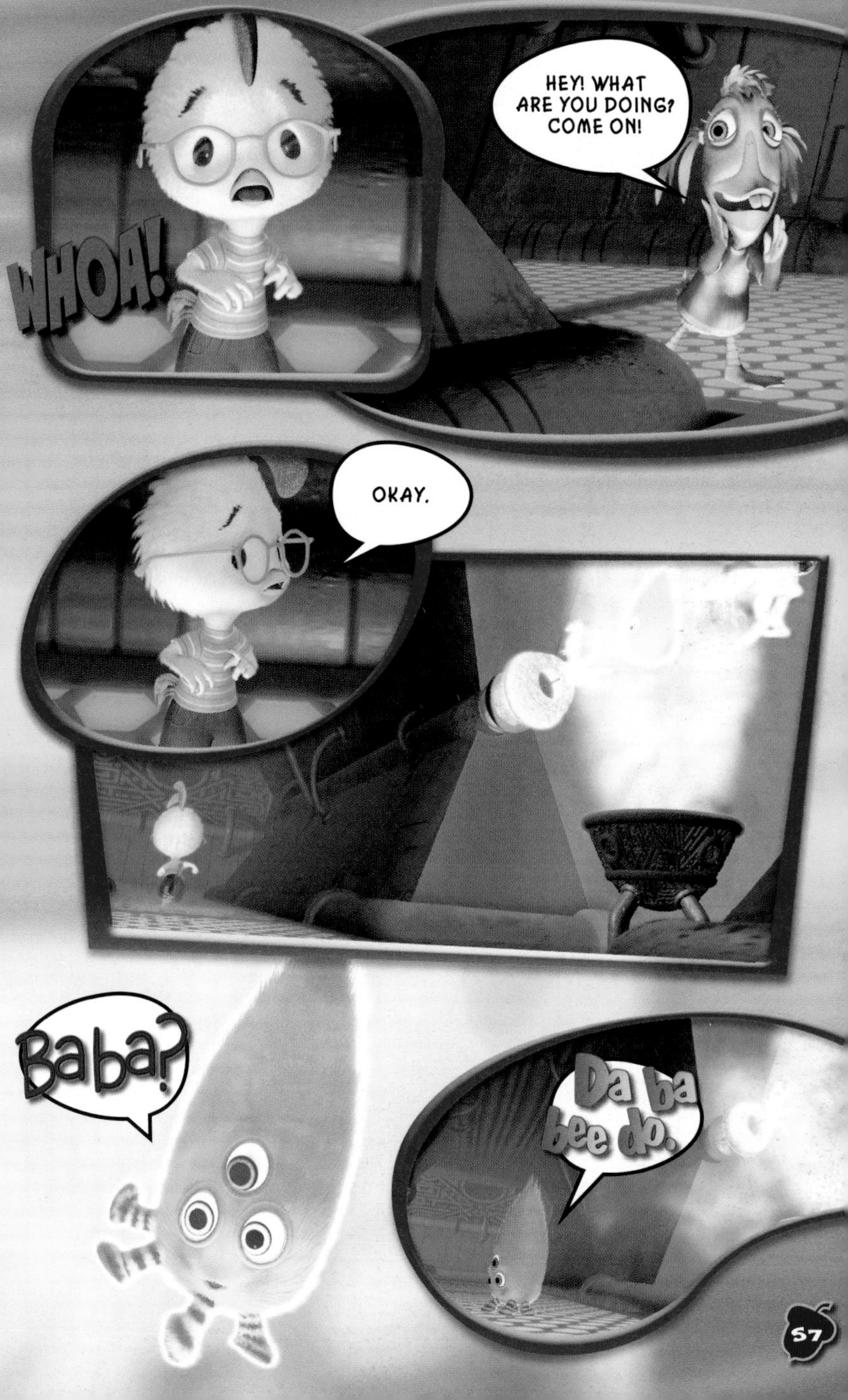
WHOA!
HEY! WHAT ARE YOU DOING? COME ON!
OKAY.
Baba?
Da ba bee do.

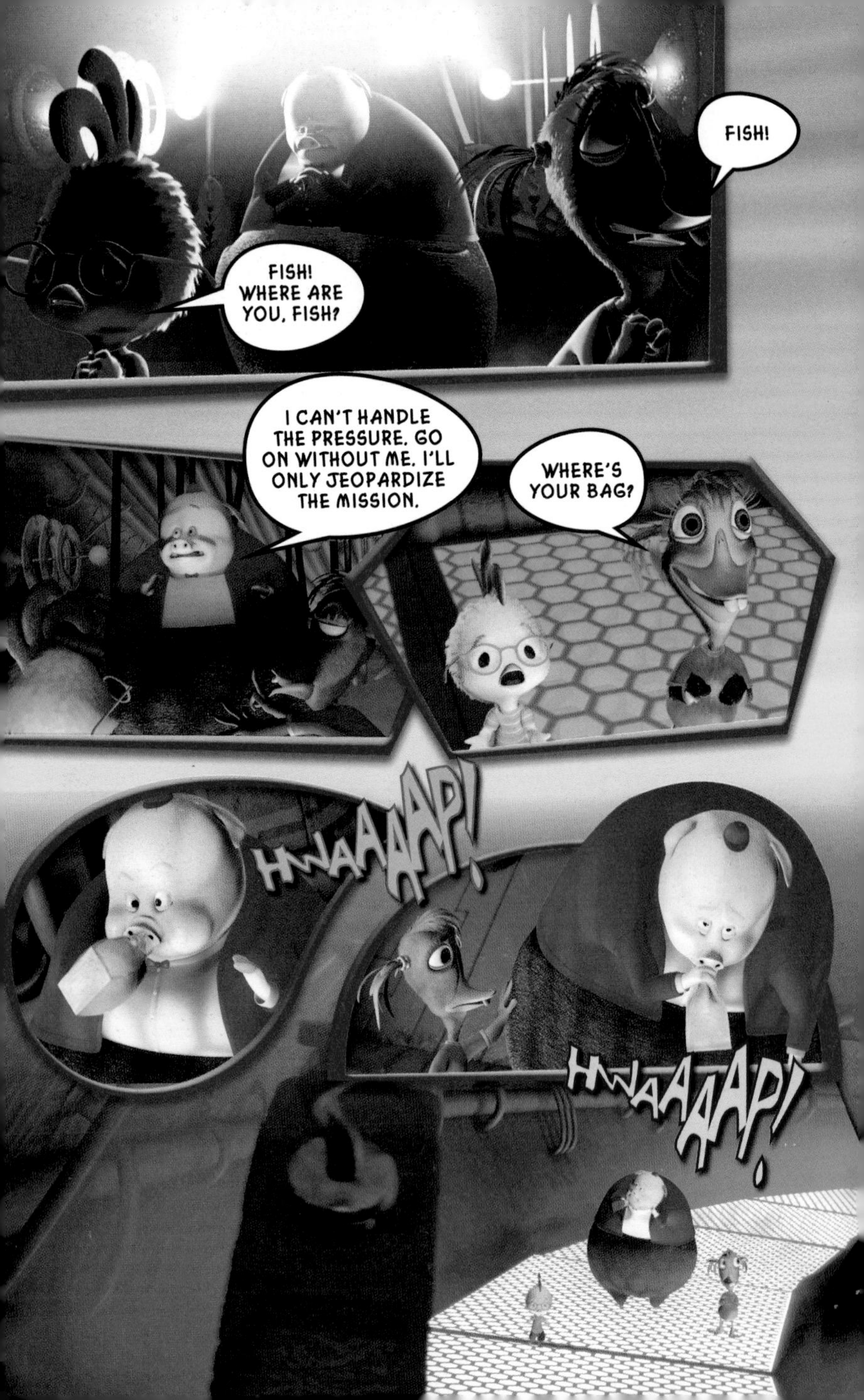
FISH!
FISH! WHERE ARE YOU, FISH?
I CAN'T HANDLE THE PRESSURE. GO ON WITHOUT ME. I'LL ONLY JEOPARDIZE THE MISSION.
WHERE'S YOUR BAG?
HWAAAAP!
HWAAAAP!

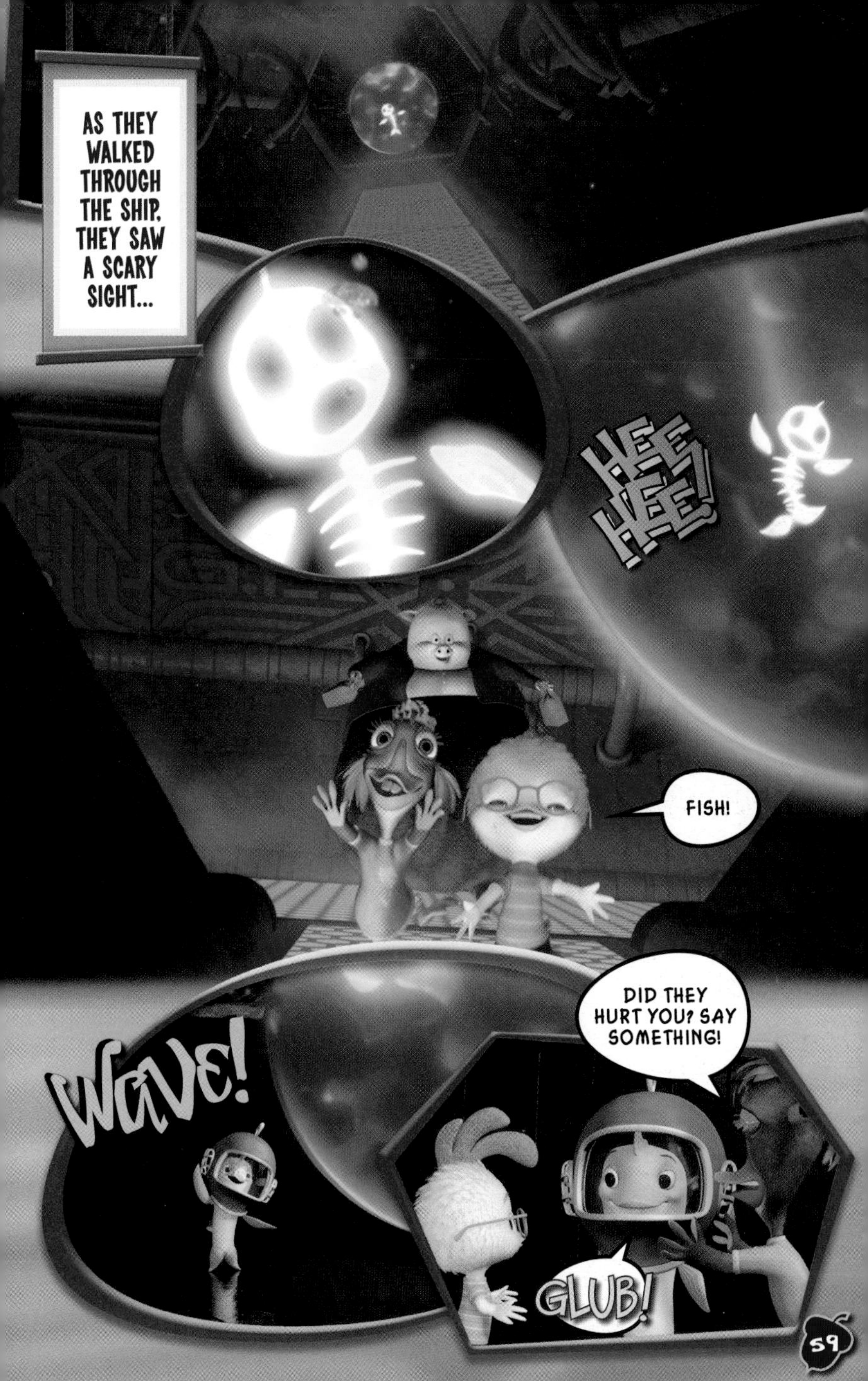
AS THEY WALKED THROUGH THE SHIP, THEY SAW A SCARY SIGHT...
HEE HEE!
FISH!
WAVE!
DID THEY HURT YOU? SAY SOMETHING!
GLUB!

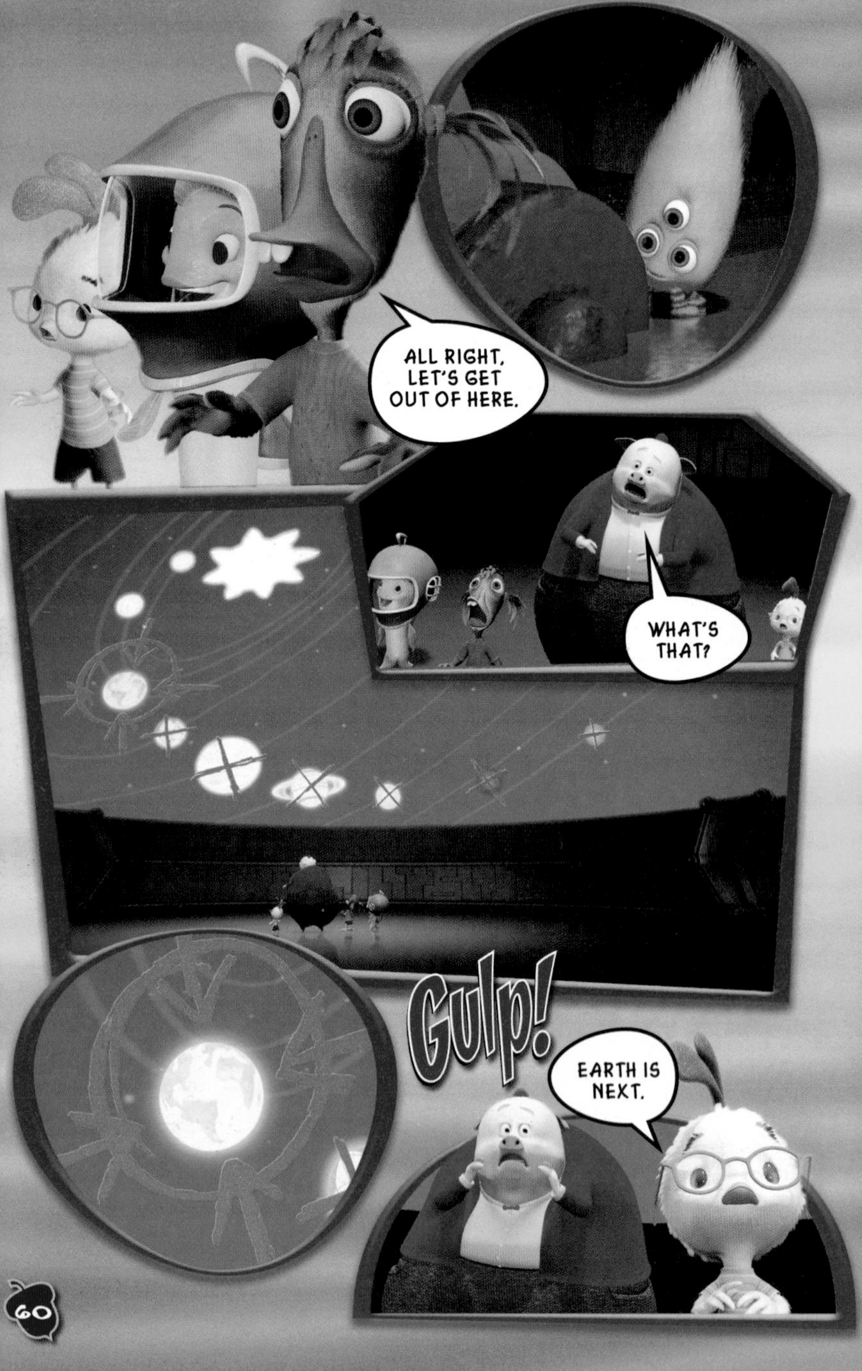
ALL RIGHT, LET'S GET OUT OF HERE.
WHAT'S THAT?
GULP!
EARTH IS NEXT.

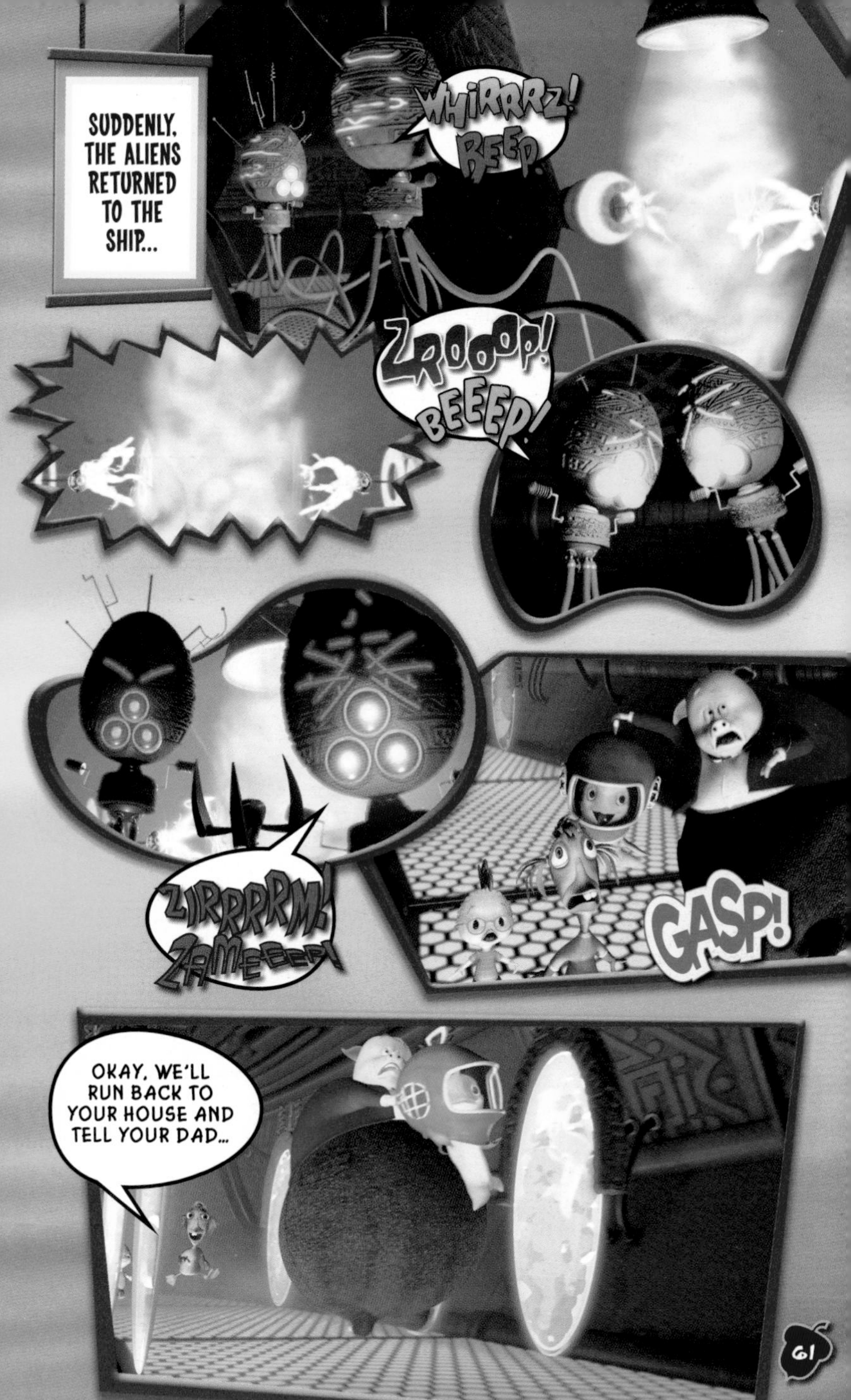
SUDDENLY, THE ALIENS RETURNED TO THE SHIP...
WHIRRRZ! BEEP
ZROOOOP! BEEEP!
ZIRRRRM!
GASP!
OKAY, WE'LL RUN BACK TO YOUR HOUSE AND TELL YOUR DAD...

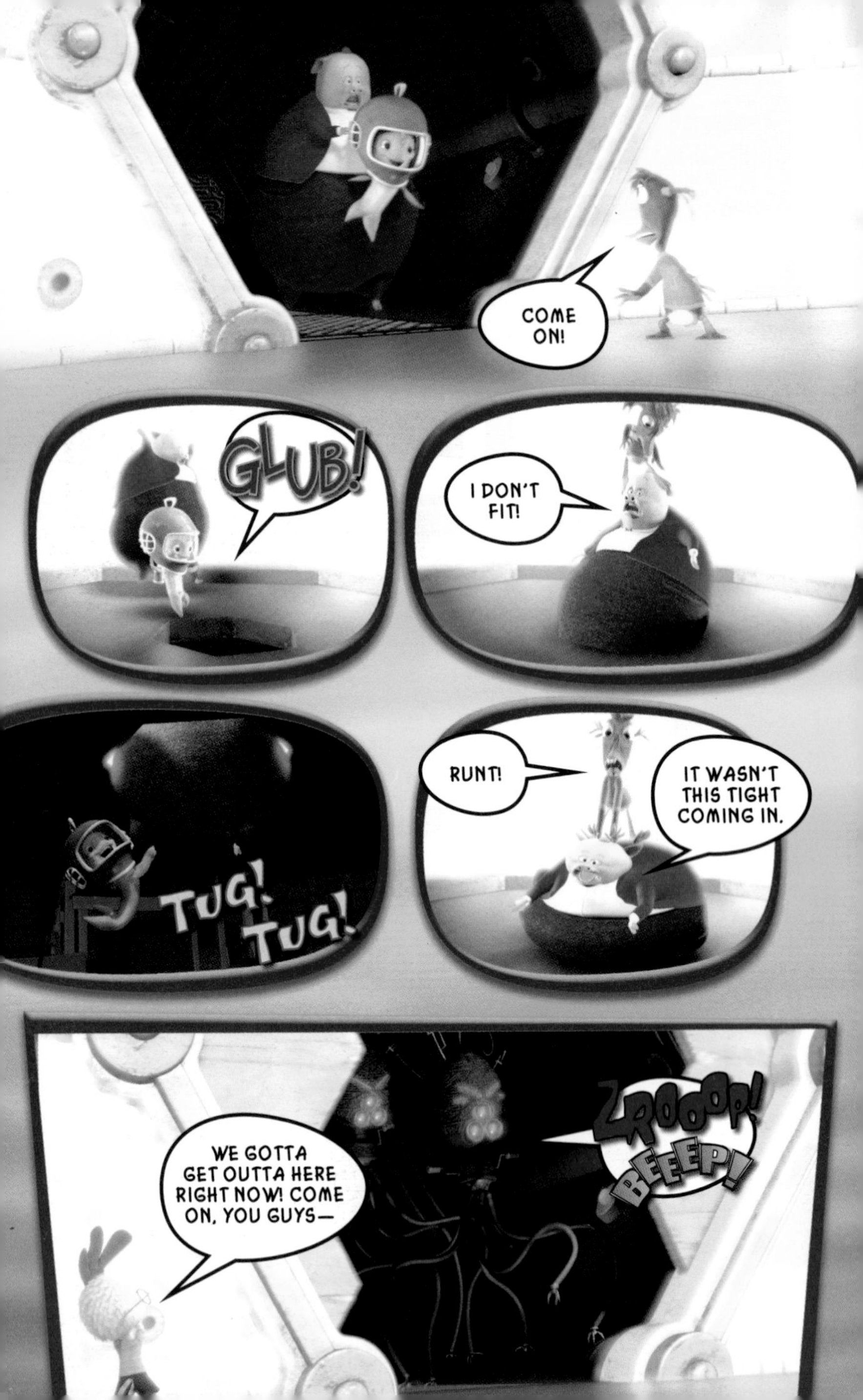
COME ON!
GLUB!
I DON'T FIT!
TUG! TUG!
RUNT!
IT WASN'T THIS TIGHT COMING IN.
ZROOOOP!
BEEEP!
WE GOTTA GET OUTTA HERE RIGHT NOW! COME ON, YOU GUYS—

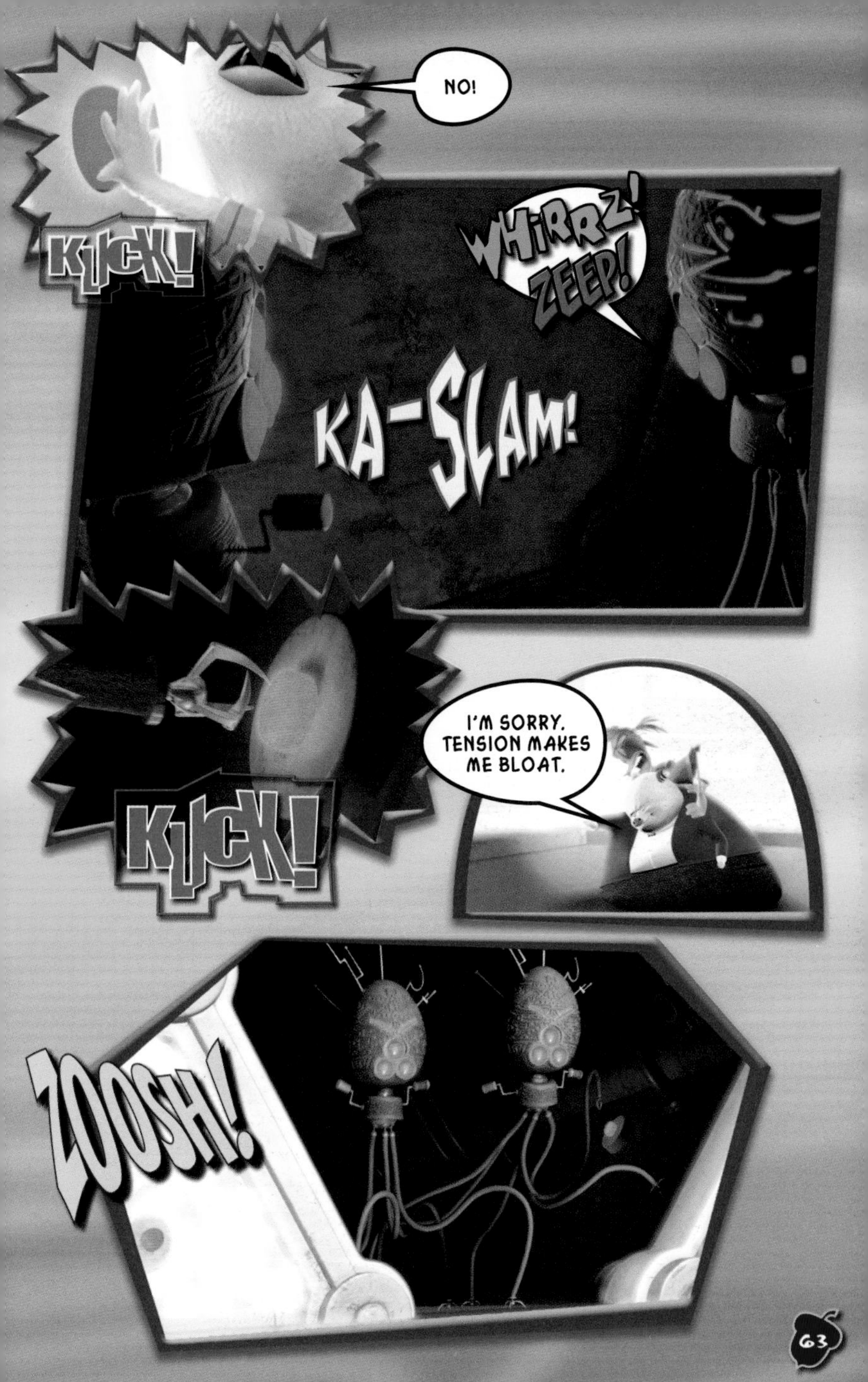
NO!
KLICK!
WHIRRZ! ZEEP!
KA-SLAM!
KLICK!
I'M SORRY. TENSION MAKES ME BLOAT.
ZOOSH!

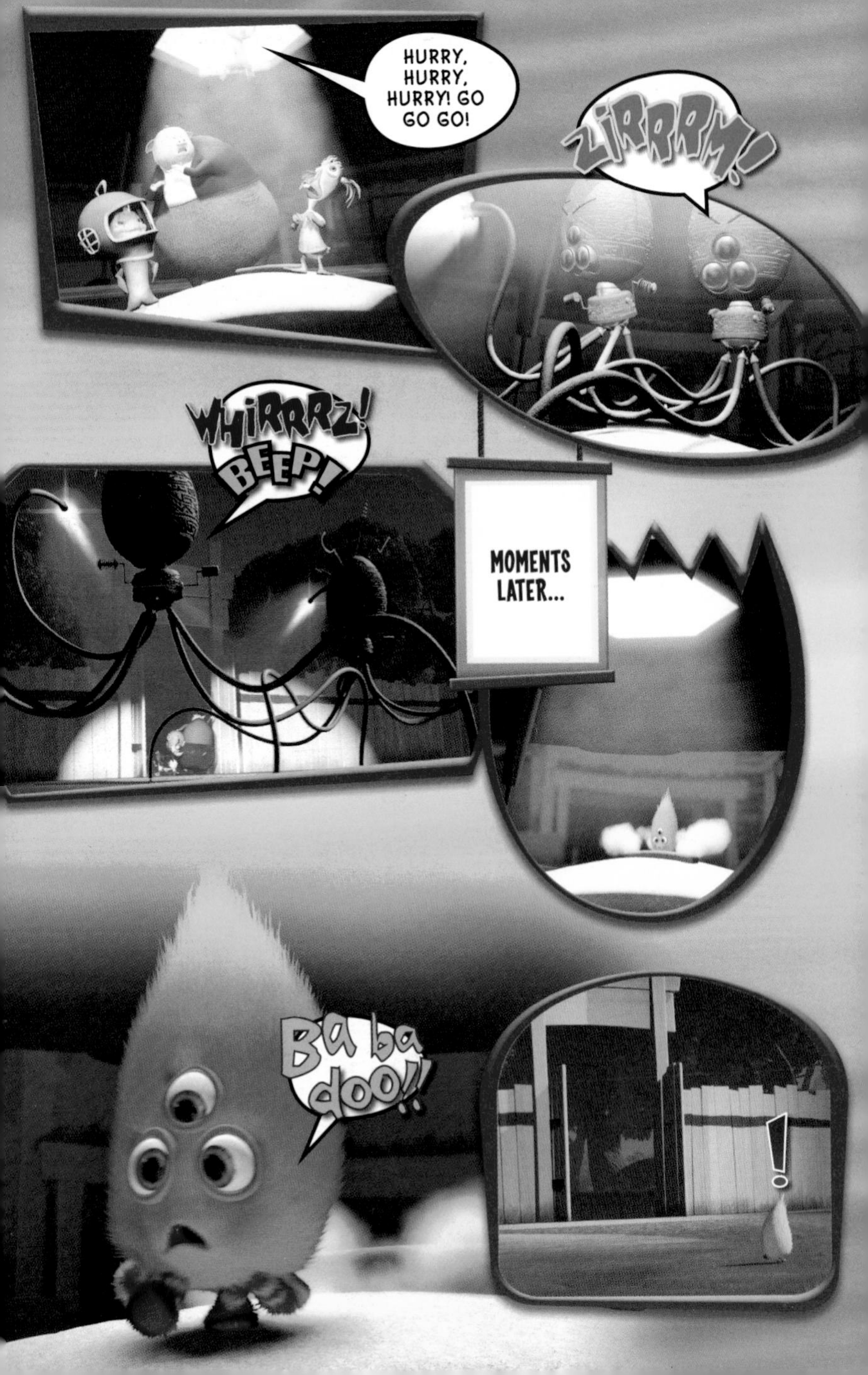
HURRY, HURRY, HURRY! GO GO GO!
ZIRRRM!
WHIRRRZ! BEEP!
MOMENTS LATER...
Ba ba doo!!
!

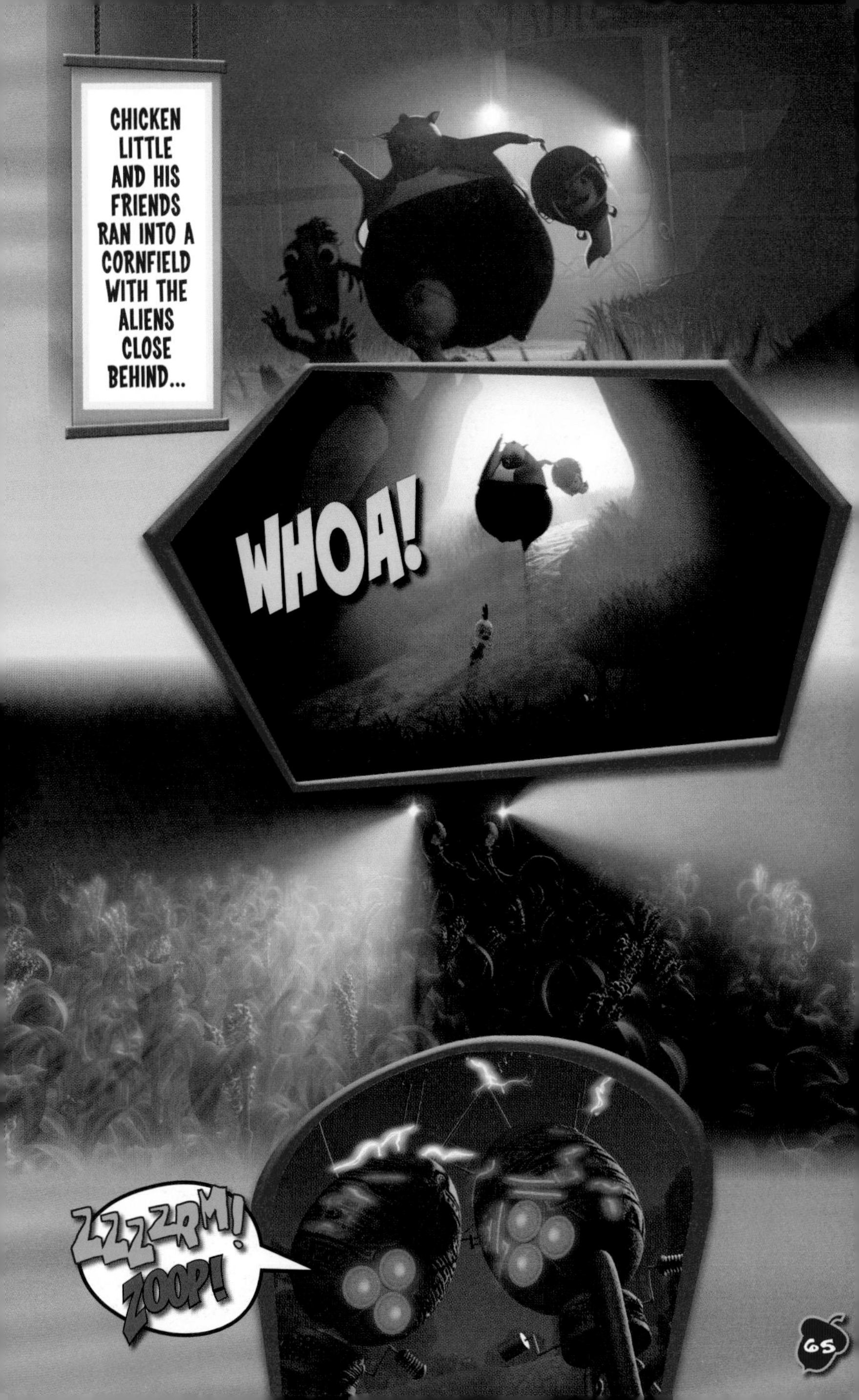
CHICKEN LITTLE AND HIS FRIENDS RAN INTO A CORNFIELD WITH THE ALIENS CLOSE BEHIND...
WHOA!
ZZZZRM! ZOOP!

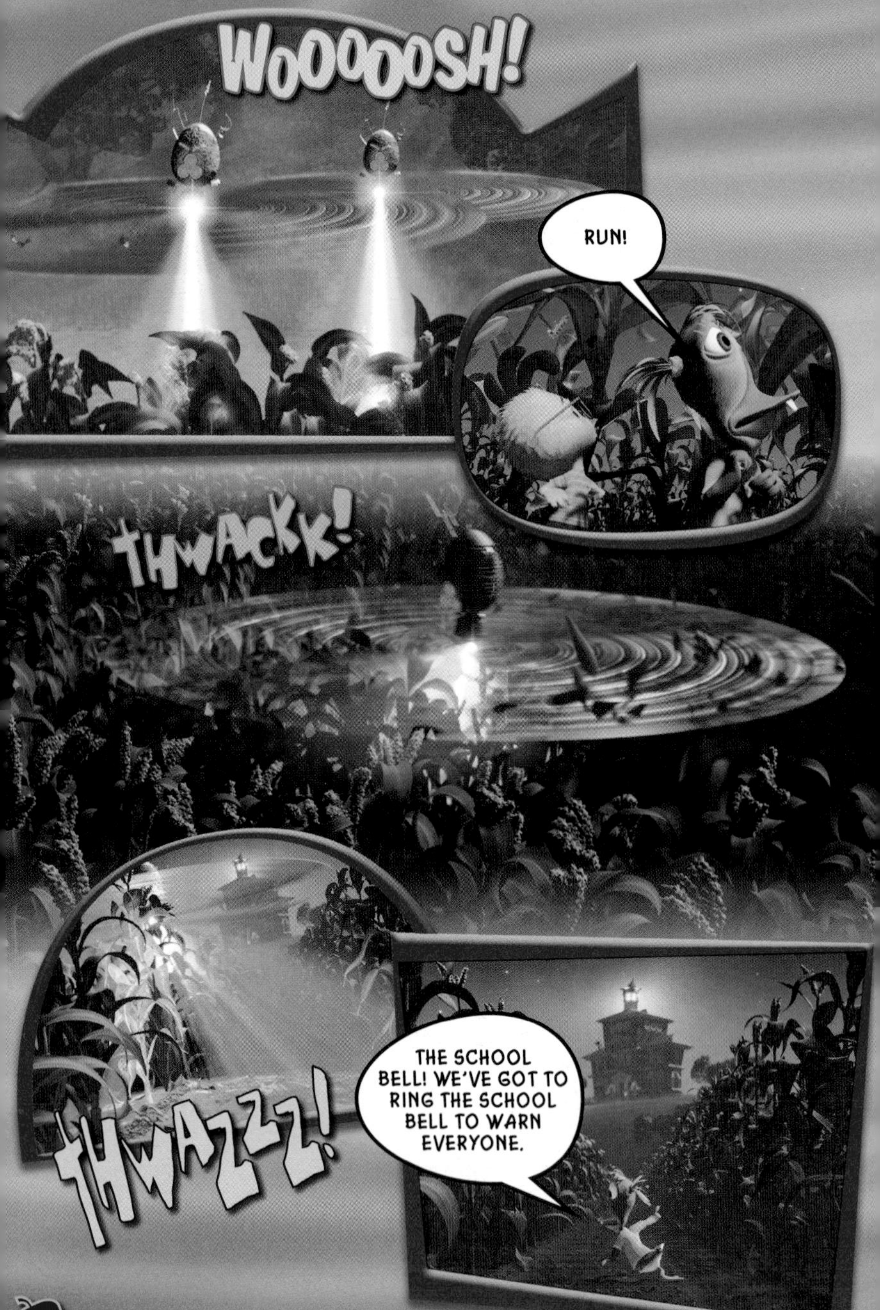
WOOOOOOSH!
RUN!
THWACKK!
THWAZZZ!
THE SCHOOL BELL! WE'VE GOT TO RING THE SCHOOL BELL TO WARN EVERYONE.

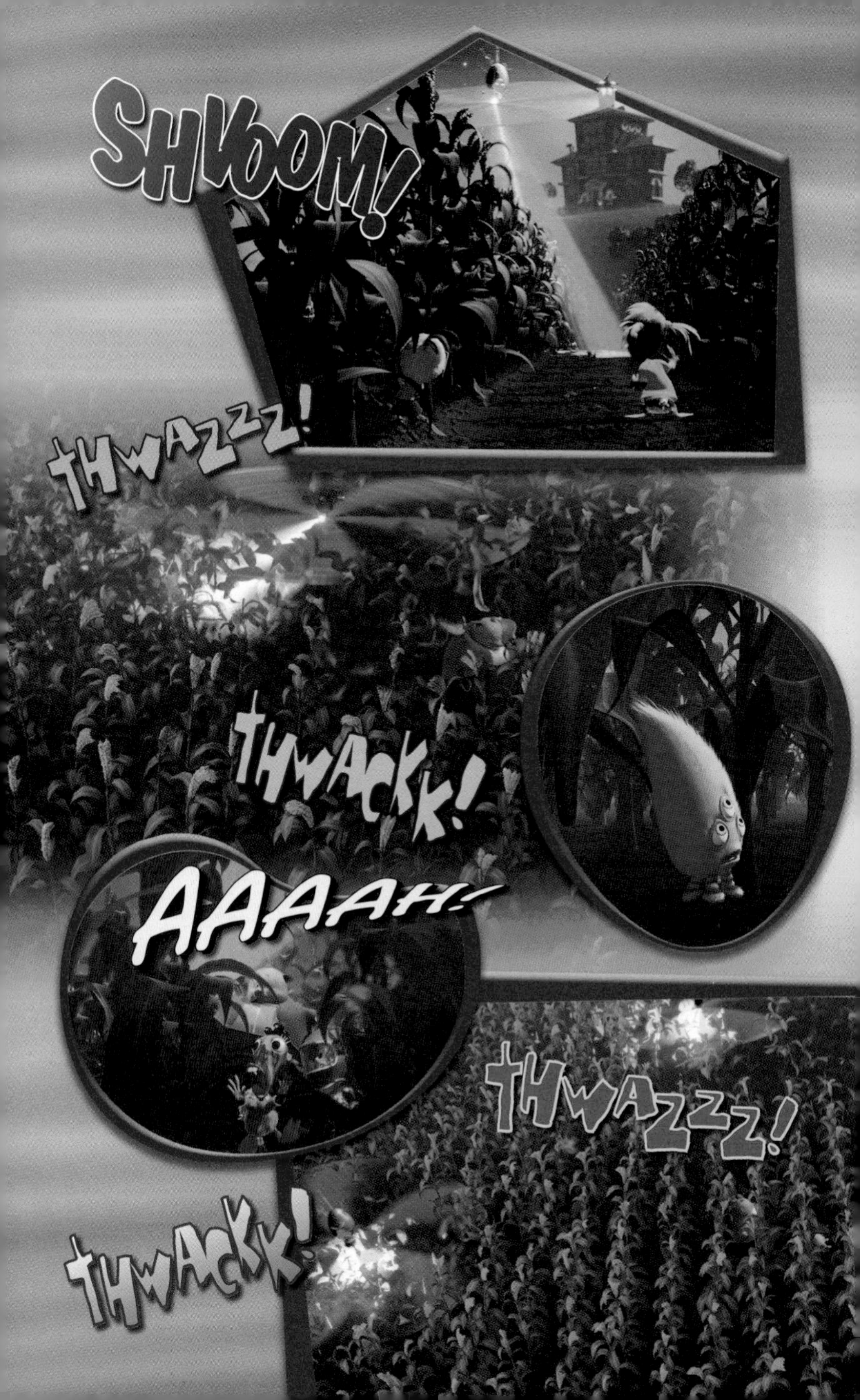
SHVOOM!
THWAZZZ!
THWACKK!
AAAAH!
THWAZZZ!
THWACKK!

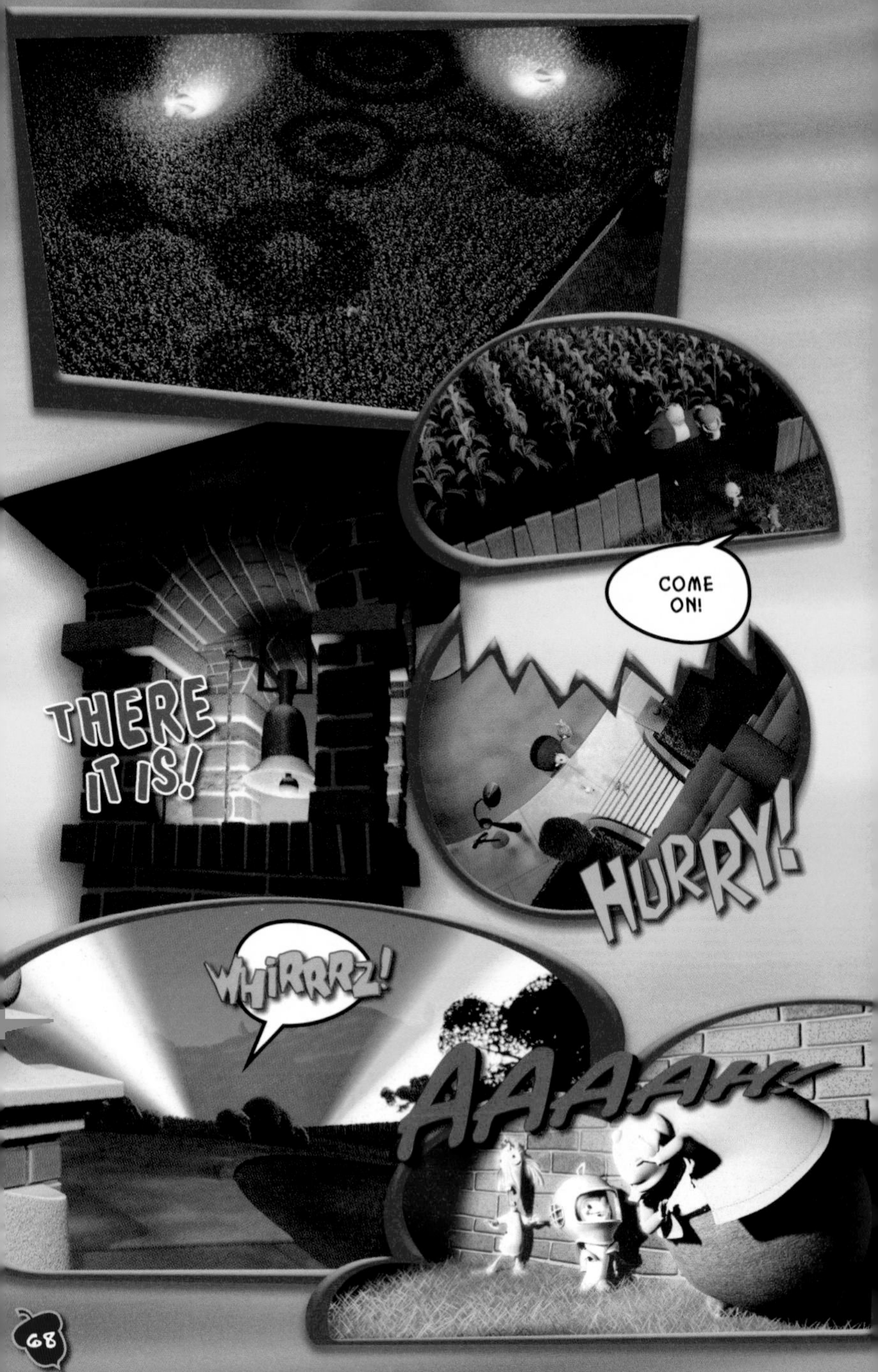
COME ON!
THERE IT IS!
HURRY!
WHIRRRZ!
AAAAAH-

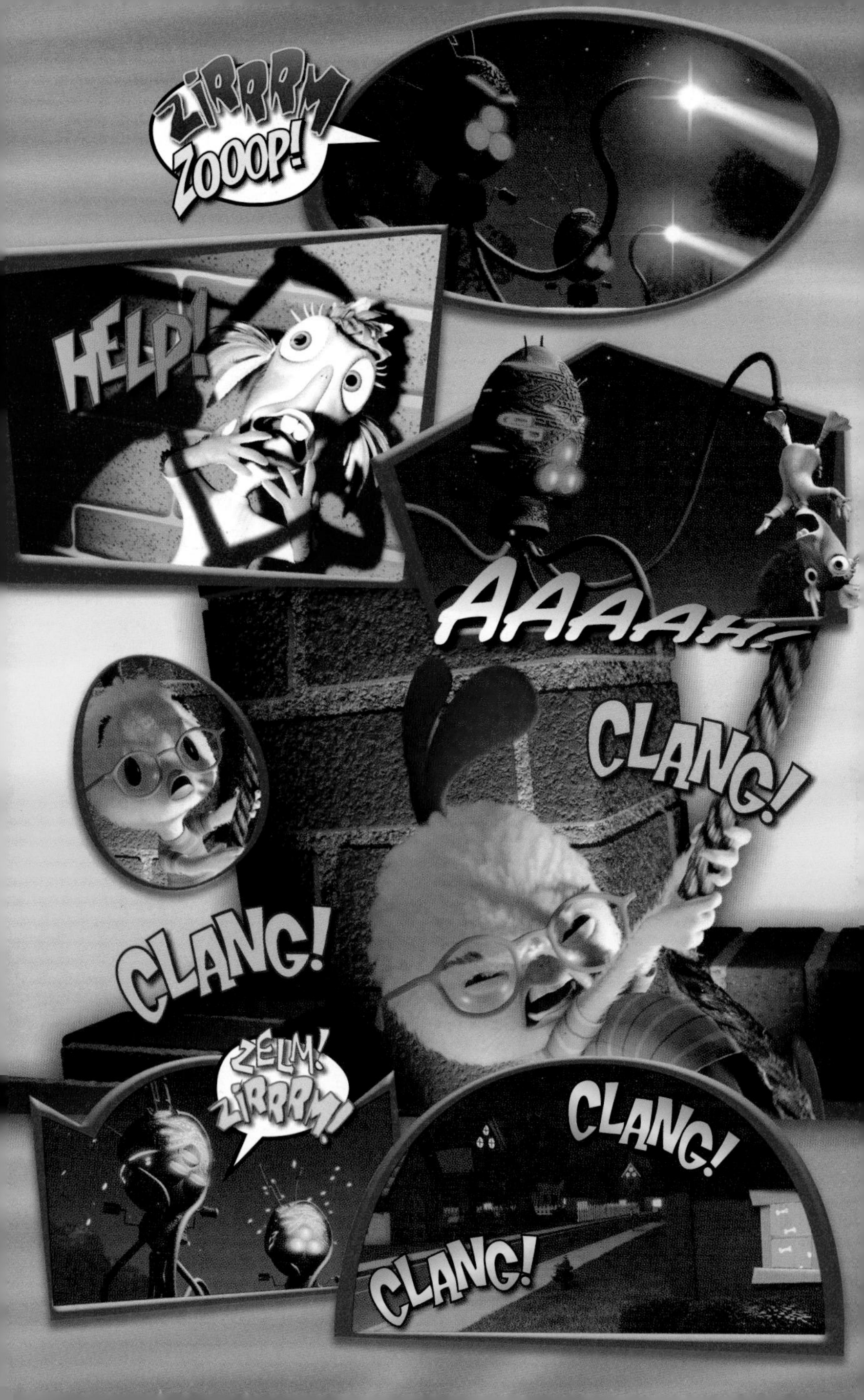
ZIRRRM
ZOOOP!
HELP!
AAAAAH!
CLANG!
CLANG!
ZELM!
ZIRRRM!
CLANG!
CLANG!

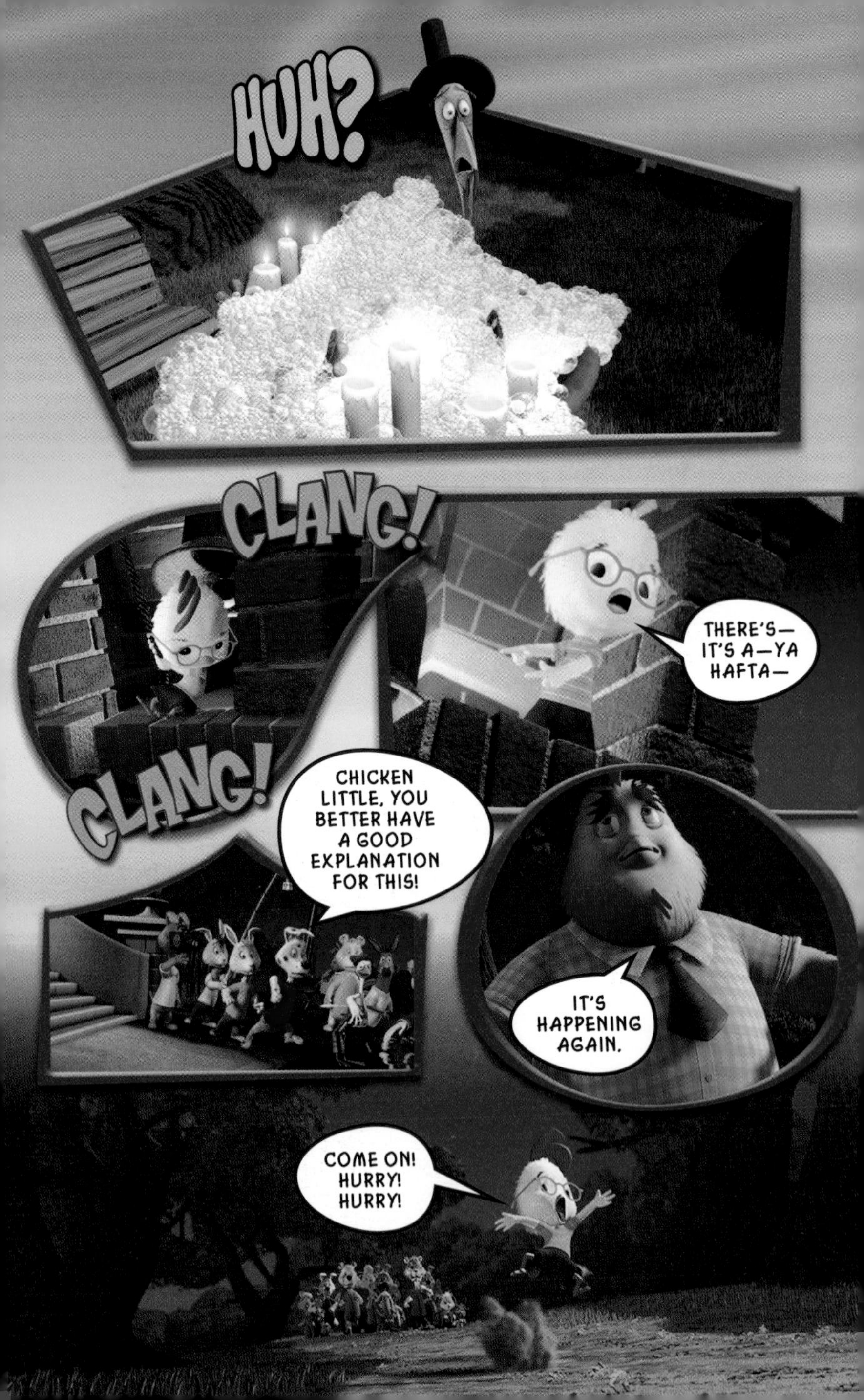
HUH?
CLANG!
CLANG!
THERE'S— IT'S A—YA HAFTA—
CHICKEN LITTLE, YOU BETTER HAVE A GOOD EXPLANATION FOR THIS!
IT'S HAPPENING AGAIN.
COME ON! HURRY! HURRY!

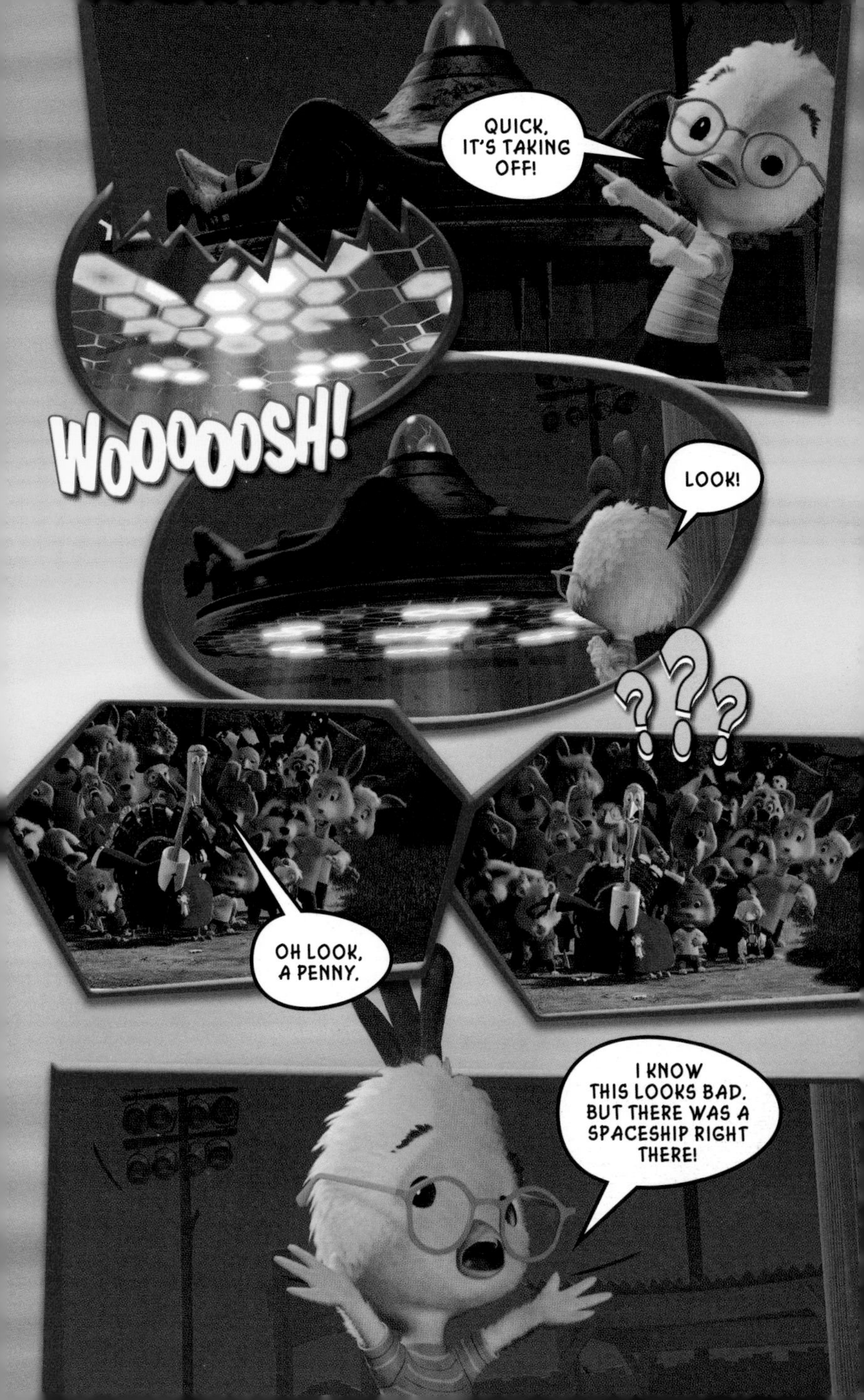
QUICK, IT'S TAKING OFF!
WOOOOOSH!
LOOK!
???
OH LOOK, A PENNY.
I KNOW THIS LOOKS BAD. BUT THERE WAS A SPACESHIP RIGHT THERE!

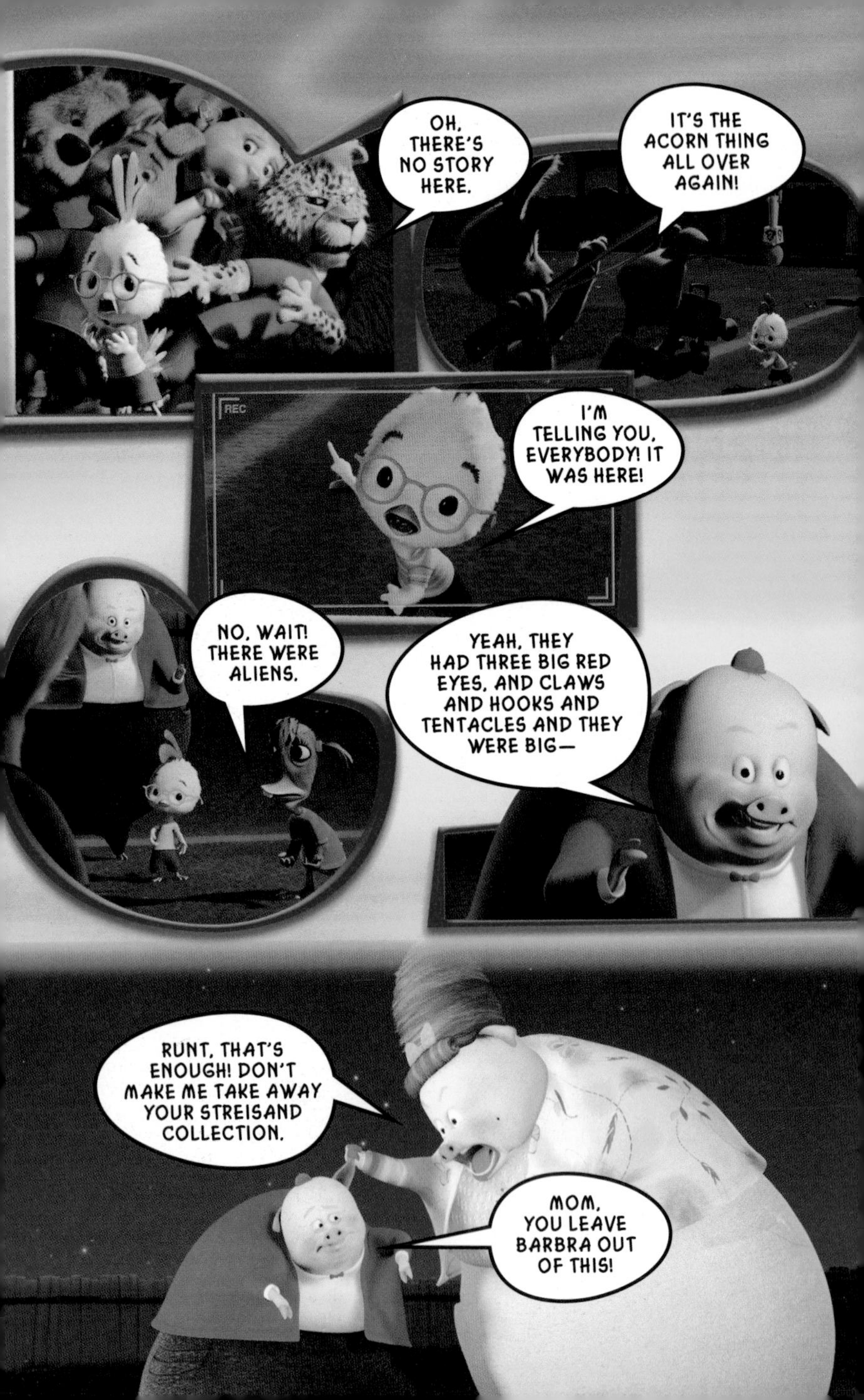
OH, THERE'S NO STORY HERE.
IT'S THE ACORN THING ALL OVER AGAIN!
REC
I'M TELLING YOU, EVERYBODY! IT WAS HERE!
NO, WAIT! THERE WERE ALIENS.
YEAH, THEY HAD THREE BIG RED EYES, AND CLAWS AND HOOKS AND TENTACLES AND THEY WERE BIG—
RUNT, THAT'S ENOUGH! DON'T MAKE ME TAKE AWAY YOUR STREISAND COLLECTION.
MOM, YOU LEAVE BARBRA OUT OF THIS!

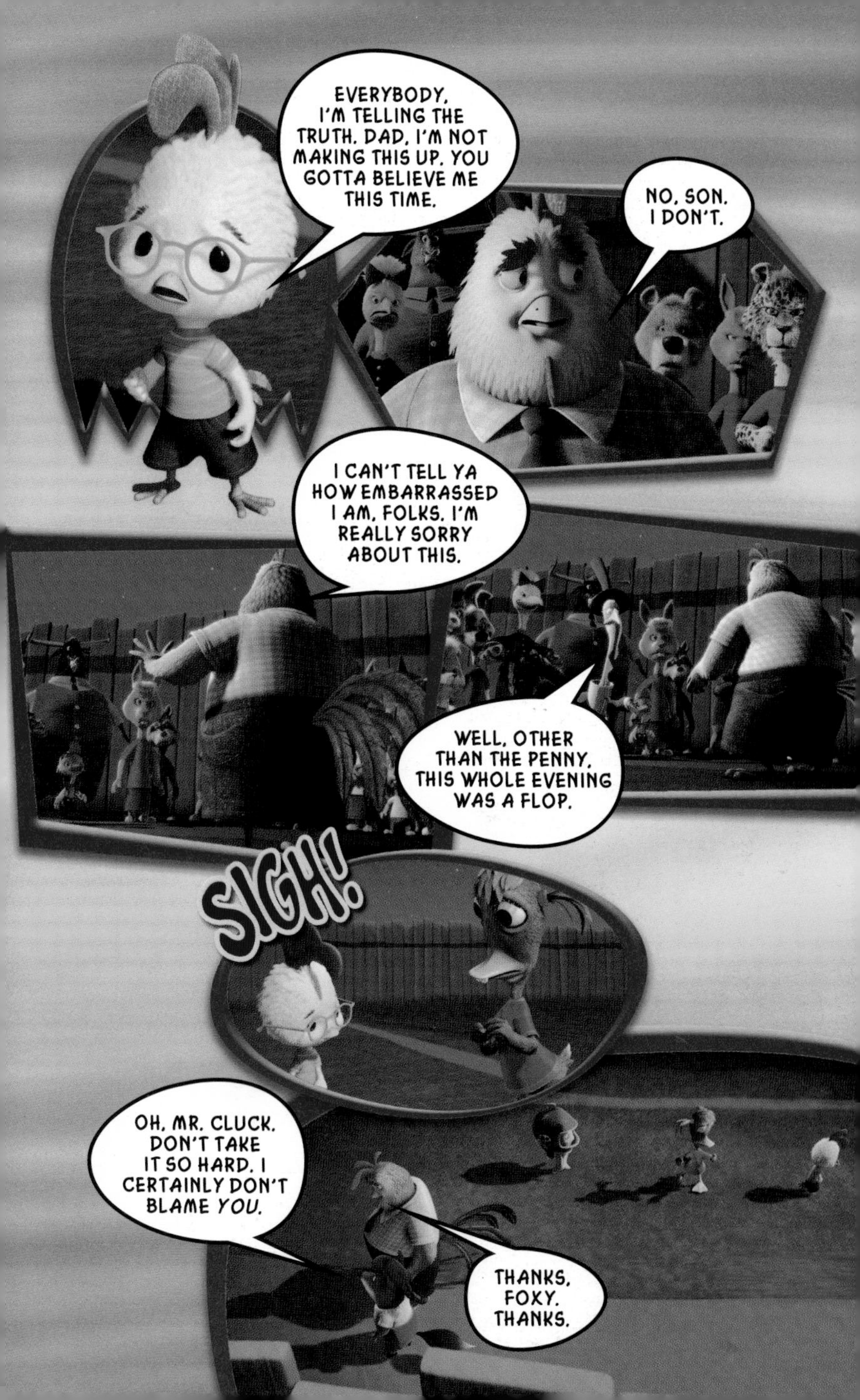
EVERYBODY, I'M TELLING THE TRUTH. DAD, I'M NOT MAKING THIS UP. YOU GOTTA BELIEVE ME THIS TIME.
NO, SON. I DON'T.
I CAN'T TELL YA HOW EMBARRASSED I AM, FOLKS. I'M REALLY SORRY ABOUT THIS.
WELL, OTHER THAN THE PENNY, THIS WHOLE EVENING WAS A FLOP.
SIGH!
OH, MR. CLUCK. DON'T TAKE IT SO HARD. I CERTAINLY DON'T BLAME *YOU*.
THANKS, FOXY. THANKS.

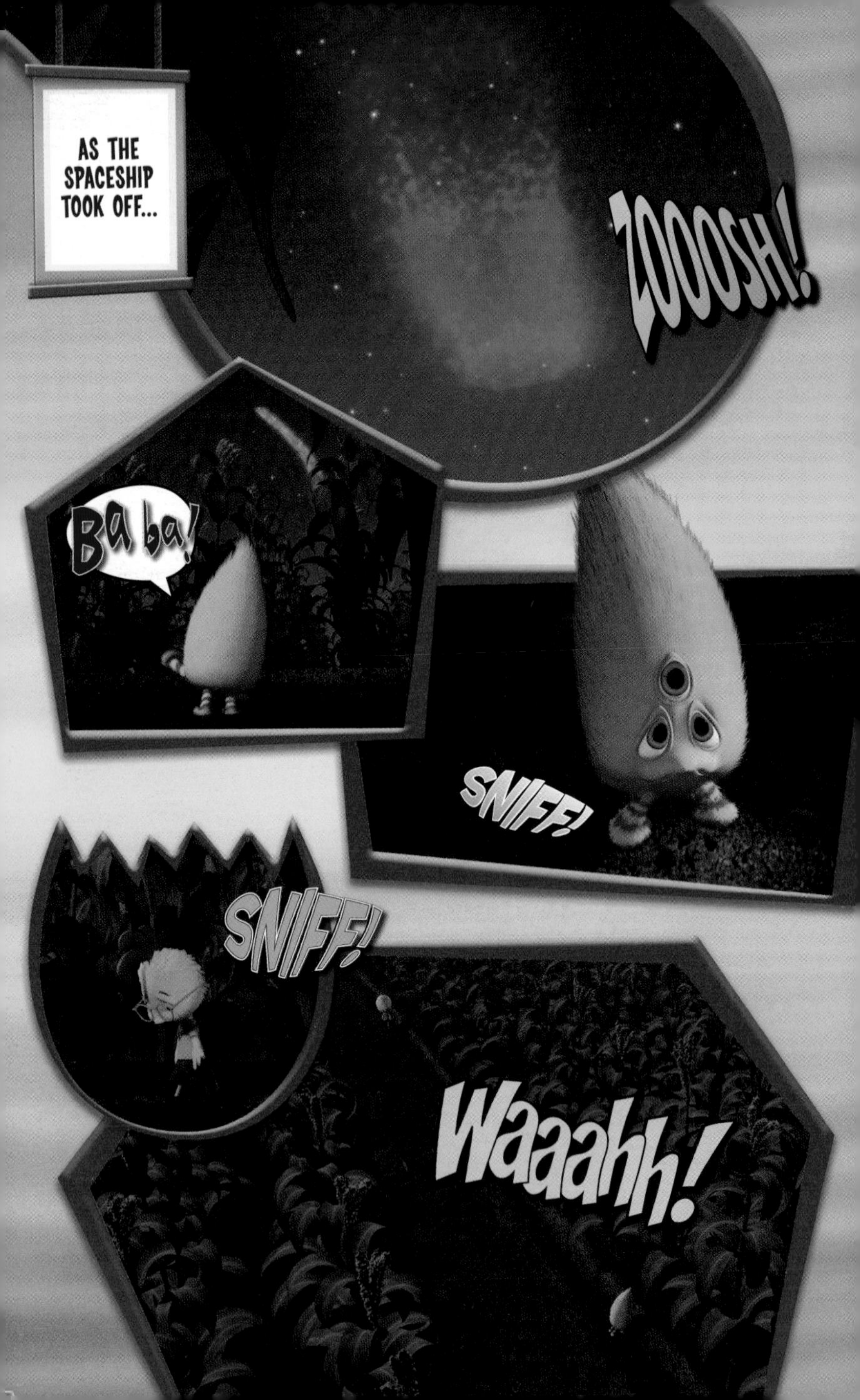

AS THE SPACESHIP TOOK OFF...
ZOOOSH!
Ba ba!
SNIFF!
SNIFF!
Waaahh!

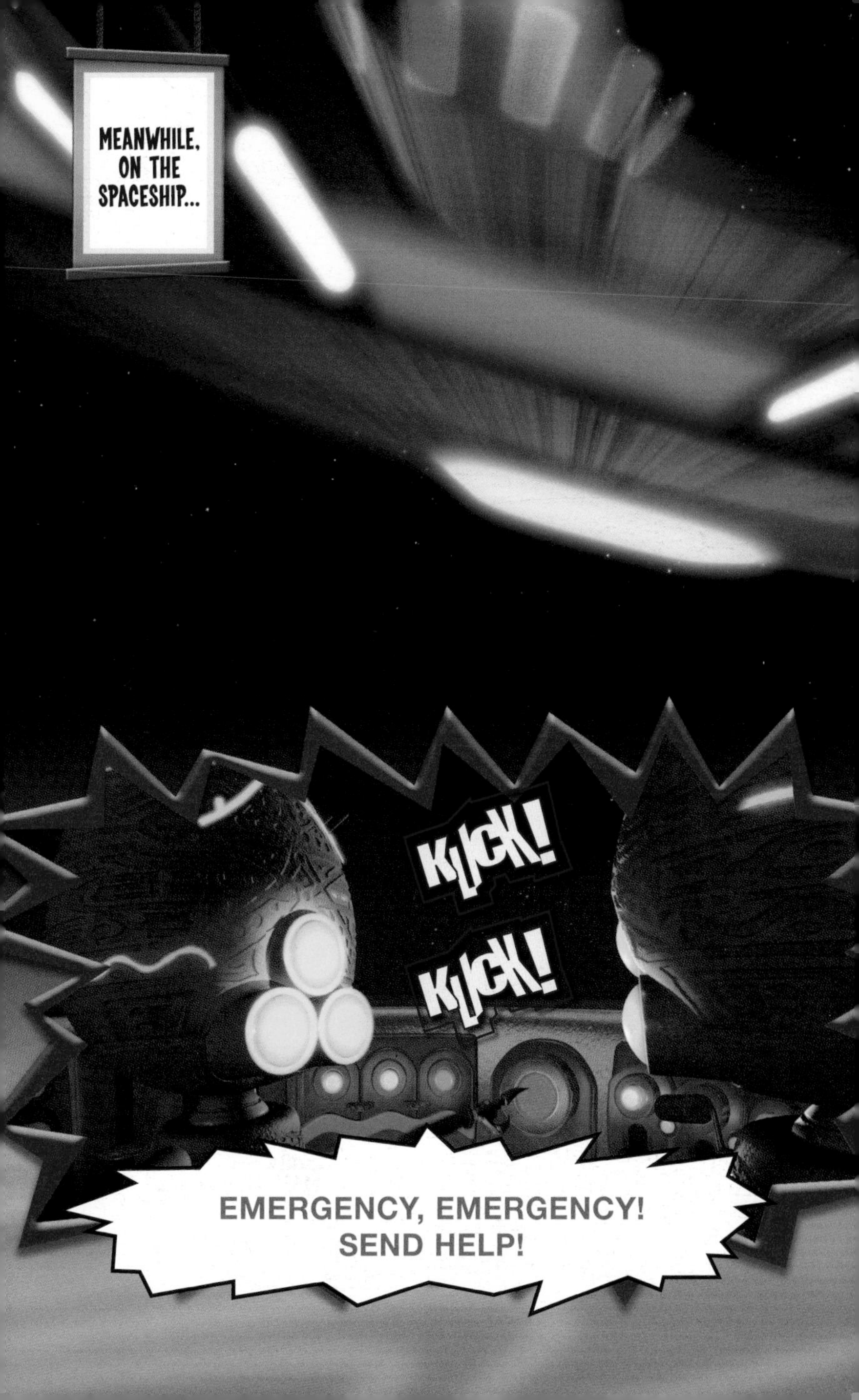
MEANWHILE, ON THE SPACESHIP...
KLICK!
KLICK!
EMERGENCY, EMERGENCY! SEND HELP!

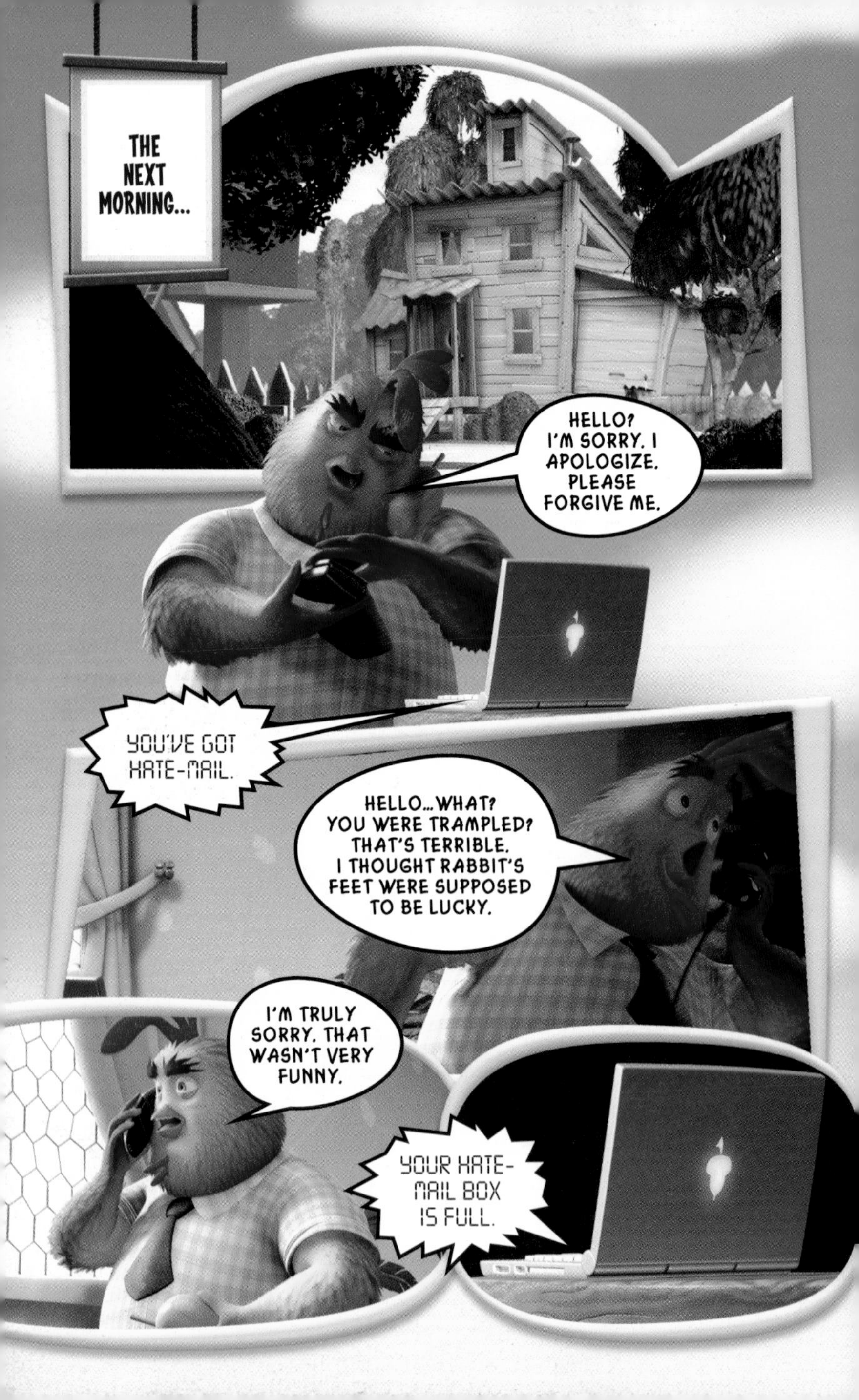
THE NEXT MORNING...
HELLO? I'M SORRY. I APOLOGIZE. PLEASE FORGIVE ME.
YOU'VE GOT HATE-MAIL.
HELLO...WHAT? YOU WERE TRAMPLED? THAT'S TERRIBLE. I THOUGHT RABBIT'S FEET WERE SUPPOSED TO BE LUCKY.
I'M TRULY SORRY. THAT WASN'T VERY FUNNY.
YOUR HATE-MAIL BOX IS FULL.

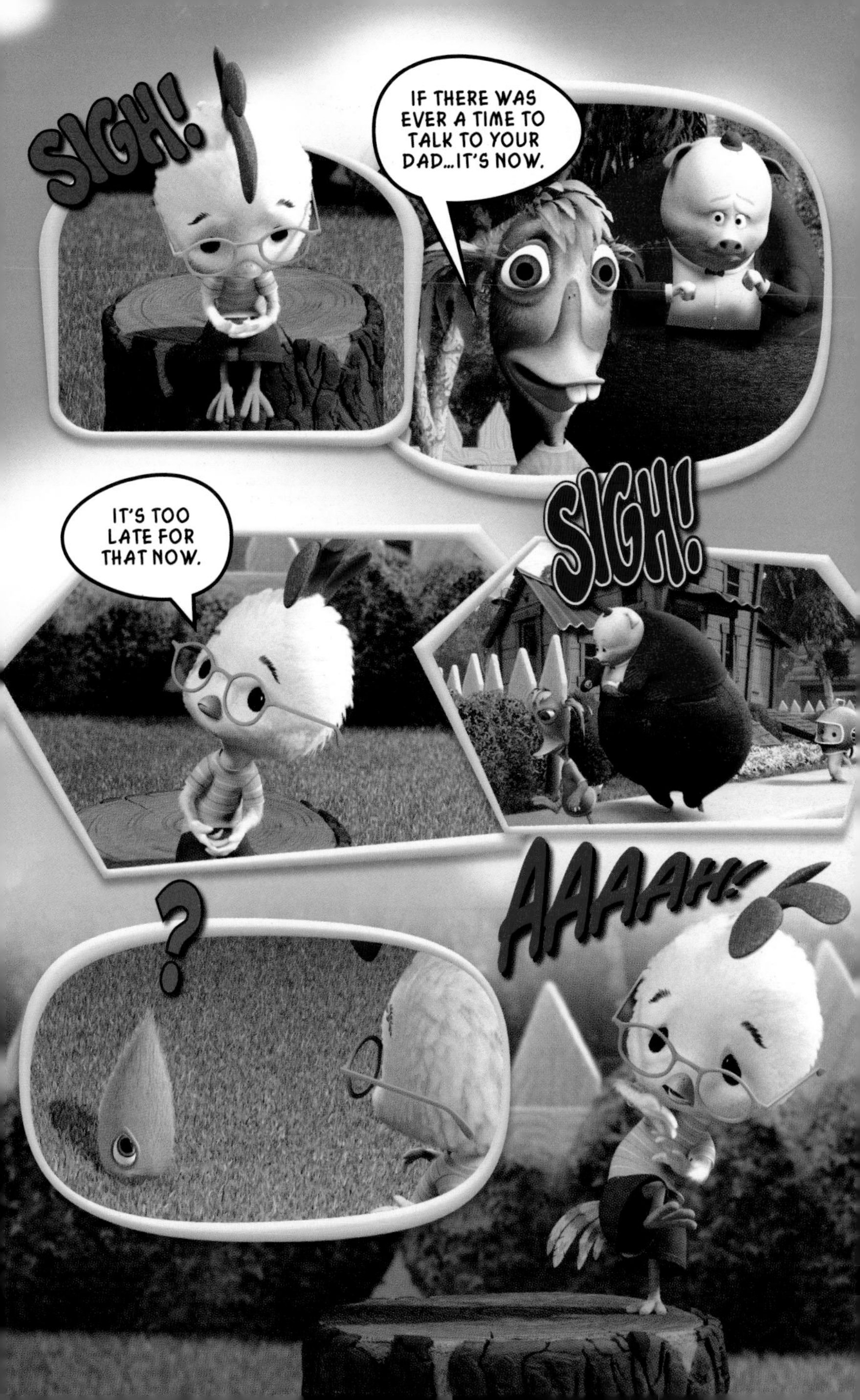
SIGH!
IF THERE WAS EVER A TIME TO TALK TO YOUR DAD...IT'S NOW.
IT'S TOO LATE FOR THAT NOW.
SIGH!
?
AAAAH!

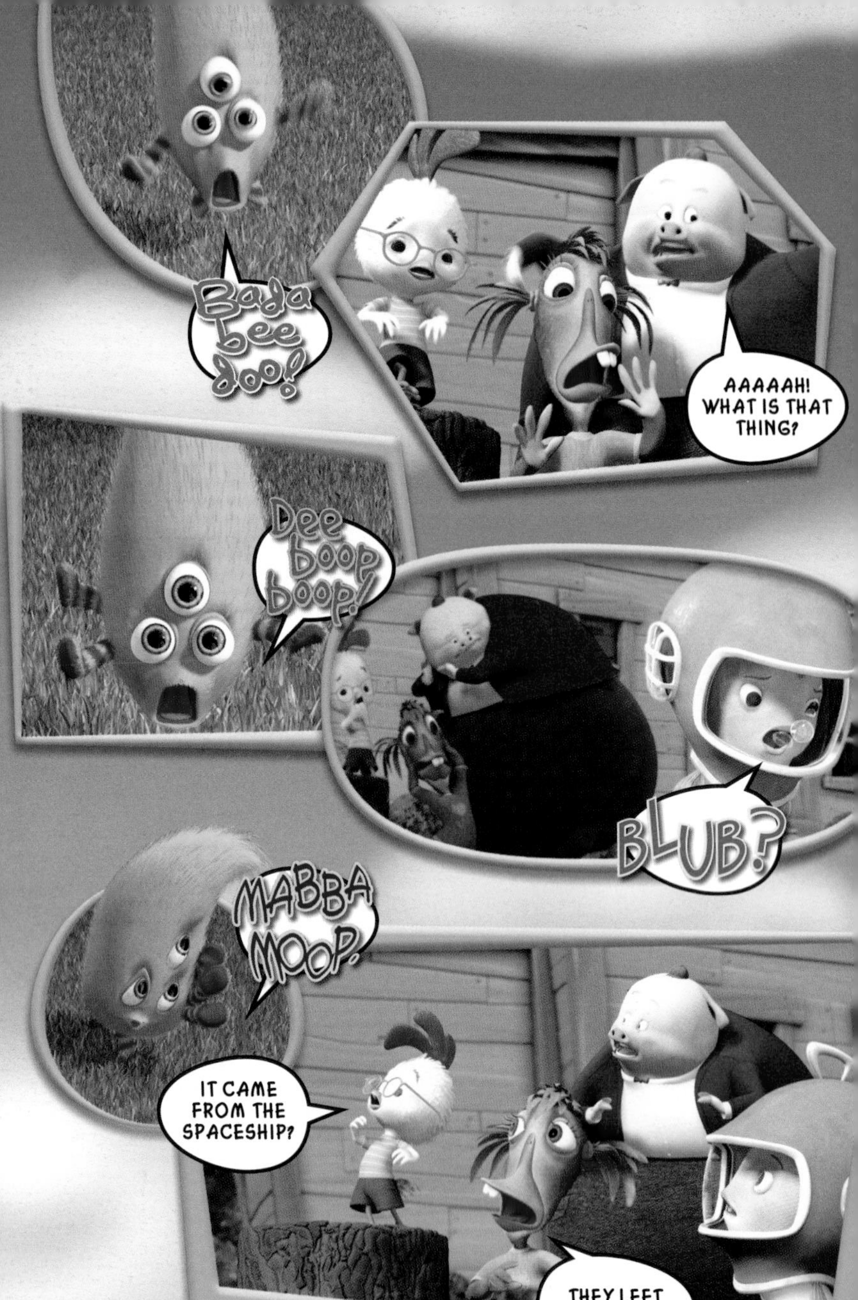
Baba bee doo!
AAAAAH! WHAT IS THAT THING?
Dee boop boop!
BLUB?
MABBA MOOP.
IT CAME FROM THE SPACESHIP?
THEY LEFT HIM BEHIND?

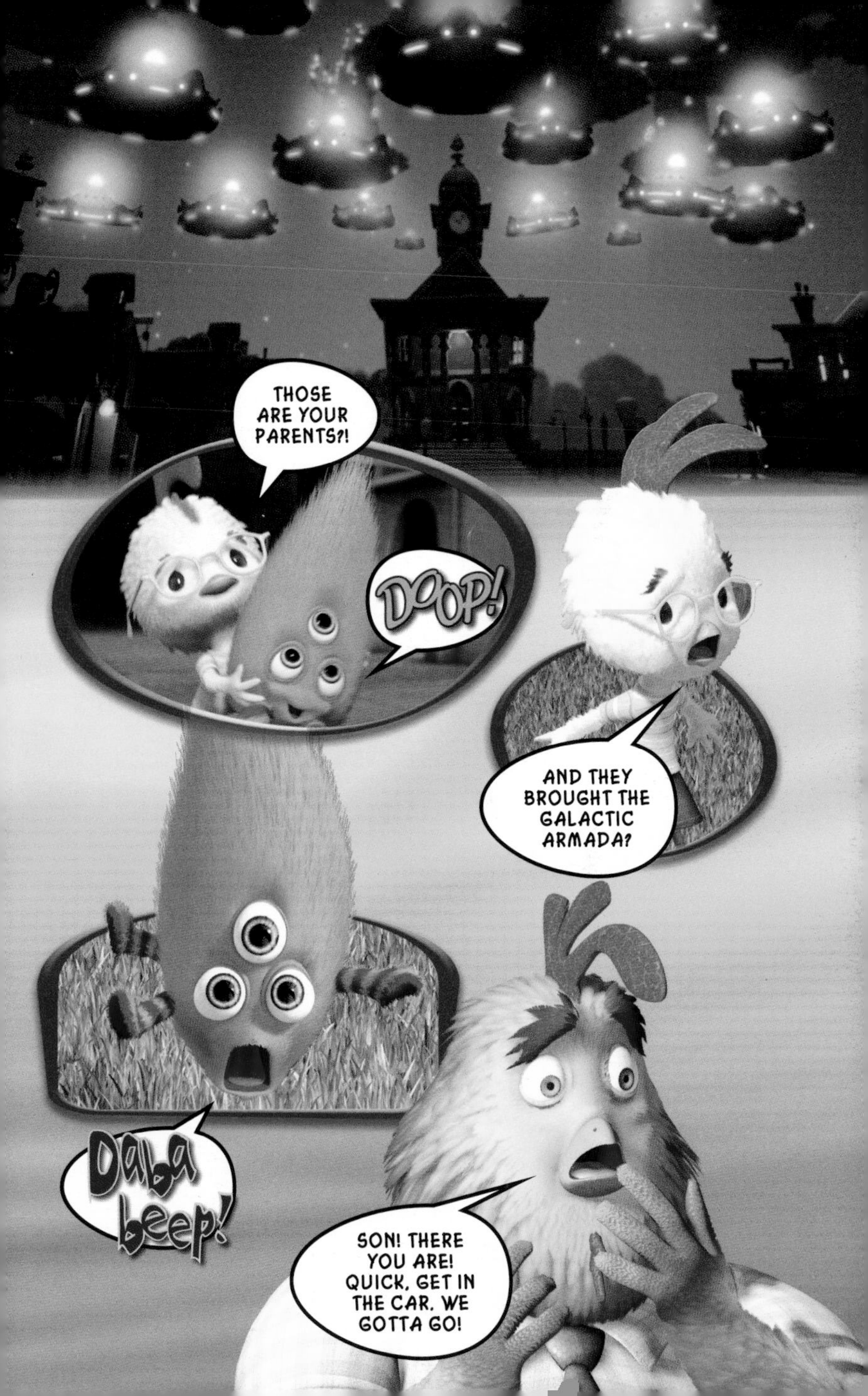
THOSE ARE YOUR PARENTS?!
DOOP!
AND THEY BROUGHT THE GALACTIC ARMADA?
Daba beep!
SON! THERE YOU ARE! QUICK, GET IN THE CAR. WE GOTTA GO!

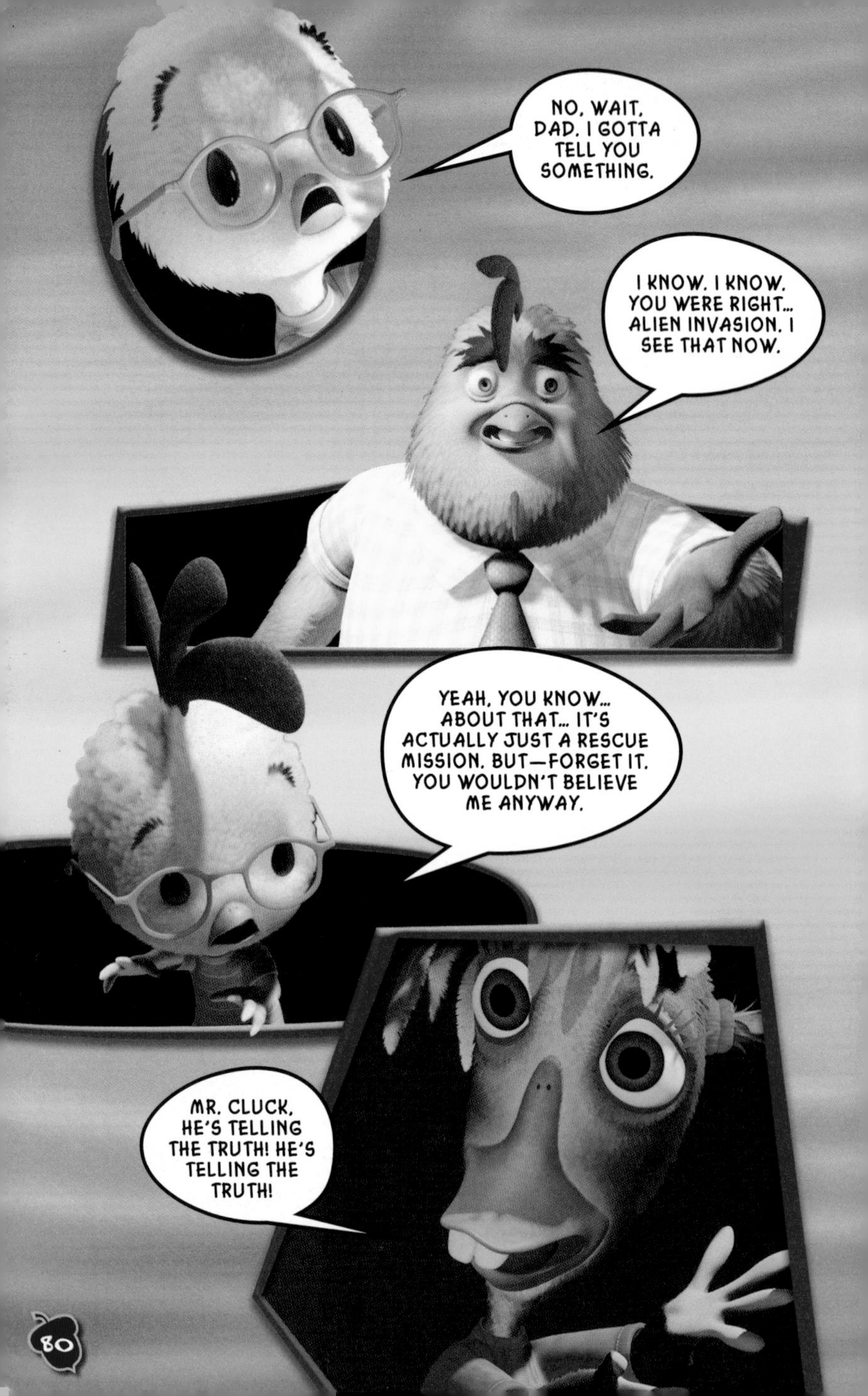
NO, WAIT, DAD. I GOTTA TELL YOU SOMETHING.
I KNOW. I KNOW. YOU WERE RIGHT... ALIEN INVASION. I SEE THAT NOW.
YEAH, YOU KNOW... ABOUT THAT... IT'S ACTUALLY JUST A RESCUE MISSION. BUT—FORGET IT. YOU WOULDN'T BELIEVE ME ANYWAY.
MR. CLUCK, HE'S TELLING THE TRUTH! HE'S TELLING THE TRUTH!

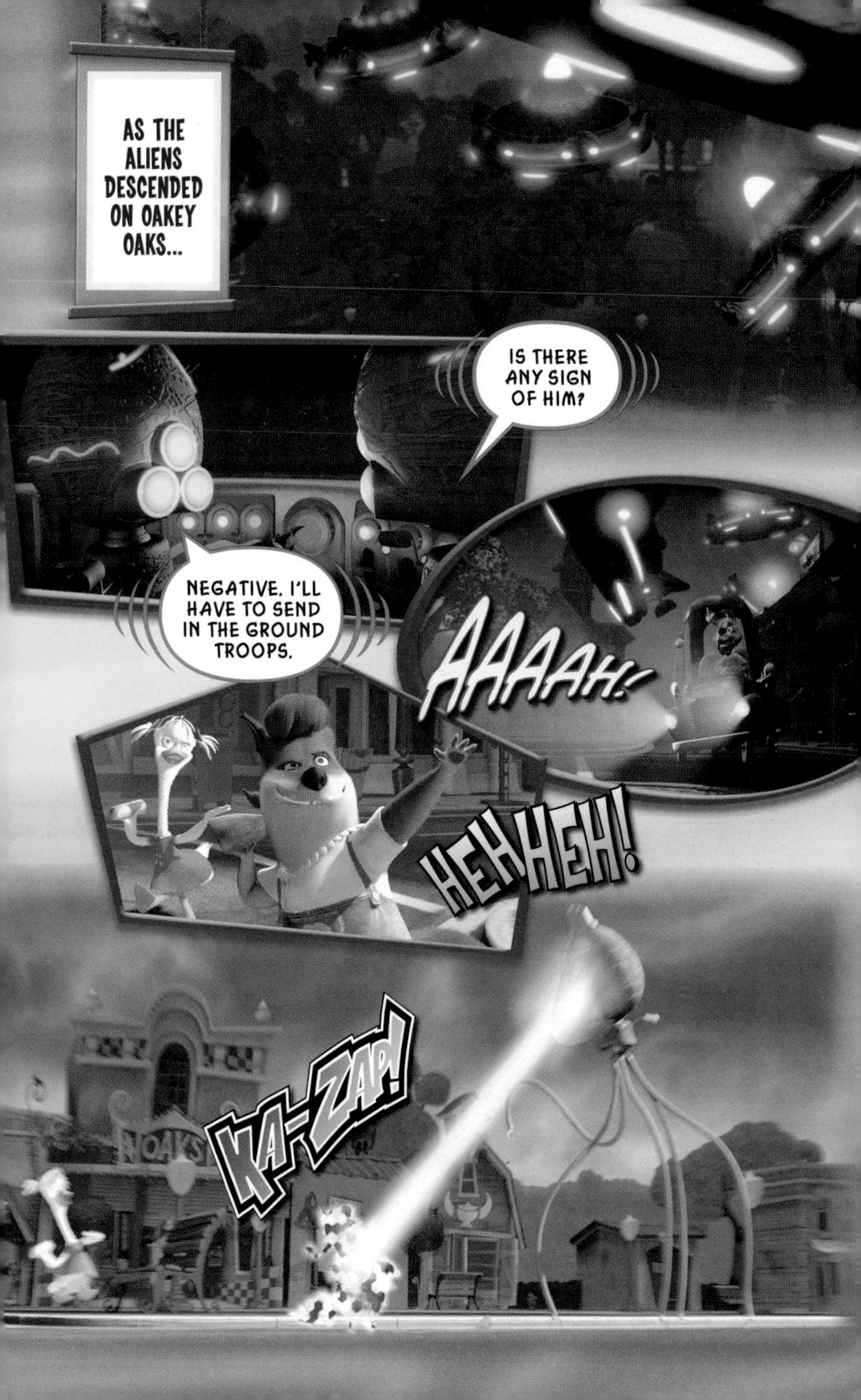
AS THE ALIENS DESCENDED ON OAKEY OAKS...
IS THERE ANY SIGN OF HIM?
NEGATIVE. I'LL HAVE TO SEND IN THE GROUND TROOPS.
AAAAH!
HEH HEH!
OAKS
KA-ZAP!

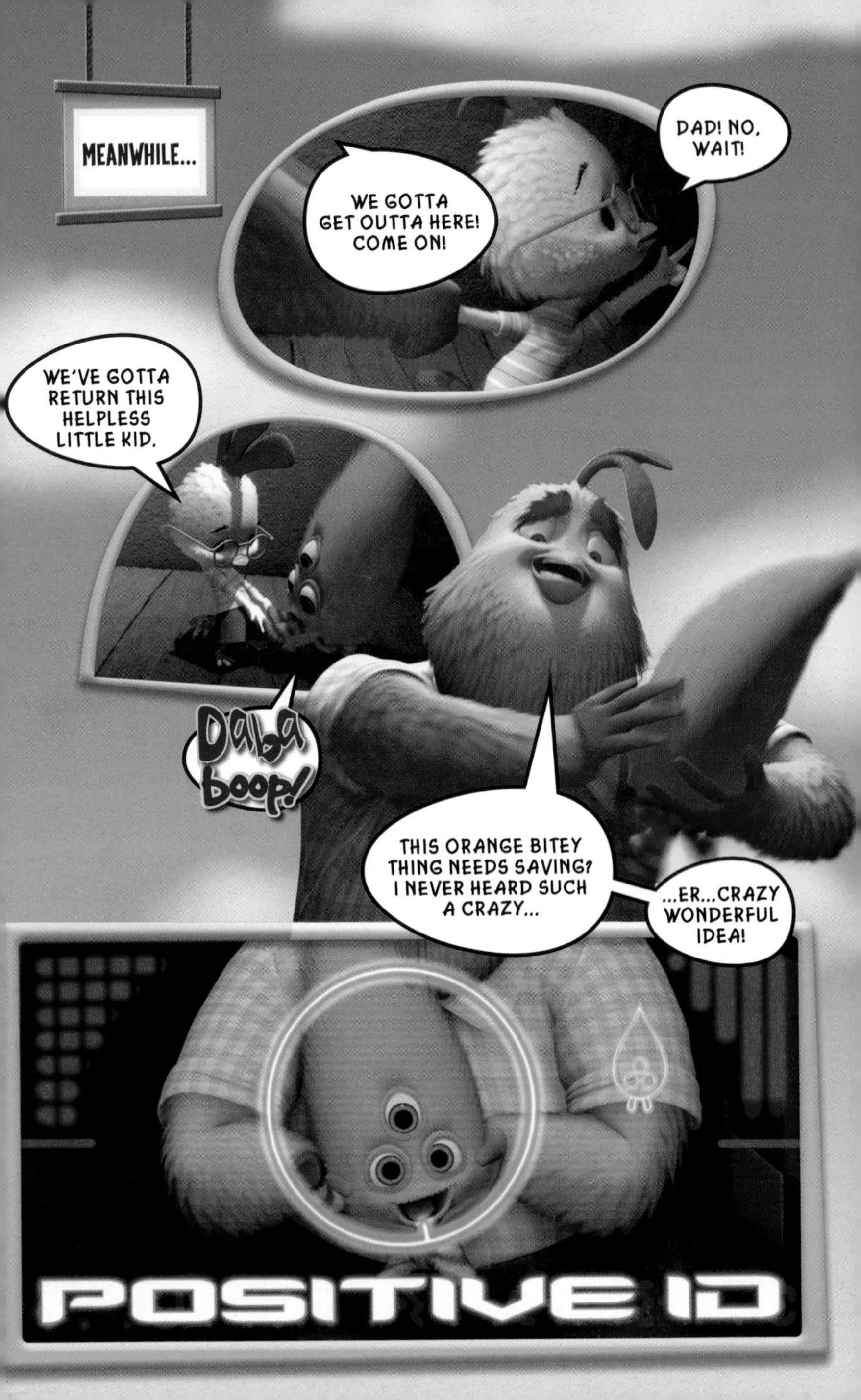
MEANWHILE...
WE GOTTA GET OUTTA HERE! COME ON!
DAD! NO, WAIT!
WE'VE GOTTA RETURN THIS HELPLESS LITTLE KID.
Daba boop!
THIS ORANGE BITEY THING NEEDS SAVING? I NEVER HEARD SUCH A CRAZY...
...ER...CRAZY WONDERFUL IDEA!
POSITIVE ID

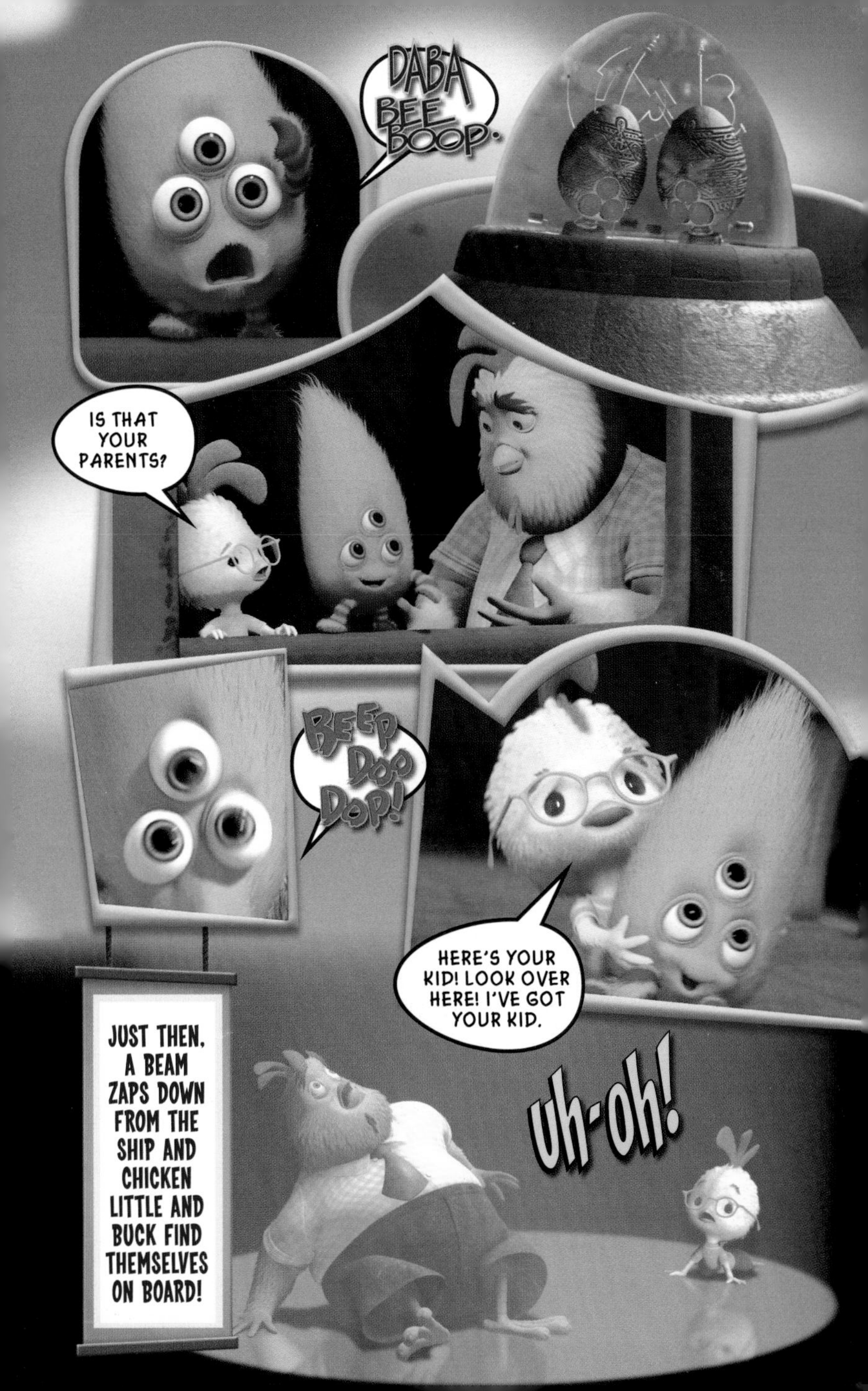
DABA BEE BOOP.
IS THAT YOUR PARENTS?
BEEP DOO DOP!
HERE'S YOUR KID! LOOK OVER HERE! I'VE GOT YOUR KID.
JUST THEN, A BEAM ZAPS DOWN FROM THE SHIP AND CHICKEN LITTLE AND BUCK FIND THEMSELVES ON BOARD!
Uh-oh!

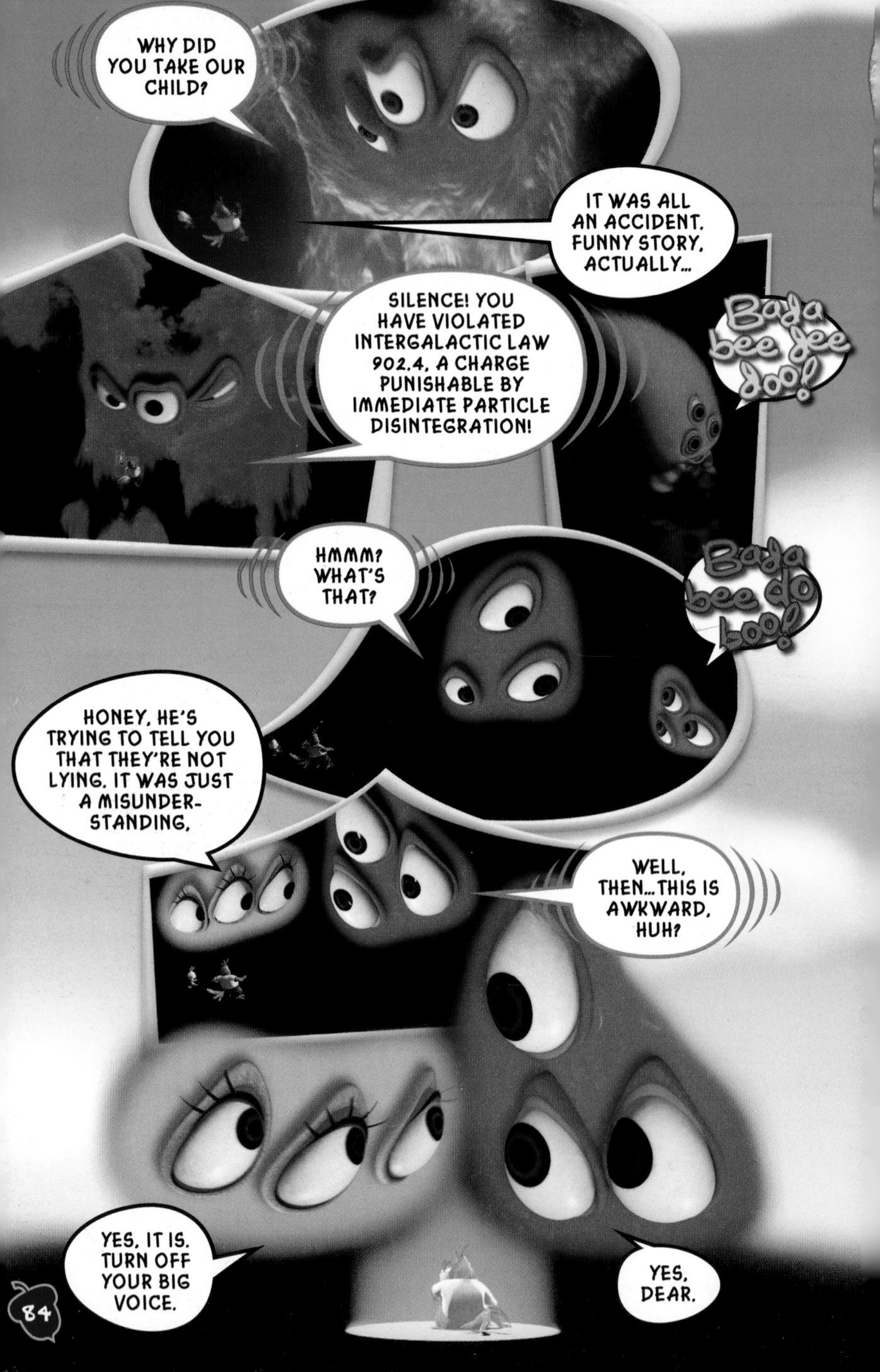
WHY DID YOU TAKE OUR CHILD?
IT WAS ALL AN ACCIDENT. FUNNY STORY, ACTUALLY...
SILENCE! YOU HAVE VIOLATED INTERGALACTIC LAW 902.4, A CHARGE PUNISHABLE BY IMMEDIATE PARTICLE DISINTEGRATION!
Baja bee jee doo!
HMMM? WHAT'S THAT?
Baja bee do boo!
HONEY, HE'S TRYING TO TELL YOU THAT THEY'RE NOT LYING. IT WAS JUST A MISUNDER-STANDING.
WELL, THEN...THIS IS AWKWARD, HUH?
YES, IT IS. TURN OFF YOUR BIG VOICE.
YES, DEAR.

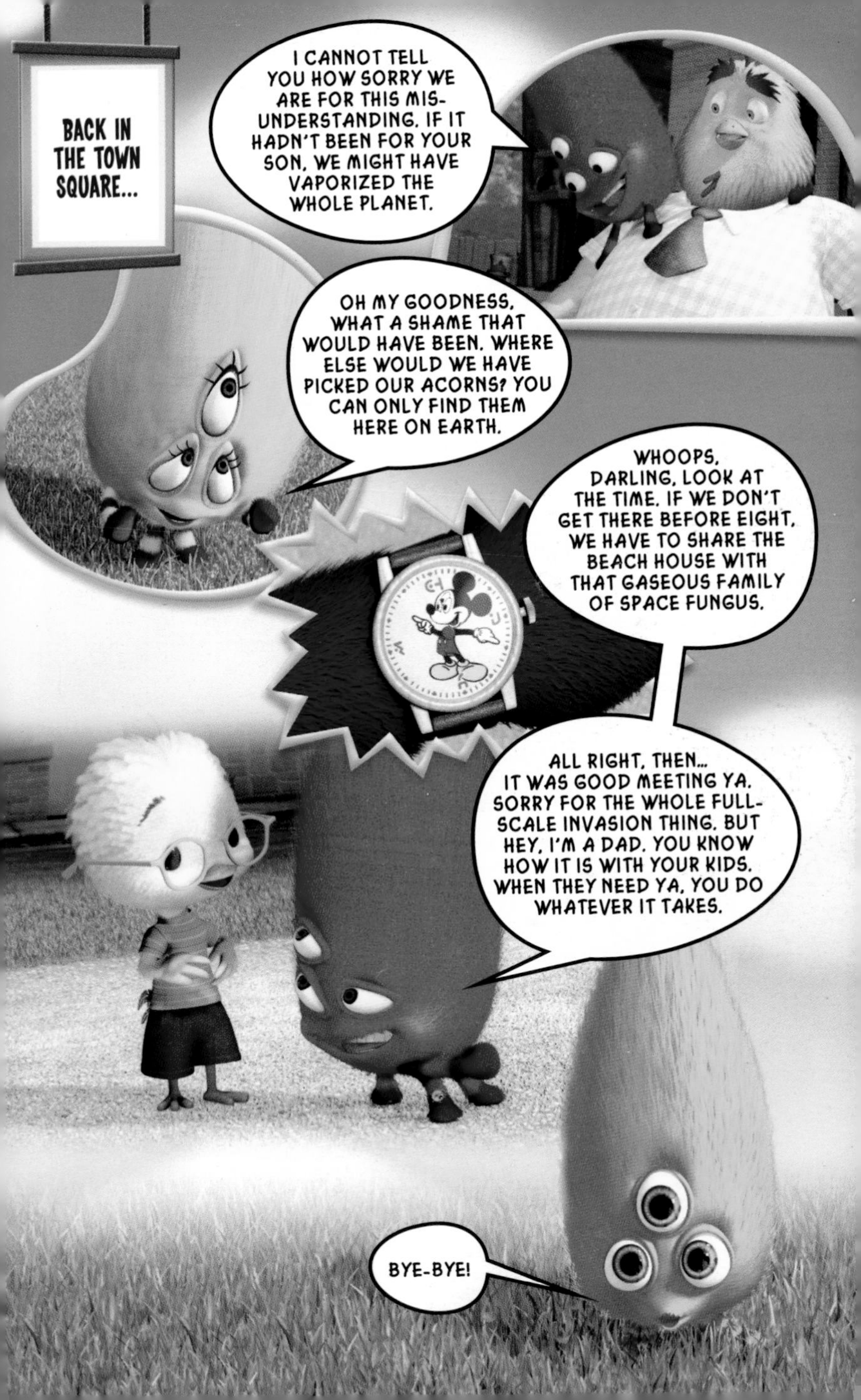
BACK IN THE TOWN SQUARE...
I CANNOT TELL YOU HOW SORRY WE ARE FOR THIS MIS-UNDERSTANDING. IF IT HADN'T BEEN FOR YOUR SON, WE MIGHT HAVE VAPORIZED THE WHOLE PLANET.
OH MY GOODNESS, WHAT A SHAME THAT WOULD HAVE BEEN. WHERE ELSE WOULD WE HAVE PICKED OUR ACORNS? YOU CAN ONLY FIND THEM HERE ON EARTH.
WHOOPS, DARLING, LOOK AT THE TIME. IF WE DON'T GET THERE BEFORE EIGHT, WE HAVE TO SHARE THE BEACH HOUSE WITH THAT GASEOUS FAMILY OF SPACE FUNGUS.
ALL RIGHT, THEN... IT WAS GOOD MEETING YA. SORRY FOR THE WHOLE FULL-SCALE INVASION THING. BUT HEY, I'M A DAD. YOU KNOW HOW IT IS WITH YOUR KIDS. WHEN THEY NEED YA, YOU DO WHATEVER IT TAKES.
BYE-BYE!

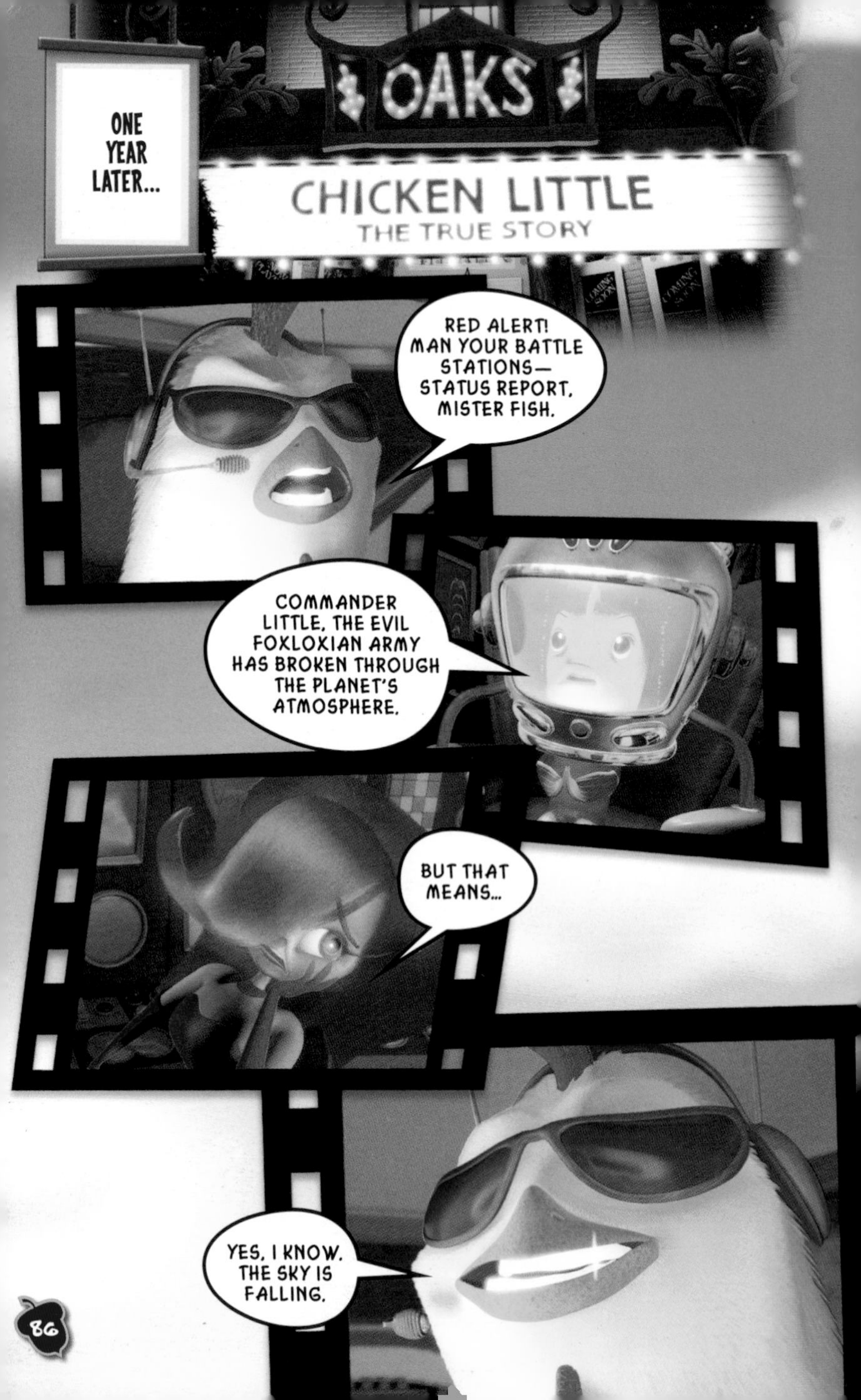
ONE YEAR LATER...
OAKS
CHICKEN LITTLE
THE TRUE STORY
RED ALERT! MAN YOUR BATTLE STATIONS— STATUS REPORT, MISTER FISH.
COMMANDER LITTLE, THE EVIL FOXLOXIAN ARMY HAS BROKEN THROUGH THE PLANET'S ATMOSPHERE.
BUT THAT MEANS...
YES, I KNOW. THE SKY IS FALLING.

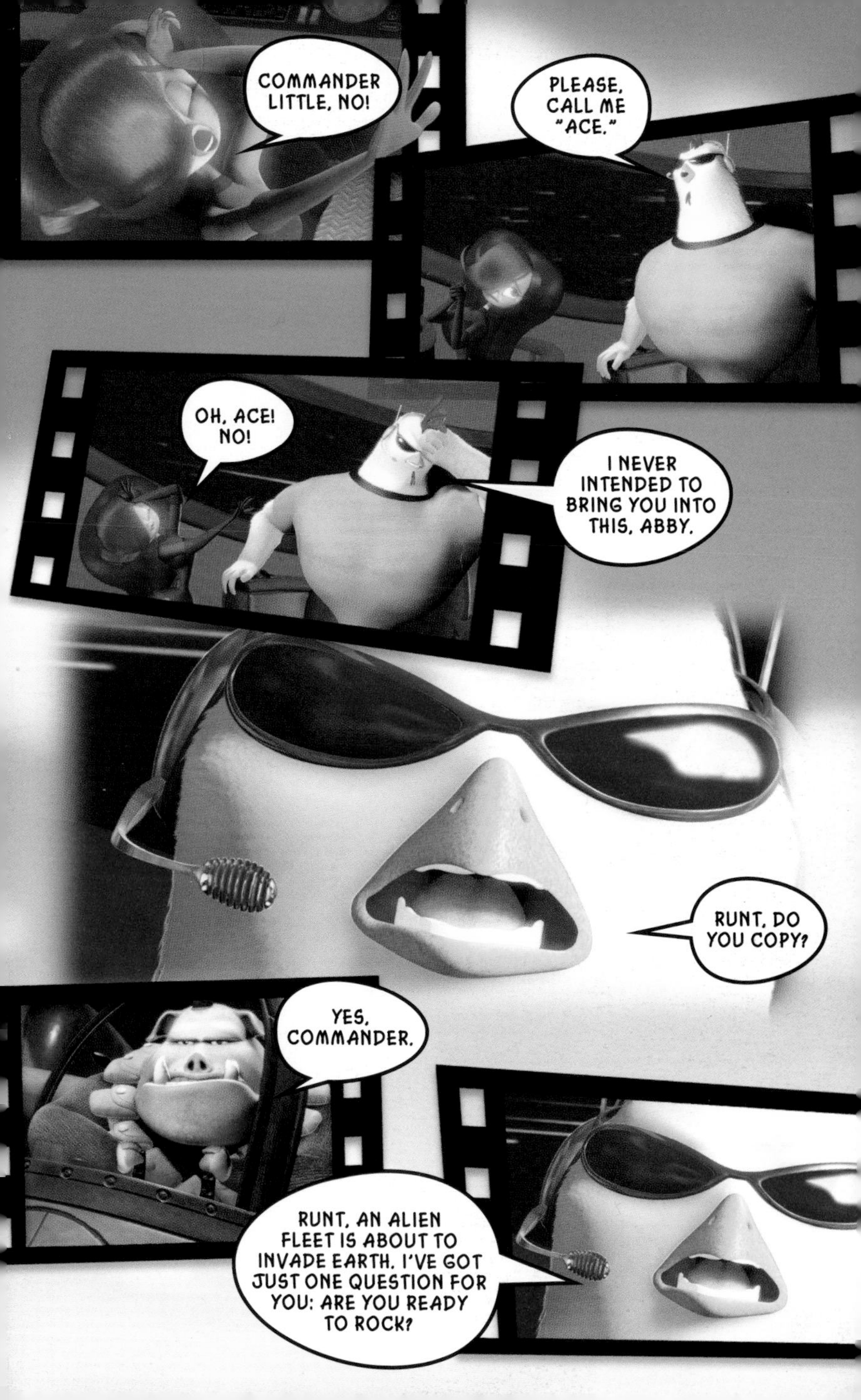
COMMANDER LITTLE, NO!
PLEASE, CALL ME "ACE."
OH, ACE! NO!
I NEVER INTENDED TO BRING YOU INTO THIS, ABBY.
RUNT, DO YOU COPY?
YES, COMMANDER.
RUNT, AN ALIEN FLEET IS ABOUT TO INVADE EARTH. I'VE GOT JUST ONE QUESTION FOR YOU: ARE YOU READY TO ROCK?

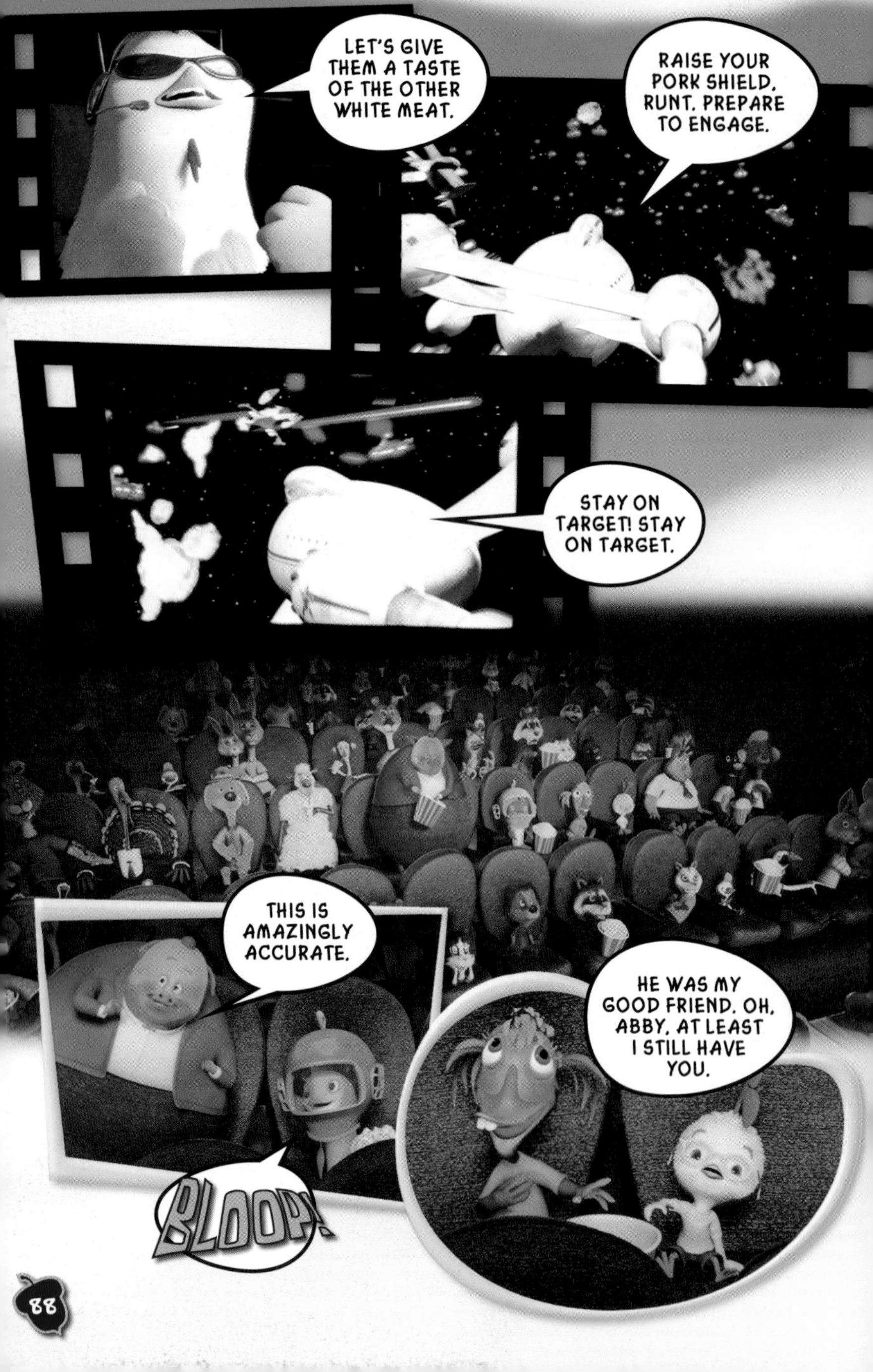
LET'S GIVE THEM A TASTE OF THE OTHER WHITE MEAT.
RAISE YOUR PORK SHIELD, RUNT. PREPARE TO ENGAGE.
STAY ON TARGET! STAY ON TARGET.
THIS IS AMAZINGLY ACCURATE.
BLOOP!
HE WAS MY GOOD FRIEND. OH, ABBY, AT LEAST I STILL HAVE YOU.

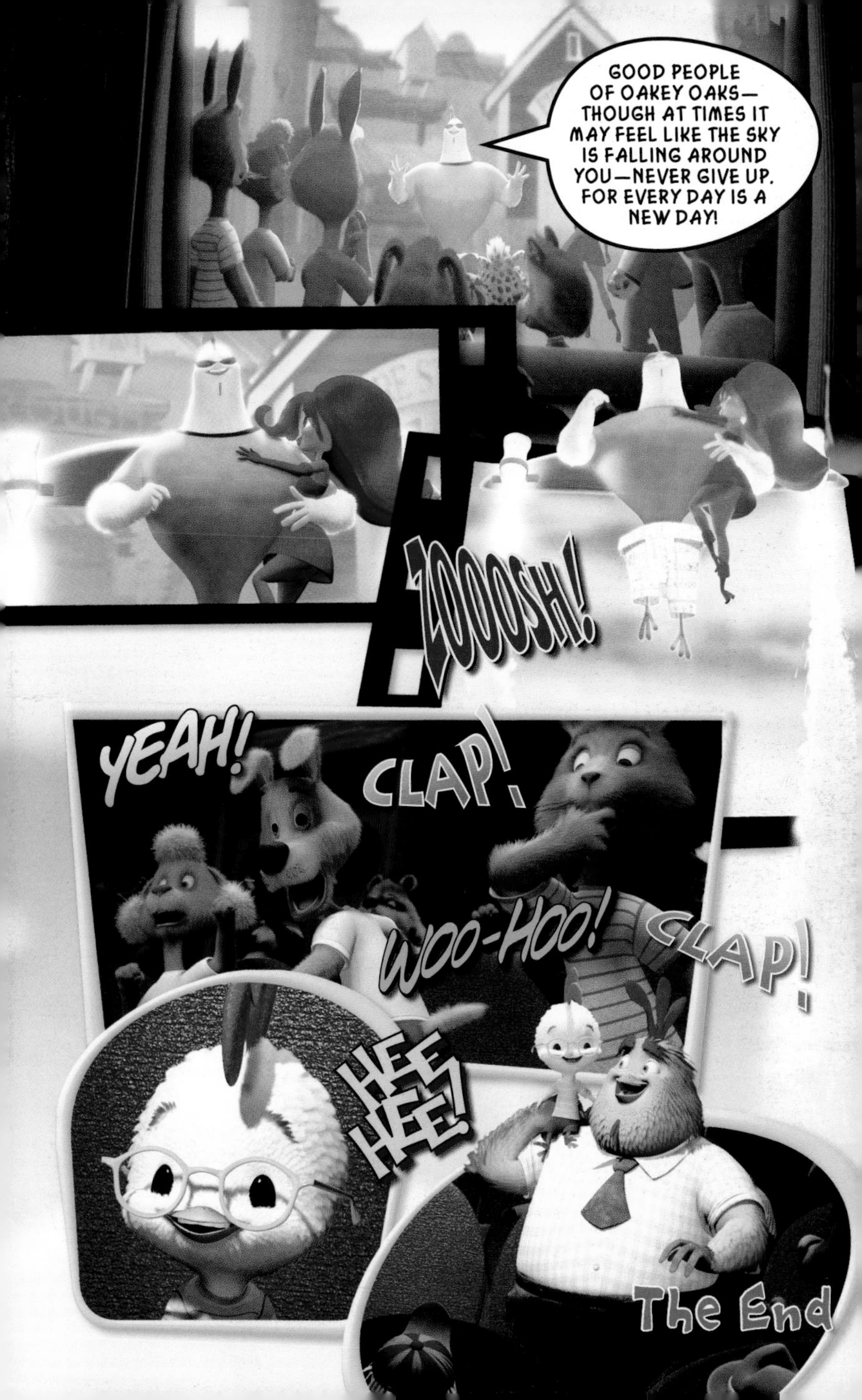
GOOD PEOPLE OF OAKEY OAKS—THOUGH AT TIMES IT MAY FEEL LIKE THE SKY IS FALLING AROUND YOU—NEVER GIVE UP. FOR EVERY DAY IS A NEW DAY!
ZOOOSH!
YEAH!
CLAP!
WOO-HOO!
CLAP!
HEE HEE!
The End